TWIN LIES

A NOVEL BY

LAUREEN
VONNEGUT

Skorpion Press

TWIN LIES, a novel by Laureen Vonnegut

First Edition, May 2011

Copyright © 2011 Laureen Vonnegut

Book Layout and Formatting by Pedernales Publishing, LLC. www.pedernalespublishing.com

ISBN: 978-0-9835271-0-7

Printed in the United States of America

Acknowledgements

Many, many thanks to Jose at Pedernales Publishing, GT at Gorilla Suit Productions, Chloë for her twin image, all my advance readers, all my advice givers (even though it may not all have been taken, it was appreciated). And to Pluto, *el gato negro*.

This book is dedicated to all the dopplegängers of the world.

TWIN LIES

CHAPTER 1

I AM A LIAR

I am a liar.

And I don't mean little white lies. These are lies of vast proportions, lies about the vital parts of life...the worst lies a person can tell, the highest betrayal. And Toby suspects nothing. The magnitude of what I have done strikes me and darkness edges into my vision.

I throw open the door and take deep breaths of chilly air. I lean against the terrace wall, and in the distance the Golden Gate Bridge floats above a layer of opaque clouds. Next to me my prize irises rise, straight and strong. I rub a blue-black petal between my fingertips and it gleams disturbingly in the early sunlight. The softness feels so pure, so real that tears drop down my cheeks. My neighbors can see me, but I can't stop crying. I snap off the flower and run into the kitchen, juice seeping out of the torn stem into the palm of my hand.

I take the shears and press the tip of the blade into my skin, slowly drawing the blade along my arm. A red line appears, the skin splits, and a thin line of blood runs down to the underside of my arm. A drop falls to the countertop, red against the white tile. It hurts. I want it to hurt. When there is pain, I know which twin has been left alive and which one lays buried beneath the grey marble stone.

The doorbell rings and a few seconds later Toby turns the key and opens the door. For some reason Toby has always done this, as if he is afraid he will catch me in the middle of something embarrassing. My self-mutilation is new, maybe it's something he willed on me by insisting on ringing the doorbell every time he enters the house. I am a great believer in the power of suggestion.

Toby sees my scars and scabs and doesn't ask. I like this about him. I wrap a paper towel around my arm and head to the bathroom. Warm water flows over the wound, leaving a swirl of pink water going around and around the drain. I open the medicine cabinet and rub on some antiseptic. My expression in the mirror looks happy, white teeth showing in a slightly ashamed mouth, lips puckering into a cheerful whistle.

The door slams shut. 'Lamb Chop, I'm back,' he calls.

I shake my head at his silliness and emerge from the bathroom. In the beginning, I pitied him for suspecting nothing of my lies. Over time the pity fermented into a loss of respect. Sometimes the pity provokes tenderness and I want to go to him and hold his sleek head protectively in my arms. This is why lies never work in marriage: Once someone lies, the other person is diminished in the liar's eyes. The two are no longer equal.

I have been lying for so many years that I don't know where the truth stops and the lies begin. I never intended to hurt anyone. The lies were created purely out of guilt, and in the beginning I desperately needed them to keep Dahlia alive.

Toby and I have known each other since we were twelve. We are not the same, yet we are. Shouldn't he be aware enough to sense something is wrong?

He stands fit and sweaty in the kitchen, running shoes discarded under the table. He looks past me and around me for Lorna. Lorna bursts through the door and hurls herself at Toby. He picks her up and they hug in a tight knot. I stand to the side and grin falsely. Their shiny black hair blends together. Like little otters.

Lorna slides to the ground and says, 'Good morning, Mama.'

She hands me her Harry Potter lunchbox from yesterday. I hear the apple rolling around inside. She hates fruit, and the same bruised apple has been inside for a week. I take out the apple and replace it with a banana, even though I know it will come back blackened this afternoon. She doesn't think to throw it away and tell me she has eaten it, which is what I would have done as a child.

I make her favorite peanut butter and strawberry jam sandwich, slathering on the chunks of fruit in hopes that she will gain some nutritional value. Cheese and crackers, a bag of nuts, and a napkin. I find a red marker and draw a heart on the napkin, and in the middle I write, '*I love you – Mommy.*'

Upstairs, the shower runs. I open Toby's wallet and take out fifty dollars. I find my purse, unzip the little side pocket, and add it to my stash. The wad is growing, and when it reaches a thousand I will deposit it in my safe deposit box. I know this adds to my foundation of lies, but it is only the thought of what I have collected, and a new future, that keeps me from plunging the garden shears deeper.

CHAPTER 2

ONE GOOD AND ONE BAD

We were twelve when we first met Toby. His mother, Mrs. Winston, bought the big ranch-style house next door and she mailed us an invitation for lunch instead of walking across her deck, through a few weeds, and along our driveway. No one had ever seen or heard of a husband, so it was only Toby and Mrs. Winston living in the house. The house had five bedrooms and a black swimming pool shaped like an eight.

Chloe, our mother, picked out our red A-line dresses and we felt sophisticated, kind of Jackie O. We walked over to Mrs. Winston's house, although Chloe said she would like to have driven to make Mrs. Winston feel silly for mailing her invitation. She made us walk the long way around the gardens, down the driveway, past the mailboxes and then back up their driveway, which we thought was even sillier.

Mrs. Winston opened the door and was surprised to see there were two of us, in addition to Chloe.

'Twins,' she said, slightly disapproving. 'Identical.'

'Yes, Dahlia and Hetta.' Chloe pushed us in front of her. 'Nearly conjoined, like Siamese twins. Even I can't tell them apart.'

Mrs. Winston stared. What Chloe meant is that we were a *we*. We learned early to share and be one because when we were in the womb, we shared both a placenta and an amniotic sac. Only one percent of twins do this. We were nearly conjoined. We could have strangled each other with our umbilical cords. Chloe showed us photos of Chang and Eng Bunker, the two famous twins joined at the hip. They were born in Siam, the old Thailand and travelled with P.T. Barnum's circus. Sometimes it seemed it might as well have been us.

We walked in through the cool house. Mrs. Winston had installed air conditioning, although she had added skylights in every room. The house felt empty, with very simple furniture and all of it shades of white. In fact, Mrs. Winston herself was dressed in white. We were like a flock of excited parrots next to her calm paleness. She took us to the back patio where there was a lunch table set for four. She clapped her hands and there was the sound of someone walking along the corridor. A figure appeared inside, behind the screen door. The sliding door itself was left open, air conditioning blasting.

'S'il vous plait, un autre plat pour les...twins,' Mrs. Winston said.

A maid slid open the screen and stood in the doorway, dressed in black and white, frilly apron and starched white hat perched on her blond head. All the maids we knew were dark with thick black hair, not blond and willowy with thin ankles. Our maid wore Daisy Duke cut-offs and a T-shirt that read, 'Divers Do It Deep.'

Chloe narrowed her eyes at the maid and touched her forehead as if one of her migraines was creeping its way into her head. Toby walked into the room and stood, staring back and forth, comparing the two of us: our eyes, ears, fingernails. We both chewed on our nails.

Chloe cleared her throat. 'Your maid is French?'

'Swedish, but I don't speak Swedish.'

'I bet only one of you has a cut on your knee.' Toby pointed to my right knee and then to Dalia's, which was unmarked. We both smiled and she pulled up the corner of her dress. There was a scab there, leftover from a week ago. Toby's mouth fell open. If one of us tripped and hurt themselves, sure enough within a day or so, the other would do the same on the opposite limb. Those sorts of things were always happening to us.

'We're mirror twins.' She explained.

'What's that?'

'We are alike in the opposite way, like if you face a mirror.' I explained.

We walked over to the big glass patio door and stood in front of it, the three of us. He stared at us with his cool green eyes and looked into the reflection of the glass. His mother watched us, her heavy eyelashes dipping. We put out our right hands and touched the left hands of our mirror images. Four of us stood in front of him.

'If these images were our mirror twins, and we were right handed, our twin would be left-handed.'

We faced each other and touched our hands together in the same way. 'One of us is right-handed and the other left. You see, we are the opposite, rather than the same.'

'One good and one bad,' he said.

'Toby, stop. Show the girls around.'

We ran down through the backyard and whooped. It was a warm and lazy day, the smell of grass and warm earth hovering in the air. Toby took us to the barn behind the house, full of hay bales for Mrs. Winston's horses. We climbed onto the bales and Toby shoved one to the side and we saw a tunnel into the middle of the stack. He crawled in first and we followed. It was dusty inside and smelled a little of mildew. The hay was prickly on our legs, but when we stopped in an open space, the hay had been trampled down and was soft. Several bales above had been removed and light streamed in from the top.

Toby rummaged in his pockets and took out a pack of rolling papers. He produced a plastic bag from one of the hay bales and began to roll a cigarette with the dried grass in the bag.

'What's that?'

Toby didn't answer. He licked the edge along the cigarette and twisted the ends. He stuck it in his mouth and found a lighter stashed under one of the bales. He lit an end, inhaling. He coughed a little and handed it to us.

After we smoked some and coughed a bit ourselves, he said, 'It's peppermint tea.'

Then we laughed and laughed and convinced ourselves we had gotten high off the peppermint tea.

'Let's show him.' Dahlia said.

'No,' I hissed at her.

Toby spit into the palm of his hand and carefully put out the cigarette. His dark straight hair flopped over one green eye. 'What?' he asked. 'You have to show me.'

I glared at Dahlia and turned and crawled back through the hay until I stepped outside. Recently I had noticed a split in our *we* whenever we argued, and it terrified me more than anything. I stood outside the entrance and glared at her as soon as her head popped out.

'I'm not going to show him without you.'

We stared at each other, her eyes seeing her, my eyes seeing me.

'You make us freaks.'

'We are not freaks. We are interesting. Boys like twins.'

'We are like that cat with six toes. Or the man with three nipples.'

'Stop it. Toby's not like other people, we can show him.'

'We don't know him.'

'Don't you think he's different?'

'I...I like his eyes.'

'Eyes are the window to the soul. Come on...'

Dahlia held out her hand. I smiled. We became we again. We inched our way back to the hay room. We sat cross-legged, fingers entwined with Toby directly in front of us. We untied each others shoes, slipped them off. We rolled down each other's socks and removed them. Our toenails were pale pink with sparkles in them that caught the stream of light from above. We stretched out our feet in front of Toby.

At first he didn't see anything. We wiggled our toes and his face changed. He leaned toward our feet, close, until a lock of his shiny hair brushed the tips of our toes. We held hands tightly. This was the moment of truth: will he think we are freaks, like the six-toed cat? His eyes jumped back and forth. He reached out a finger and looked up at us to see that it was all right. We both nodded.

He touched our toes and we felt a spark. He pulled our toes apart and touched the web growing between. His fingertip started at the bottom, near the base of the toes and slowly moved up to the tip, between the two nails. Our legs shivered. He looked at us with disbelief and what we thought was disgust. We pulled our feet back and yanked on our socks, embarrassed, regretful, until we saw we had misunderstood him. His eyes shone at us in awe, and something more: his twelve-year-old heart had split in two, a side for each of us.

CHAPTER 3

THE EARTH MOVES

The Golden Gate Bridge is empty — deserted at 5:00 p.m., prime traffic time for the World Series. San Francisco vs. Oakland, but still, how can everyone in the Bay area be watching the game? The air is freakishly sultry without the slightest breeze. I smile into the warm air, feeling it move along my bare arms, privileged to witness such a surreal evening.

It doesn't matter how many times I drive over the bridge and into San Francisco, I always feel a magnetizing surge of energy. The absence of traffic will make me early to pick up Lorna from her gymnastics class and allow time for a quick walk on the beach. I speed past the ticket takers who have their tollbooth doors open, radios blaring. A man in a convertible, driving next to me, winks conspiratorially and I grin back, as if the two of us share an intimate secret.

The smile has not faded off my face when my car jumps. It twists and shakes. I slam on the brakes and the car chatters sideways and stops, but continues to bounce. Madness. I leap out of the car and the ground is shaking. I look at my tires, my mind slow to grasp what is happening, until I look back at the bridge and I see it swaying like a giant swing set. I fall to my knees and look around quickly to see if I am under something that can fall and crush me. My schooling taught me to stand in a doorway or crawl under a desk, it never told me what to do if I were in an earthquake on top of a bridge off-ramp.

The ticket takers run out of their booths, waving their arms. Two of them fall to the ground. The bridge is designed to move twenty-seven feet. I never thought I'd see it, surely it will crack. The ground stops moving, the bridge still swings awkwardly. Alarms shrill into the otherwise total silence. Nothing moves, there is an eerie stillness. Then the sirens start. Wailing from all directions. Several black clouds puff into the sky over Oakland. The sharp smell of my sweat tells me how frightened I am.

I run to my car, jump in and pull back into the right lane. The Marina District is now smothered in angry, billowing smoke. I take the first exit, searching for cracks in the road that would swallow me and my car. My legs are shaking, somehow managing to hit the pedals at the right moments. Mine is the only car on the road.

This is it, what I have been preparing for for years. I didn't know this is what I was waiting for, but now that it has happened, it is as if it were part of my plan all along. I drive not toward Lorna, but toward Fort Funston, where in the back of my brain, I've stored the knowledge of the perfect cliff. There are no traffic lights working and only a few cars driving cautiously. The drivers look at each other through the windshields with wide eyes.

When I get to the Fort's parking area, I am relieved to see that it is empty. I open the trunk and remove some of the clothes from my gym bag. Sweatpants, T-shirt and a zippered hoodie. My heart is beating so powerfully that I can hear nothing else, not even the slam of the trunk. I run down the hiking path to the ocean and veer off the main trail onto a small ragged track, for the more adventurous hikers who like a splash of water on their faces. I've been walking along these paths for years now. The track twists past the sign — *Hikers stay on designated paths / fine $250* — down the hill, steeper and steeper. I feel the pebbles crunch under my sandals, yet still no sound reaches my ears.

I stop above the perfect cliff. A sharp incline juts straight down to the water, ending in the jagged rocks. A slight miscalculation could make a foot slip, a body thrown off balance could waver, arms flailing, legs scissoring, before the plunge onto the rocks.

This cliff has been waiting for me for years. The currents below are violent, they strip victims of their clothing and destroy their bodies.

I unbutton my shirt and throw it over the edge. The red linen hangs in the air like a kite until it slowly drifts back towards me, landing three feet away. I pick it up and wrap a rock inside it and throw it again. This time it falls into the water, the red disappearing under the waves. I slide off my skirt and wrap a sandal inside of it. It hits the edge of a rock and bounces down. On impulse I unhook my bra and fling it away. It catches a breeze and traipses sideways across the rocks until a wave swoops up and claims it. The last sandal goes straight into the water. I stand nearly naked before the Pacific Ocean.

This is it. I feel light, as if I could float over the cliff and follow my red shirt. By freeing myself of my life, I have freed myself of her.

I put on my yoga clothes, shaking so hard it is nearly impossible to put my foot through the leg of my sweatpants. I have to sit down and try to calm myself. It's not just the earthquake, or the escape. A twin no longer. Remus killing

Romulous. A vanishing twin, fourteen years too late. Deep
breaths. I put my head between my knees and stare at the
ground. A twig blows under my legs and I watch it quiver in
the wind until it flies away.

She's gone.

I open my purse and remove the fake ID I always
carry with me. I have five of them now, but this is the one
registered with my bank. My safe deposit key is tucked away
inside the little snap area. I take it out and put the cord
around my neck. This is the most important part of the
plan. I open the cash partition of the wallet. Seven hundred
and ninety-one dollars. Plus the fifty from Toby's wallet and
the rest from my savings in the bank. I take out the money
and toss the wallet back into my purse.

I stand and wind up to throw my purse into the ocean,
but at the last second remembering that I wouldn't be
walking along the path with my purse, I would have locked
it in the trunk. I snatch it back to my chest. I am sure that if
someone investigates my death, they will find discrepancies,
but I am relying on other deaths of a more brutal nature.
And with the strong currents, there is a high probability my
body would never be found.

The parking lot is still deserted. I open the car and toss
my purse in the trunk. I rummage around for my gym shoes
and next to them is my Zanzibar box. Bigger than a bread
box, smaller than a carry on bag, in the shape of a treasure
chest with nearly a dozen drawers of varying sizes. I bought
it the previous weekend from a beautiful young boy at the
flea market. He ran after me holding out the box, without
saying a word. I was prepared to turn away until I saw the
intricate carving and solid brass hinges. He opened the lid
with a flourish, and my nose was hit with a peppery, orange-

blossom smell. I inhaled again and found the aroma of fresh earth and coffee. The third time it was fresh cut grass.

'A magician's box of smells,' I said.

'A Zanzibar chest, from the spice islands,' he said, and smiled a wide white smile. 'A box of lies.'

'I don't need a box of lies.'

He showed me the secret drawers and how to open them. 'You put your lies in the box and they will disappear.'

I laughed and bought it.

I grab the handle, haul it out and shove my sweatshirt into the main drawer, the passport and money into a side drawer. Slip on my shoes, slam the trunk, then I remember the car keys. The keys need to go into the ocean too. I lock the car and run back to the cliff, leaving the box at the beginning of the trail.

A huge wave crashes with momentous force, threatening to come up and over the rocks. The keys arch, landing smack in the water. Just for good measure, I make skid marks with my feet right where I would have slipped and scratch my fingers into the dirt. One more thing: my wedding ring. It skims through the air and sinks into the grey water. My lungs clench, squeezing out my breath, and I have to stop for a moment before running back. The wind is picking up and it gusts, pushing me from behind. Now there is a car on the other side of the parking lot. A couple stands kissing hard and groping. After the 1906 earthquake there was a surge of marriages and births, people bonded together by the disaster, desperate to leave a piece of themselves for the future.

I grab the box and skirt around the edge of the parking lot in the bushes. The couple is engrossed and don't notice a thing. In fact they are perfect witnesses for the car being parked there when they arrived, except I don't think they are aware of anything outside their own lips.

I run down the hill, holding my box like an oversized football. It's happening, I'm doing it. Pushed by an inside strength, a guiding force I never knew I had, I speed toward the airport. I don't let my mind rest on Toby or Lorna. They hover in the corner of my thoughts and I push them away, concentrating on the up and down of my legs as I run. Once I'm on 19th Avenue, I can hitchhike to a hotel near the airport. Away from the city center where anyone might see me.

It feels good to run, it takes out the wobbles from my legs and adjusts my breathing. In less than half an hour I am on the streets of San Francisco. There are only a few people around. A knot of people stand on a street corner listening to a hand-held radio. The signal lights are still out. People walk by me, eyes wide, making eye contact, saying nothing. There is a man standing on the sidewalk in front of me, holding the side of his head, which is bleeding.

He looks like my father, Val. I stop and slowly face him. It's not Val. He's simply a tall old man. I grimace and keep going. A block later, I stop. It occurs to me that I may never see Val again. I will be dead to him. I turn around and race back to the old man. I keep my head down, everyone I see reminds me of someone I know, someone who could identify me. He has hobbled a few steps and is now leaning against a telephone pole. There is a good sized bump on his head trickling drops of red onto the sleeve of his khaki jacket.

'Please, can I help you?'

'No, thank you,' he says with certainty.

'You're bleeding.'

He touches his hand to his head. I open the main drawer in my box and take out my sweatshirt, the only spare clothing I have with me. I hold it to his head and dab it. It looks sore. A truck stops near us and I think it's my neighbor in the passenger seat, but when I sneak another glance, the man looks nothing like him.

'Damn earthquake knocked me right over.'

'Do you live near here?'

He looks around and squints. 'Looks too clean to be China.'

'No, it's San Francisco.'

'I don't live in San Francisco.'

'Do you have a wallet?'

'Why?' He looks at me suspiciously.

'I'm not going to rob you, I'm trying to help you.'

'You have to be careful in this neighborhood.'

I would like nothing more than to walk away from him, but I feel as though I am walking away from Val and this keeps me standing in front of the old man. I wave my sweatshirt at a car driving towards us, trying to hide my face behind the old man at the same time. When the car slows down near the stop sign, I knock on the window. A Volvo with a lady and a kid in the front.

'Can you please take us near the hospital?'

I can see the lady doesn't really want to go in that direction, but to refuse in front of her child would not be a good example.

'My father...has bumped his head. Thank you so much for stopping.'

The old man looks around for my father and frowns at me. Why did I lie? I don't even call my own father, father. It has always been Val. Lying comes so naturally to me — it's not even necessary and I lie.

She nods. 'Please, get in the car.'

We slide into the back seat.

'I am not so weak, am I?' The man holds up his scrawny arm and points to his bicep. 'That damn earthquake knocked me right over.'

The boy from the front says, 'He said damn, Mom.'

'He's injured, we're going to the hospital.'

'When I'm injured, I can curse?'

'Me, a grown man, thrown to the ground.' The old man holds up his arm again and flexes. 'Knocked over by nature.'

The car pulls up at the hospital, not in the emergency lane, it's full of ambulances with sirens blaring and red lights flashing. I help the old man out of the car and lean in the passenger window.

'Thank you so much...and don't worry about the cursing, it's an unusual time right now.'

'I hope your father is all right.' They wave goodbye.

We walk around the ambulances and into the door. He is gaping at the lights with his mouth open. Inside, the hospital is full of people much worse off than this old man. I seat him on top of a coffee table, next to a boy holding a bloody bandage over one eye. I go to the registration desk. There is a crowd of people around the desk: a girl clutching her arm bent at an impossible angle, a fat man covered in deep scratches who is holding onto his knee with a piece of glass protruding from it, and a lady holding a squirming child in her arms and a bloody bandage around her neck. All the nurses and doctors are wearing yellow construction helmets.

Now I am afraid that someone in the hospital will recognize me. Is that Lorna's friend's mother over by the desk? I know she's a nurse. Toby's great uncle is a doctor. He works somewhere in San Francisco. It is quite a while before I can grab one of the nurses and get a form for the old man. When I return, he is no longer sitting on the coffee table.

The boy with the bloody eye stares at me with his one good eye. Kids often see what adults cannot. When Lorna was a baby, barely able to walk, she came into our room one night with a fever. I lifted her onto the bed and she wiggled right over to Toby even though he was asleep. I think she always knew I would leave. Kids are geniuses with some things.

I tell myself she will not remember me, she is too young. She will have a photo of me and she will make memories from other people's memories and this will be the me she remembers. The thing that kills me is that it will not even be me she remembers — it will be me as Dahlia. This is what makes me able to leave Toby and Lorna, the fact that it is not me they know. I am no longer a mother or a wife or a sister. A vein in my head starts to pound and I have to grab onto the nurses' station with both hands, my head suddenly too light. A nurse leans over and tries to take one of my hands, but I can't let go of the desk and kaleidoscopic specks pinwheel in front of my eyes and I scream before everything turns black.

The back of my head hurts. I am lying on something chilly and hard. I open my eyes to see a group of people standing over me. There is a lot of blood on them. A doctor kneels next to me holding onto my wrist, checking the pulse and next to him is the young girl holding her lopsided arm. I stare at the crowd staring at me and try to take in all their injuries. I bolt upright and the doctor grabs my shoulders and tries to push me back down.

'You fainted. Nearly hit the floor,' he says. 'He saved

you.' He points to a fat man behind him, the one with the glass in his knee.

'You still bumped your head on the wall,' the fat man replies apologetically.

'The old man,' I say.

They look at each other and shrug their shoulders. I stand up and look over at the table where I left the man.

The kid with one eye tugs on my arm. 'He told me not to trust anyone and then he ran outside.'

My eyes tear and I push the kid away and stagger outside. I look up and down the street, but he is nowhere to be seen. I throw the hospital form in the trash and gingerly touch the back of my head.

I stand in the parking lot and watch the ambulances tearing into the parking lot. There is a line of them before the emergency doors, sirens wailing. I think about hitchhiking back to my car and back to my life, but my feet walk in the opposite direction, toward the freeway entrance and closer to the airport and my bank.

I will follow my plan and head south to the Switzerland of the Americas: Panama. Bank accounts, no questions asked. Crooks, bamboozlers, carpet baggers – they all flock there. And deserters. Me. Powered by dollars and Columbian drug deals, Panama City wallows in its corruption, smolders in its heat. It is there I will deposit my carefully hoarded cash and IDs. It's there I will begin a new life.

At the stoplight ahead of me, there is a group of people talking to drivers about rides. All public transportation is stopped. I have no idea how bad the earthquake damage is, but judging from the sirens and smoke billowing over the city, it must have been a big one. I stick out my thumb and stand before the light. An old four-door Chevy pulls over to

the curb, the back door swinging open. There are already
five inside, three in the front and two in the back. I crawl in.

The car sparks with adrenaline. Everyone is talking at
once, where they were and how it felt. How the earth moved
for them. I don't think anyone felt it as profoundly as I did.
I would never have had the motivation necessary to leave
on my own. I would have staggered through my life until I
killed myself.

The driver, a young girl, holds up her hand and looks at
it. 'I am still shaking,' she says.

I keep quiet. I am searching inside myself for Dahlia: Is
she still there? Is it only me now, only me to live my life and
make my own mistakes? I want to make a lot of mistakes.

A Latina woman sitting next to me sobs periodically as
she talks nonstop.

'I was cleaning the drawers in the bedroom, Senor and
Senora Dickson's room, when there was a crack like I've
never heard and a noise like the house were hit by a truck
and the whole room moved, it moved to the side and fell
and the drawers came across the room, me in front of them
and they trapped me to the wall, *sob*, there was a window
and I didn't want to break Senor Dickson's window but I
had to so I took the lampshade off the lamp and unscrewed
the bulb so I wouldn't break the bulb and hit the window
with the lamp and I screamed and a man came and he
walked right up to the window, the second story window,
and he said the street sank and he leaned in the window and
pushed the drawer away from me and helped me outside
and I couldn't breathe, *sob*, the foundation was gone and
the house was sideways and I hurt everywhere and it wasn't
my fault and I have to get home to my children but they are
in Oakland and there is no more bridge they tell me, *sob*, oh
God my children...!'

We careen down the highway, the driver holding up her hand every so often to monitor the shaking.

They drop me off at an airport hotel. The lobby is in chaos, luggage stacked in all corners and people swarming around the reception desk, yelling and gesturing. A hotel maid passes out bottles of water and chocolate bars to the guests. I hear strains of piano music and through an interior door I see the bar is packed with people, dozens of candles lit. A piano man, dressed in a shiny, square-shouldered tuxedo, plays while two women stand in front of him, arms around each other, singing an old show tune.

A young bell-boy, perhaps attracted by my yoga attire and intricately carved wooden box, approaches me. He looks me in the eye briefly and then his vision skitters across the room. He is shy, made brave by the extreme circumstances.

'Can I help you?'

'Yes, a room, please.'

'I'm sorry. They are reserved for stranded airline customers.'

'I am a stranded airline customer.'

'Can I see your ticket?'

'I don't have it. I don't even have a purse. I'm really stranded.'

He puffs out his cheeks and looks up at the ceiling.

'The ticket is at the airport. There is no electricity, so they couldn't print it.'

'Luggage?' he asks hopefully.

'This is it.' I hold out the Zanzibar box. 'My life is destroyed,' I say and my eyes tear up. It's true, my life is destroyed.

He walks to the desk and talks to the manager in a short sleeve dress shirt and red power tie. The manager looks up at me and I catch his eye, hoping the tears are still shimmering in my eye. The bell-boy walks back to me.

'There really are no rooms, you can see for yourself.'

He motions to all the people in the lobby.

'But where will they go?'

He shrugs, avoids my eyes and walks off.

A radio, must be battery powered, feverishly runs on about the Marina, sunk in some areas, Victorian homes tipped over and flames everywhere. The Bay Bridge collapsed, the Oakland freeway pan-caked. I will be one more person lost in the devastation. My escape has been planned for years, but the quickness with which I drove and abandoned my car, my family, my life…it shocks me. I didn't know if I would have the guts to do it. And maybe I don't. Maybe in the morning I will go home. I can imagine the tears and hugs, their faces tight with worry.

I don't know what to do with myself so I cross the room and slump down next to a table with an enormous flower arrangement. On the other side is a young couple resting their heads together, eyes closed. The flower arrangement seems so normal, so out of place in the upheaval that I want to knock it over.

Someone shakes me on my shoulder and I open my eyes to find the bellboy handing me a sandwich and a bottle of water. He moves on, passing them around to the people in the lobby who have settled against the walls and on the floor. I eat my sandwich and immediately after realize that I have no idea what I ate.

The next morning I wake curled around my Zanzibar box. I hear the sound of jets landing one after another. The airport has reopened. Sirens continue to pierce the air. I try not to let my mind wander and concentrate on calmly,

methodically making a list of what I have to do. Bank.
Supplies. Airport. The sun seems to have a dark filter over
it, a doomsday veil blocking out the real light and once
I smell the smoke and see the dark cloud of it above, my
panic returns.

Across the overpass is my bank and next to it is one
of those huge discount import stores, the ones that have
everything from canned salsa to chipped ceramic Santas.
To get there I have to go across the overpass, I don't see
any other way to get to the other side. I stand at the cusp
of the overpass and gaze to the other side, envisioning the
collapse, the disintegration the same as the Bay Bridge. I
walk to where the bridge starts and line up my toes on the
last piece of concrete attached to land. My heart pounds and
I feel silly, but it's not like it's an impossibility – yesterday
it happened. Then I run like hell. About half way over, my
shaking legs give out and I stumble to my knees, my box
thudding onto the ground. I hit the cement hard and pull
myself over to the rail, gasping. A man driving by stops and
leans out of his car.

'Hey, you need some help? You okay?'

His hair is disheveled and it looks as though he is
wearing his pajama top. I shake my head no and wave him
on. When I am calm enough to stand, I restart my venture
over the overpass. This time there is no panic, in fact I am
ultra calm. One foot in front of the other, back straight,
arms tight until I reach the other side.

Inside the bank it's quiet, only a few people in view. I
fill out the request form for access to my safe deposit box
and head for the teller. A squeaking noise follows me across
the floor and it is only when I reach the teller and the noise

stops that I realize it is my shoes on the marble floor. The young woman behind the counter glances up with a worried look. She has large breasts that rest on the counter and her bra is too small, they bubble over the edge of material and I wonder if there are red marks on them at night, after she has removed the straps. She takes my form and my fake CA ID. Melissa Irine Kensington. Died as a child in 1969. Reborn in 2005, courtesy of the library death records and my cunning lies at the passport office.

'Miss Kensington, please follow me.'

Her shoes hit the floor with a crisp clack. I follow behind trying to walk so my shoes don't squeak so loudly.

'I hope your family was safe yesterday,' she says.

'No family...just me in my home,' I reply. Lying again for no reason. I feel empty after my breakdown on the overpass. 'A couple of pictures off the walls, shaken, but no problems. And you?'

'It was just horrible. I arrived home and my nanny and kids were locked in the basement. She's from Kansas and apparently thought it was a tornado, so she took them down there and the door shut and they couldn't get out. Can you imagine?'

She opens the door and unlocks the security box and places it on a narrow table in the middle of the room.

'My husband was at the game. He said when those grandstands moved, the man next to him peed his pants. They all thought they were dead.'

She doesn't want to leave, she wants to talk it out. Everybody needs to tell their story. I wonder if anyone will ever hear mine.

'Can you imagine, you pay a fortune to go to this game thinking you're going to a historical game when it turns out the only thing historic is the earthquake.'

She realizes I haven't said a word for a while and blushes.
'I'm really sorry, I can't seem to stop talking.' Her eyes well
with tears. 'God help us...' She blinks her eyes rapidly and
walks out.

I open the security box and take out the IDs. Five of
them. Four passports and one more CA ID. This is the one
I will use to travel to Panama. Then I take out the envelope
with the cash. $33,700. Plus the remaining $841 from my
wallet. I stare at everything. This is my new life. Not a mint,
but enough for a start. The money is wrapped inside a white
plastic grocery bag. I flatten the bills so they fit into the
bottom drawer of my Zanzibar box and tuck the IDs into a
side drawer. Nothing is visible from the outside, but it feels
as though I am flaunting a lot of cash, inviting a robbery.
I buzz to be let out and woman reminds me to renew my
contract for the security box.

The parking lot for the store next door is full. Helicopters
cruise the periphery of the smoke, circling outside San
Francisco. Inside the store people are swarming, buying
bottled water, batteries and bandages. It's not a war, I want
to yell – it was an earthquake.

There is a large underwear section. I stare at the bras. I
picture the amount of money I have and how big my bra will
be to fit it all inside. I grab several size DD's and head for
the changing rooms where the sales lady counts the hangers,
unlocks the door and doesn't blink at my choice of bras.

I hook the massive bra around my torso and take
a handful of cash and shove it into one of the cups and
frown. I am not one of these women who yearn for Pamela
Andersons. I put on my old T-shirt over the new bra.
No, I will need a new shirt to accommodate my two new
additions. I am not a large woman and these breasts look

obscene. However, I do see the appeal, they make my hips appear miniscule and I feel like a walking sex organ.

The store also has a section of clothing, not much, a dozen oversized T-shirts in bright yellow, my least favorite color. The seams are not perfect and they twist off to the side, but for $6.99, I take one. X-large. A cotton skirt, a tank top, toiletries and a few pairs of underwear. And a pair of hot pink flip-flops. Scissors. The idea of becoming a new person makes me giddy.

Back at the hotel, I realize I don't have any luggage. My wall has been claimed so I find a new space and sit down. I pull open the drawers in my Zanzibar box and shove the toiletries into the top drawers. In the middle section I put the skirt and underwear. I manage to squeeze the flip-flops together and fit them into one of the narrow deep drawers. It all fits, barely.

I sneak into the staff bathroom and look at the scissors. They are encased in the kind of plastic that you need scissors to open. There is nothing in the room that can pierce the plastic. I try heating up the plastic under hot water and ripping it open. I jam it into the door lock and twist it. It cracks.

In one of those women's magazines I read that the easiest way to cut hair into layers is to pick it up in a ponytail above your head and cut straight across. I pull my hair up and freeze, looking at myself in the mirror. This is it. This to me is the limit — if I do this, there is no going back.

I start cutting. The scissors don't work very well, cheap and not sharp. As I hack away, I feel the split ends already. When I am done, I have a large pile of light brown hair on the floor and a ragged hair cut, shorter in the back near the crown of my head. Screw that magazine.

Standing in front of the mirror, I put on the bra. The bra stands out on its own, it's made of heavy elastic material. I take the money out of the envelope, bend it in two and shove it in. My boob is lopsided. The second method works better: roll the bills into sort of a cone shape with the pointy part facing out. Shoulders back, a little heaving of the breasts, it works.

The sirens haven't stopped. Even in the bathroom I can hear them. I stuff toilet paper in my ears and look at myself in the mirror and this makes me cry. I cry for all the dead and maimed and homeless and broken. And I cry for myself and my family. I cry for my twin.

It's a horrible thing I've done. The grief I will cause my family and friends. Grief has an odd effect on people. It binds people and throws unlikely couples together. I can only hope it will throw Toby and the nanny together. Disasters bring out emotions. Toby may crack open in a moment of vulnerability.

I splash cold water on my face, avoid my eyes in the mirror and square my shoulders. I pick up my Zanzibar box and walk out the door.

CHAPTER 4

TOBY TALKS

When I think back on the day I met the twins, I can replay the details over and over in my head like a movie. I bet if I asked Dahlia for her version, the details would be completely different. Memory is distorted by retelling and I've gone over that day so many times — God knows what sort of facts I've concocted. I'd like to ask Dahlia, but I won't.

We don't talk about anything from the past...it's as if our childhood never existed.

I was twelve years old, new kid in the neighborhood, and my mother thought she'd do me a favor by introducing me to a friend. A neighborly lunch. She did not account for two girls next door, let alone twins and the effect twins have on young boys. I was so intrigued by the two of them I couldn't keep quiet. I asked them a million questions: 'Do you have the same dreams?' 'Can you read each other's minds?' 'If I pinch one, can the other feel it?' They frowned at me with duplicate frowns, with identical muscles moving in their foreheads. I zoomed in on their eyebrows and even the hairs sprouted from the same pores.

My mother sized up their mother as soon as she walked through the doorway to our house, while Chloe took her time, darting glances in my mother's direction and squinting her eyes when my mother spoke. Our mothers were both modern opinionated women and they would have been great friends if they hadn't both been alpha females. The twins' mother was a cool intellectual and she had no time for my mother's catty comments, her jokes about the neighbors, her put downs of the local fashion. The first time the twins called their mother Chloe instead of Mother or Mom, my mother's nostrils flared in resentment. I knew they would never be friends.

From that afternoon on, my mother wore full battle gear whenever she was around Chloe: polished nails, blood red lipstick, coiffed shiny locks, and tight skirts that showed off her shapely calves. My mother was 'racy'. Coco. She loved her men and she loved her vodka. And she loved me — she was jealous as hell.

My mother arranged for two weeks in Saint Petersburg the winter I met the twins. She wore a white fur coat with a hood and drank shots of vodka every night. She flirted with the waiters, the maitre d', the chef. She poured me a vodka and when I told her I didn't like it, she mixed it with orange juice and ice and handed it back to me. I became boisterous and joked with her as if she were one of the twins. She laughed hoarsely and told the waiter I was a bad boy. When we went to bed, she clutched my arm, called me Pumpkin, saying she couldn't sleep alone. I leaned over and threw up.

A year or so after I met the twins, one chilly autumn day — the kind of day that as an adult saps your strength and makes you shiver, but as a child energizes you and you run and leap and shout — we collapsed on the lawn. We sat panting and watched the twins' father, Val, raking the red and yellow leaves into a pile to burn for a bonfire party that evening.

Dahlia lay back with a piece of flat grass between her thumbs making a shrill whistle. Hetta sat perfectly still with her tongue sticking straight out into the air, drying a tiny white canker sore. Chloe had told her to rinse her mouth with hot salt water, but those twins were rebels and didn't like anyone telling them what to do. Hetta felt me looking at her and opened her eyes wide. We gazed at each other and she slowly withdrew her tongue back into her chapped lips, between her even white teeth. I felt a tug in my groin and inhaled sharply — my first erotic memory.

Hetta asked, 'When was the first time you knew there was no Santa Claus?'

She was always asking these types of questions that made people stop and think and chuckle. The twins were raised with no religion, no belief in Christmas, yet they still had Santa.

Val gathered the leaves into one huge pile, singing an old show tune. My mother said she didn't trust a man who knew all the words to *West Side Story*. But I noticed it didn't stop her from standing too close to him and touching his arm with her red fingernails. Val tossed the leaves in the air and struck a pose. Neither of the twins looked at him. He was always in the spotlight, even if he was alone.

It had occurred to me that even though he was tall and old and handled the rake with dexterity, he was still a child himself. He didn't belong in the adult category, yet he was too old to be one of us.

'The only reason we had Santa was because Dad liked to dress up as a fat man and say *hohoho* to impress all his friends sitting in the living room sipping bourbon and mocking us,' Dahlia said loud enough for Val to hear her.

He walked over and sat on the grass and swatted at Dahlia's feet with the rake. 'Don't tell me you didn't enjoy it.'

'I am not saying that we didn't enjoy it at the time, but I am stating why you did it, which had nothing to do with us.'

Val stood up angrily. 'I don't know where you learned to read minds...we should put you in a circus and make some money off you.'

Dahlia's animosity toward her father was just getting started at that point. Those two were just too much alike and when we dislike a quality in someone that we have ourselves, we detest them for it.

'I live in a circus,' Dahlia taunted.

He turned and strode back to the house. Stuck to the back of his pants was a stick, straight up and down the middle of his ass, with a red leaf attached to the top, waving with each indignant step. Dahlia started laughing so hard she couldn't speak. She pointed and we looked and laughed, rolling around on the grass. He threw us a disappointed look before slamming the door.

I liked Val. Maybe it was because I didn't have a father. At least they had one and even if he wasn't around much, he tried to be with them when he was there. My father sent my mother bank deposits two times a year. He had another family, a real family that lived in the same house as him and shared dinners and family squabbles.

There was a tinkling of a bell and a muffled thump in Val's pile of leaves. Hetta, who had been facing the pile, jumped up and stared with her eyes wide, a clear white circling the warm brown center. She looked up into the sky and I followed her gaze. A bright sky, unblemished except for a few white wisps streaked across the center and a hawk circling above.

'It fell from the sky.' Hetta's face was drained of color under her summer tan.

'What fell from the sky?'

'I don't know. You heard it too.'

We stared at the pile. The leaves shifted and something cried softly.

'Oh God, it's alive,' said Dahlia.

Hetta backed away. 'It's from outer space.'

The twins held onto each others arms. I grabbed the rake and moved some of the leaves away. There was a yelp and a small animal ran out of the pile and under a low patio table. There we found a curly-haired black dog with a white patch over one eye. It wore a collar that jingled faintly as it cowered, shaking, its eyes moving back and forth, tail thumping the ground.

Hetta looked up. 'That dog fell from the sky.'

'Don't be silly,' I said.

'I saw it. It dropped down. Where do you think it came from? The tree?'

We looked back at the leaves and up. There wasn't a tree branch growing over the pile. Anyway, how would a small dog get into the tree? Hetta crawled under the table and held out her hand to the dog. It growled and flattened against the stone wall. She murmured to it in a low voice and it sniffed her carefully before sticking out its pink tongue and anointing her with its saliva. 'We've never had a dog before.'

'It's not your dog,' I pointed out. 'It has a collar.'

They both glanced sideways at me and then ignored my comment. After a few moments the dog sidled over and took refuge in Hetta's lap. Dahlia slid under the table and the two of them stroked the dog. She held up her hand and it was smudged with blood.

'It's hurt,' she said.

Chloe walked out of the house carrying one of those thick books written by someone foreign. She was never without one of them tucked under her arm or held up to shade the sun. She was dressed in tight black trousers with a sheer blouse, a large stone at her throat and deep pink lipstick. She looked great, but not right for a bonfire party. It was something I'd noticed before: when they threw parties, she wore an outfit that was out of place. When I look back on it now, it must have been a rebellion against Val and his hordes of jovial friends. She bent over and looked under the table. She tossed the book on the ground and crawled under there with the twins, not caring about the knees of her tight black trousers.

The three Carter women huddled under the table with the little black dog for a long time. I lay on my stomach across the table and hung my head upside down to watch them. They looked so cozy under there, and happy, as if all they needed in the world was themselves and a table to huddle under.

Eventually the puppy forgot his recent trauma and began to frolic and roll onto his back. Chloe inspected the puppy's wounds and shook her head. She crawled out from under the table and looked up at the sky. It looked the same, wispy clouds in a brilliant blue.

'There's the culprit,' she said and pointed at the hawk circling above us.

'The bird?'

'It's a hawk. This little guy was its dinner.'

We watched the bird circle above us. It made me dizzy to watch it. I imagined I was the puppy, caught in the hawk's sharp talons, struggling in the sky, the trees and houses specks below me.

'We can keep him, can't we?' Hetta asked.

'He's someone's pet.'

Dahlia tilted her head back. 'But the hawk could have come from anywhere.'

We all looked back at the sky as if it held the dog's address.

'We need to clean his wounds.' Chloe examined his scraped paw and the cut on his mouth that made him look like a blood-sucking vampire dog, then she went into the house for some antiseptic.

We sat cross-legged in a circle with the puppy in the middle. The puppy sniffed a few times at his wounds, tried half-heartedly to lick them and then forgot about them. He loped around and climbed onto our legs and peed on Hetta's shoe. She didn't mind, she laughed and threw the shoe into the middle of the lawn.

'We'll name him Bird,' Hetta declared.

'You can't name a dog Bird,' I said.

Dahlia took Hetta's hand in hers and they both looked at me. 'His name is Bird,' Dahlia said defiantly.

'Where's the collar?' I asked.

The twins looked at each other and shrugged.

'The collar with the bell?'

I pinched one of them on the arm and the other one grabbed her arm as if she were in pain. I fell in love — again. It happened often with those two. Each day I fell in love over and over. As an only child it seemed so perfect to get two instead of one. If only I could have predicted that the two great shames of my life would be connected to those twins.

'You can't tell anyone.'

'Who the hell would I tell?'

Dahlia held out her clenched fist and dropped the collar and bell into the palm of my hand. I examined the bell. It had writing on it. Muffin. On the back was an address. I squinted at it, it sounded familiar.

'Isn't this where —'

Hetta grabbed the collar from me. 'You can't tell.'

Dahlia dug into the dirt in front of us with her nails, scraping at the leaves and soil. The puppy joined in and when she had a small hole, Hetta dropped in the collar. They piled the dirt back in and pounded it down with the heels of their hands and sprinkled leaves over the top.

'I won't.'

'Promise us,' Dahlia said.

'Jesus Christ, I promise.'

'Seal it.' Hetta grabbed my arm. 'In honor of Bird.'

We all looked at each other.

'Stick out your tongues,' I ordered.

The twins stuck out their tongues at me. Goddamn it, even their tongues were the same. I leaned into the circle and we all touched tongues, waggling them around like tiny eels.

'In honor of Bird,' I said.

'In honor of Bird,' they repeated in unison and smiled happily.

The hawk circled above and later on I would recall this as one of those pure bliss moments that only comes along a few times in life.

Once I was introduced to those twins, I held every girl and woman I met up to their image. I wonder if this is what happens to pedophiles — they get stuck with their adolescent sexual desires and never grow beyond them, even though their bodies age and their hair falls out.

In my pubescent mind, I had it all figured out that I could have sex with both the twins. I saw no obstacle in this: first Dahlia — she was more adventurous — and then

Hetta later, when she was ready. I would wait forever for her. She was the one I loved. Dahlia refused to see me after the death. I hung around their house, swinging on the tire under the oak tree or sitting on the edge of their lawn, tears bouncing down my cheeks. I could still cry then.

My guilt ate away at me. I never told anyone what I had said to Hetta before she ran in front of that truck. The only other person I've ever said I love you to was Dahlia, when she told me she was pregnant — and then I slapped her. I had never realized that the childhood memory of Hetta slapping me, after my first ever declaration of love, was so fresh in my mind after all those years.

And so attached to the words I love you.

That's the first shame of my life and no one ever knew what happened that night. How can a boy tell someone that seconds after he confessed his love, the girl ran straight into the middle of the street and killed herself? They called it an accident. It wasn't a goddamn accident. I killed her by uttering three words. She turned around and looked at me and darted straight into those two blinding headlights. Brakes howling, the driver screaming at her and the odor of burning rubber that I still smell in my dreams.

The night of Hetta's death I sat on the grass, in the no man's land, between my house and theirs. The crickets were loud, screeching, and I welcomed the noise, it helped to block out the replay of Hetta that reverberated in my mind. I watched her bedroom window and rocked back and forth without blinking. Dahlia's guilt could only rival mine. She would blame herself for leaving Hetta alone with me. She would blame herself for the extra bond that opened between us when Hetta was sick. She would see herself as the ultimate murderer.

I must have fallen asleep because I was awakened by something in the garden. The night was lit by a perfect half moon. The noise started again and I swept my eyes through the shadowed garden seeing nothing. Then I saw her. She was under the massive oak tree in their garden, doing something to the swings. I moved into a crouch position and crawled toward her so that if she did anything dangerous to herself, I would be there.

I saw from her ghostly glow that she was naked. It looked so natural in Chloe's garden, as if it were grown for nudity. Even with the blow of Hetta's death, I felt myself grow so hard that the urge to throw off my clothes and shove myself deep into Dahlia was nearly uncontrollable. But then I saw her methodically sawing the rope off the swing seats. Her skin shifted under the moonlight and I saw how vulnerable human bodies are. No thorns or fur or armor. Her skin was so thin I could nearly see her blood and bones. I wanted desperately to protect her.

When the second swing fell to the ground, she stood for a moment and then went to the tree and climbed it. She straddled the big branch that ran horizontal out from the trunk and began to chisel at it with a tool. She seemed to be digging a hole and when she finished, she plucked off some moss and shoved it into the hole. Then she swung her legs behind her and lowered herself down onto the tree limb, wrapping her arms around it. She didn't cry or make a noise. She just lay there motionless. I stood and started toward her, but her naked vulnerability and distrust of my own primitive urges held me back, so I sat quietly and watched over her.

After an hour or so, she sat up and climbed back down and drifted over the lawn to the house and up to her room where she turned off the light. I know I shouldn't have, but

I did. I climbed her tree and pulled out the moss from inside the hole. Inside were two tiny stones. I held them up to the moon and could see through them. I put one back inside and took the other one. It felt as though I had a part of Hetta in my hand.

I meant to tell Dahlia next time I spoke to her. How was I to know it would be an eternity?

On the morning of Hetta's funeral, I kept watch on Dahlia's bedroom window and saw her move from one side to the other, pausing in the middle to gaze outside. I knew she would try to kill herself. I watched until there was no more movement in her room and I ran into the house. It was quiet inside, I don't know where her parents were. I found her in Hetta's room, in Hetta's closet. She was held up by a belt and her face was purple. When I released her, her arms and legs convulsed like we did when we choked each other for fun, but this time her eyes did not open. They took her away to the hospital where no one could see her and that was my last visit with her, unconscious and nearly dead.

Chloe withdrew when Hetta died. Physically she was there, she removed the lacquer from the floor and repainted walls, but when I spoke to her, she looked through me, puzzled, as if I were something she had forgotten about and couldn't quite remember. I'd see her staring at a fencepost or the door for an hour or so, no expression on her face, in a trance.

I tried to engage her by going to the library and checking out books with foreign names, anything French, Spanish or Russian. I left the books around her house to see if she would pick them up or start to read them, but she left them untouched.

I never regretted our affair. At the age of seventeen I was in love with all of them, all those Carter women in one way or another. Chloe was the leader of the pack at that time. Those twins adored her. When I first had sex with Chloe, it was as though I had sex with all of them at once, it was that powerful. As an adult, when I look back on the situation, it must have driven Chloe mad to see the twins growing up so beautiful and sexy, just as it will drive me mad when Lorna reaches puberty and all I want to do is protect her from boys like me.

After Hetta's death, I turned into a monster fueled by whiskey and drugs, vicious to my own mother straight through to her death. She died four years later in a quick bout of cancer and I swore I would never leave the house. I vowed to live there forever, wishing I had been a better son, one who her made her tea with two sugars and milk, and took her glass bottles to the recycling plant when the box was full. Instead, I drank and smoked and whored, flaunting it all in her worn face while she was still alive.

This downhill spiral stopped when I saw Dahlia at Chloe's funeral. She saved my life just as I saved hers so many years ago. I knew she would never say no if I proposed — she didn't. Dahlia had changed, she never did go back to the girl I used to know before Hetta died. I guess I never went back either. It was a case of needing something so badly and then when I got it, it wasn't at all what I had imagined.

I used to worry that Dahlia would run off again like she did before. I was so impressed that she could just make a decision, leave everything behind and start a new life. What an admirable talent. I wish I could do the same, but the guilt will never leave me, even if I run as far as Timbuktu.

I tried to love Dahlia and I think I had her fooled, but Hetta lived between us all those years. Hetta had been the glue that kept the three of us together, smoothing out arguments and laughing away our petty grievances. Hetta was the one I lived my life for and the one I saw in my future. Hetta was the one I loved. Dahlia always seemed so tight inside, as if she were going to split in two. The only way to tell them apart was to tease them. Dahlia would spit right back, but Hetta, she'd get a little flustered and sometimes she'd blush.

I don't know why Hetta charged in front of that truck. I've replayed the scenario a million times in my head and in my nightmares. I hear the words from my lips — *I love you.* I feel the slap of her smooth hand on my cheek and I hear the sounds of her feet crushing the dry leaves as she runs out onto the road.

The other shame of my life is Lorna. Not Lorna herself, but her conception — Can a man rape his own wife? What I did to Dahlia because she wasn't Hetta. She could never be Hetta. It's because of Lorna that life righted itself, so it can't be too bad, can it?

Can it?

When Dahlia died in the earthquake I felt the guilt all over again. Every time I lay down in my bed, Hetta's face in the headlights appeared before me. If I started to drift off, her slap would fling me out of my bed. If Madeline the nanny hadn't been around, I don't know how Lorna would have eaten or made it to school. She took charge of the household as though she had been preparing to her whole life. I see so much of the twins in Lorna that sometimes I feel they are living inside her.

CHAPTER 5

PANAMA, THE BEGINNING

Cars line the airport curbs. I step out of the taxi and look north where a shifting black cloud plumes over San Francisco. I look away, guilty for deserting my city in its time of disaster. My city and my family. I am doing what those shysters on the news do, the ones who fake their deaths to get out of debt or dead marriages. My eyes snake back to the dark sky. The end of the world. The end of my world.

Inside, the airport is chaos. Poor San Francisco. A bad earthquake and all the immigrants and Midwesterners want to abandon ship. People are wide-eyed, nervous, they want eye contact, they want to commiserate about the disaster. Emotions are raw and everyday masks are dropped from faces. I stand clutching my box and looking around.

Luggage and children are stacked in one pile, with the adults patrolling the outside like pioneers encircling their wagons. Bodies are sprawled against every wall, people resting their heads on purses, sweaters, necks kinked onto their bags. One woman is sitting cross-legged on her coat practicing yoga.

I find the Air Panama counter. No lineup. Panamanians are not trying to escape. They are braver than most. The man behind the counter has thick grey-speckled hair and direct-line eye contact with my breasts. I slouch below the counter and place my fake ID on the counter and ask for the first flight to Panama City. He types away efficiently.

'How many bags are you checking?'

Shit. The bag again. Makes me immediately suspect. 'None. Carry on.'

He leans around the corner of the counter and looks at my box.

'Running away?' he frowns.

I drop my passport, I pick it up, I drop my cash, I pick it up, and then I realize he is asking me this not because he thinks I am fleeing my family, but because he thinks I am fleeing California.

'No, no,' I protest and laugh shrilly. 'Just a holiday.'

'A holiday,' he grins. 'Don't miss Casco Viejo. It's not for everyone, but you look like the type who would enjoy it.'

'I look different?' This is fine, just so I don't look like myself.

'These people,' his eyes dart around the airport, 'they're deserters. In a war, the maximum penalty is death. They should be banned from returning, even for a holiday.'

'Good riddance,' I say. 'Can I have a window seat?'

The security line is long and I steal glances at everyone while trying to avert my face. Once again, everyone looks like someone I know. Aunt Celia has a face recognition problem. It's not that she doesn't recognize faces, it's that she recognizes everyone and every person she sees on the street looks like a celebrity or a neighbor. She can pick out the tiniest detail on someone. For example, she'll say, that guy, the one with the hot dog, he looks like George Clooney. And I'll say, are you nuts? No, she'll say, look at his

mouth. I'll stare at his mouth chewing on the hot dog and
then I can see a little something that reminds me of George.
Then she points out that between his nose and nonexistent
upper lip, the skin puffs out, almost an over-bite, just like
George Clooney's puffy upper lip, and *wham*, suddenly the
guy looks exactly like George. The power of suggestion.

Even if men do not stare directly at my breasts, it is
obvious they are aware of them in their peripheral vision. I
find myself slouching around my box, acutely aware of my
large yellow breasts.

Do big boobs put men in a better mood? Men are smiling
at me more than before, expecting me to smile back and
then I realize they are flirting with me. And I smile back.
Flirting, flirting. As I smile and smile, the terror of what I
am doing curls my stomach into a knot. If they find my extra
passports they will search me and discover the money in
my bra. What is the penalty for money smuggling? Multiple
IDs? Would they be able to find out who I really am?

As the Zanzibar box disappears through the x-ray
machine, I start to perspire. My new bra is not made of
natural fabric and pools of sweat gather under my arms and
in the center of my chest. I look down and notice that my
breast on the right has moved sideways. I attempt to shift if
over to the left, but I see a guard staring pointedly at me. I
look away. Several drips make their way down my ribs and
lodge into my already damp waistband. I stare back at him
and wink lewdly. He blushes and looks away and I nudge
the cup back into place.

And then I am through. On the other side. I look back
at the people still in line and I don't care if they recognize
me anymore. It's happening, I'm really doing it. The
momentum of the earthquake, the destruction, the frantic
energy pushes me on and reveals strength I never knew I

had. There is one more step and that is getting on the plane. I could still go back through the security gates. I am still in California.

The airport televisions continue to flash scenes of homes tilted off their foundations — the 880 freeway collapsed, vandals stealing car radios while the dead lay in their cars. To avoid the news, I board as soon as the gate is open. I step from the tunnel into the plane and the tension increases. It's hard to breathe. My muscles feel so tight I can't walk normally.

My seat is near the front of the airplane and when I try to lift my Zanzibar box, I find it has become too heavy for me. I stand there grasping the leather handle, staring at the shelf before me. My palms are sweating. I wonder if I've had a stroke or something. I remain motionless until the old man seated next to me stands and slides the box easily into the overhead. I sit down next to the old man who winks at me with pride. He is wrinkled and shrunken, his mouth stretches into a grin showing a row of perfect teeth that look too big for his jaw.

As the plane wheels leave the ground and the acceleration force pushes me against my seat, the tension that has been knotting my body washes away in one great surge. I close my eyes and let my mouth drop open. I sense the old man looking at me. I open my eyes and he winks again.

'Have you been to my most beautiful country before?' he asks. 'Monkeys, mangos, and real Indians.' He opens his eyes wide. 'The Kuna.'

'Real Indians?'

'They even have their own government ruled by their chief.'

'I've never been to South America.'

He frowns. 'Central America. The US, Canada and

even Mexico are North America. You are going to Central America.'

I squint and imagine a map. 'Oh, I am so sorry, of course.'

He rummages through his bag and picks out a five-day-old newspaper and proceeds to read, obviously finished with such an ignorant North American.

I shift my bra and it rustles. His eyes slide in my direction, but he doesn't turn.

I stare out the window and clench my eyes shut at the sight of the Bay Area growing smaller and smaller as the airplane ascends. This departure has been planned for so long, yet it could have easily never happened. My eyes stay closed, stinging, until the stewardess offers me a drink.

Flying into Panama City I see the dark squiggle of the canal and a dozen huge cargo ships lined up to pass through the narrow strait. The sun is heading down and the Caribbean Sea is an astonishing green with dots of white sand islands, and further out the dark azure of reefs. I feel the thrill of travel and adventure that has lain dormant through my entire marriage.

The plane taxis to a stop and the door opens. We walk down the steps and the passengers head toward a low white building. It's sweltering and waves of heat rise from the tarmac, filling my nostrils with air so thick there is no room to breathe. My shoes press into the asphalt as if I am walking on a sponge.

Taxi drivers besiege me, waving their hands and pointing at their taxis. I take a few steps back and point to a clean-shaven one with a crisp white shirt tucked into his pants. As I climb into the taxi, I notice he has only one eye.

I'm not sure where to tell him to go. My plan never progressed further than Panama City and a bank. And a new life. But in all my planning and scheming I had never envisioned what this new life might entail or where it would begin.

I tell the driver to go to Casco Viejo. He looks at me in the mirror with his one eye and squints. Or maybe it's a wink.

'Is this somewhere I shouldn't miss?' I ask.

'*Que?*'

'Never mind.'

He speeds through the traffic. We pass rundown buildings, swarms of people crossing the streets against red lights, water-pocked walls, trees with trunks as big as houses. Everyone on the street is carrying something, from plastic bags to babies to an old typewriter to an iguana. The driver stops at a corner and fixes me with his one eye in the rear view mirror.

'*Donde en Casco Viejo?*'

'*Un café.*'

'No cafés in Casco Viejo,' he says. 'I take you to a very nice hotel in the center.'

'I don't want to go to a very nice hotel in the center, where I am sure you will make a very nice commission.'

'Casco Viejo is full of *putas* and *cabrons*.'

'There must be one café in Casco Viejo. Take me there. Or just drop me off on a street.'

The taxi does not move. 'You can leave the taxi now.'

'What?'

'We are here.'

'Jesus Christ.'

He crosses himself. I get out and throw ten dollars at him through the taxi window. At the end of the street I see blue that I think must be the ocean. I head towards it, swinging my box. A bedraggled man with over-plucked eyebrows and tight jeans passes by, my first Panamanian transvestite. His thin shirt is open, baring his emaciated chest. A kid, maybe eight years old, follows me skipping and singing, 'Hoooola hola, hoolaa,' in a high-pitched, remarkably on-tone voice, to the tune of *Ave Maria*.

At the end of the street are a park and a high seawall lined with Asian looking trees with vibrant orange blossoms. There are life-size human sculptures made from iron, posing in a variety of positions. A straggly cat sits in the lap of one of them. I stroll along the water's edge and climb the white stairs to look over the Pacific Ocean. Three men in sweat-stained shirts are repairing the wall and they put down their tools to watch me. A light breeze hits me with the smell of fresh salt from the sea.

I sit down on the wall and dangle my feet over the edge. It's peaceful on the wall. The sounds of the city are distant: horns honking, trucks rattling, a motorcycle revs its engine. Here the dominant sound is the water lapping against the wall. Below several large rocks poke out of the ocean. The scraggly cat joins me and sits watching the fish darting below.

I turn and face Casco Viejo. I see streets lined with decayed buildings and every once in a while a painted one, bright blue or yellow. A faded red awning juts out above a storefront and beyond it, strung across the street, are several wires with laundry dancing in the wind. I need to think about a new life. But then I am reminded of my old life and I have to stop thinking about any lives.

The sun is low and a slight chill blows off the water. I remove my sweatshirt from the big drawer and put it on. On the front, over my misplaced heart, is a big misshapen stain. I rub at it and it feels slightly damp and then I remember wiping the old man's head wound with it. All I can smell is a metallic tang of blood. The old man may be dead by now and I am wrapped in his blood. I whimper and try to throw off the sweatshirt, but the hood strings catch and tighten and it won't pull over my head and I panic and struggle and lose my footing, falling sideways until my body hits the water.

I swallow a mouthful of water and cough. The water is cold and my arms are tangled in the sweatshirt and despite the buoyancy of the sea, I find myself struggling to stay afloat. I see the lights of some boats in the distance and the darkness of the water. The wall in front of me seems impossibly high. The thought of drowning in the same way Dahlia did, first makes me smile and then howl until I remember the money in my bra and I clutch both hands to my chest causing me to sink straight down.

The water is dark with spots of light above like stars from an underwater world. I can feel the cold beginning to wrap around my body. Salt stings my eyes. There is an explosion of bubbles next to me and I see another body and two hands reach out to me. I keep my hands pressed to my chest and let the person drag me over to the rocks below the wall. He hoists my body up onto the rocks. I smell a rotten algae stench and try to get a grip on the rocks, but they are covered with slime and I slide back into the water. This time he gives me an extra push so that I can scramble up the rocks on my stomach. I can feel the bra full of sodden money pushing against me and I roll over.

I lie there shaking. He pulls himself out of the water and sits panting several rocks down from me. It's dark now and all I can see is the outline of the man.

'Talk to me,' he says.

I blink the sting out of my eyes and stare at his dark form.

'Answer me or I'll give you mouth to mouth.'

I try to answer and choke and vomit up some water. He crawls up, flips me over on my stomach and I cough some more. A pair of women's shoes appear near my nose. I sit up and drape the half-on sweatshirt over my chest.

'Ella esta bien,' the woman calls out. 'She's alive.'

The two haul me up onto the seawall where I huddle, clasping the sweatshirt to my waterlogged chest. The man rests his hands on his hips, breathing hard. A crowd has gathered and they talk among themselves darting glances in my direction every so often.

'What the hell were you doing?' the man asks. His voice is deep with a rolling accent that warms me and stops my shivering. 'It looked as though you were fighting yourself.'

'It was my arms. They were stuck.'

'Not a suicide?'

I look at him, trying to see his face. 'Not a suicide.'

'I don't believe in suicide. I'd throw you back in if that were the case.'

And I believe him, the way he says it. He is very still except for a watchful turn of his head that makes his hair change color like silk in sunlight. The woman stands before me, shielding me from the crowd.

'Can you walk?' She holds out a hand.

I nod. They help me to my feet and we start off, arm in arm. I can feel the man's muscles moving through our wet clothes. He pauses and looks behind us. He drops my arm and jogs back to where we were. She takes hold of my arm again and we continue walking.

We arrive at the tattered red awning down the street, which is a café with a banner declaring: Queen's Café. She opens the door with a key and flips on a light. The café is small, neat, with half a dozen tables and deep yellow walls.

Huge, old black and white photos are the only decoration giving it an old-style feel.

I get a good look at the woman. She's about ten years older than I, maybe forty or so. Everything about her is abundant. Her hair, springy and full, her voice, strong and husky, her flesh, curvaceous and dark. Stacks of flesh placed in just the right spots. A *brick shithouse* pops into my mind — not usually my terminology, but fits her perfectly. She looks me up and down and smiles broadly. I cross my arms across my chest. Is there some sort of camaraderie among big-breasted women? What have I been missing? Women with average breasts don't grin at each other in this way.

'I could see you all afternoon sitting there staring at the water.'

'I was watching the fish.'

'Whatever. Then you just jumped into the water.'

'I didn't jump into the water, I fell. It's different.' I look her in the eyes. 'Thanks.'

She snorts. 'I'm not the one who saved you, thank Oscar.'

'Where is he?'

She shrugs and pours me a glass of water that I drink in one go. Then she pours two shots of tequila and we drink them. She disappears into a back room and reappears with a pair of sweatpants and top. In hot pink. She hands them to me and points at the bathroom. I take them and flip on the light and see my sunburned face in the mirror. My hair hangs unevenly around my ears.

I hear a thunk outside in the café and then the voice. My savior has returned. I peel off my clothes, smeared with rock slime and look at myself standing in the stuffed bra. I take out the stacks of bills and blot them dry between paper towels. They are still wet and when I try to fit them back into my bra, I find they have expanded in size. I shove as many as I can into the bra and look around for somewhere to leave the rest until later. There is a bucket with cleaning supplies under the sink so I wrap the money in a rag and shove it way down to the bottom.

I step out of the bathroom and stand holding my wet clothes. It feels so good to be in something dry that I smile. The woman smiles back and shakes her head at me.

'What time do you open tomorrow? I will return your clothes first thing.'

She points to a sign in the window. 4-8 is written in big numbers. I glance around the café, no one else is here, but on the counter is my Zanzibar box. I drop my wet clothes on the floor and rush over to it. I open the drawers and find everything is still there.

'You left it on the jetty and a thief was running off with it, so he had to go back and rescue your box. He says it's from Africa.'

'The same guy?'

'Oscar.'

'Oscar. Where is he?'

'Wet. Went home.' She sizes me up again. 'So, where're you staying? There are no hotels here in Casco Viejo.'

'And the taxi driver told me there were no cafés.'

'On a holiday?'

'Sort of.'

'Well,' she puts her hands on her big hips and wiggles them. She steps toward me and holds out a hand. 'I'm Roza.'

I shake her hand. She has a strong grip.

'I'm Jillie.' I don't know why I chose such a ridiculous name. It's the name of one of Lorna's friend's hamsters.

'Jillie, nice to meet you. *Con mucho gusto.* I have an apartment my cousin manages that I rent out. You can stay there tonight and find a hotel tomorrow. I'll rent it to you for the same price of a hotel. One night. Drugs?'

'No, thank you.'

She sighs. 'No drugs allowed in the apartment.'

I'm not afraid of drugs. I have used them periodically and have been around them enough so that there is no mystery or thrill. 'I don't really do them,' I say.

'Maybe you should try.' She laughs uproariously, slaps the counter and picks up the phone.

The apartment is several blocks from the café, on a ratty street. An old electric street lamp in front of the house tilts sideways, metal rusted to a deep orange, wires protruding from the base like mechanical tentacles. Roza's cousin arrives and shakes my hand, looking away from my face. His name is Manuel and he is short, very young, with powerful long arms. He wears dark mirrored sunglasses at night.

He opens the front door, which has a metal safety door and a second regular interior door. The inside smells of citrus and smoke, not from cigarettes, smoke from a fragrant dusty wood. The walls are painted vibrant colors and the floor is terra cotta. The opposite of my house in San Francisco, my old house, with its glass and steel and stained wood.

Manuel is inspecting me through those mirrored glasses he continues to wear, even in the house. I stare back at him and it takes me a moment to realize that I am gazing in a mirror and seeing myself. Only me. I smile.

'How long you wanna stay,' he takes a step closer to me, 'mi bonita?'

'One night,' Roza says.

'We don't do one-nighters.'

'We do now.'

He sneers and lights a cigarette. Roza walks over and plucks the cigarette out of his mouth and extinguishes it under the kitchen tap.

'Let's go,' she says and pushes him out the front door. She returns in a moment and hands me two keys.

'Listen honey, I don't know what you've done or what you're running from, but I'm going to give you some advice. Slow down, take some time here and think about your next step.'

I nod gratefully. Advice is exactly what I need.

The door closes and I look around. It is basically a studio. A large studio with a loft bedroom and an open kitchen and living area with a wrought-iron balcony. There is a small lizard on the blue wall, watching me. His body is pale, translucent and he has oversized bubble eyes. His toes stretch out on the wall like fingers. Along the floor are some flakes of blue paint from the wall that I scoop up into the palm of my hand and toss off the edge of the balcony.

I unhitch the bra and mounds of soggy bills flop onto the floor. The bra goes in the trashcan. I pick up the bills and begin to lay them across the tile floor in rows. Most of them are stuck together and I have to pry them cautiously apart. I look at what my life has become and it is disturbingly insignificant.

Pure silence. Then a motorcycle whines down the street. Water trickles in a pipe in the wall. No one wants or expects anything from me. For the first time since I threw Dahlia over the cliff, I am alone. This is what it is like to be alone.

I open my Zanzibar box and inhale its fragrance. I take my toothbrush, toothpaste and flip-flops out of the center of the box. I open the little drawers on the bottom and take out my new underwear and place it on a shelf in the bedroom. Then I sit on the sofa and cover my mouth with a pillow and scream. I scream again and when I glance up the lizard is still watching me. He doesn't flinch, he has no fear.

CHAPTER 6

A DOUBLE BIRTHDAY

Birthdays, for twins, were doubly important. Not only were we double twins, mirrored and identical — we were also Gemini. It was a day more special than Easter or Christmas. We came from a single egg, a monozygote, split and divided into two identical spirals of DNA. We had the same brain wave patterns, the same mirrored toes and hair cowlicks and we even started our periods for the first time on the same day, in the same hour. Birthdays were our days.

There was a raised energy in the house, a magnetic pull that lifted spirits and pulled the corners of mouths into uncontrollable grins. It was the eve of our fourteenth birthday, and we were having a slumber party and barbecue. Bird dashed around corners and gave strange little hops in the air as if he had been electrocuted.

Upstairs Chloe sat in a white slip, in front of her vanity mirror, applying black liquid eye liner with a sure hand. Her shoulders were pale and square and her clavicle bones shifted as she slowly ran the wand along her upper eyelid and beyond the corner, just a bit to give her cat eyes even more of a cat look. When she dressed up she was stunning. Her everyday nonchalance was in direct opposition to our father's militarily-pressed shirts and carefully slicked-back hair.

She had the same kind of face as us, proportionally correct, anatomically symmetric, but unless enhanced with lipstick or mascara, nothing stood out in particular. Brown hair that could go blond in the sun or dark in the winter. Eyes that were grey next to the ocean, dark in the evening and yellow tinged on a sunny day. With one swipe of blood red lipstick, plain shifted to striking.

'Can we pick out your dress?' we asked together.

Chloe smiled indulgently and nodded. We shrieked and ran to her closet, shuffling quickly past jeans and sweaters and tailored shirts to the back of the closet where we found the dresses, chiffons and satins. We took out the silver lamé, the crocheted halter dress, the red taffeta suit and draped them across the bed. We threw off our shorts and stained T-shirts and slipped on the dresses, pirouetting in front of the mirror. The clothes hung off our adolescent bodies, but when we pinched them from behind we could see ourselves as adults with full breasts and hips and hair swept back in delicate waves.

We wanted Chloe to look glamorous, not odd. After all there would be a lot of adults at our party and there had been times in the past when we were not sure if she looked good or strange. We went further into her closet where we found a simple silk spring-green dress that shone out from the depths. Our eyes met and we unhooked it from the rack, both holding tight to the hanger. We ran back to her, presenting it with double curtsies.

Chloe clapped her hands in delight. 'The perfect dress.'

She slid it off the hanger and unzipped the side. The dress glided over her head. We held it out from her face so she did not smudge her mascara and it settled around her body without any pinching from behind. She was beautiful. She sat back down to outline her lips and choose her jewelry. We ran our hands through her necklaces and bracelets and rings and brooches. We lingered over the two stones our grandfather had given us when we were born. He died before we could form him into a memory. A large sparking ruby and a deep iridescent sapphire. Years ago we each chose our favorite gem and it never changed. Ruby for Dahlia, sapphire for Hetta. As rubies and sapphires are made of the same rock, so were we.

Once, when we were much younger, we put the stones in our mouths and Chloe was furious, she thought we would choke on them. We wouldn't have swallowed them, we were protecting them like a hen with an egg. She screamed and pinched our cheeks and made us spit them out on the bedspread. They lay there glistening like two perfect Easter eggs.

We took the red tube of lipstick she no longer used. Too orangey-red, not enough blue in the shade and we mimicked the way she outlined her lips...slowly, thickly... and then we mashed them together as though we were going to blow a big red bubble-gum bubble. We kissed the back of our hands and compared the lip prints to see if they were different, but as always, they were the same. We smiled happily in our orange-red lipstick and kissed each other on the lips like lovers.

Chloe shuttled us into our rooms and dressed us in our matching white drop-waisted dresses. Under the sheared skirt there was a cotton slip that puffed out the hem so we looked like 1920's flapper ballerinas. We loved those dresses and spent a good amount of time spinning and hopping on our toes, hoping someone would make the ballerina connection. The only one who seemed to notice was Bird, who sprang along beside us and managed to bump into a table and break an ashtray. Luckily it was an old one and we kicked it under the sofa so Chloe wouldn't notice and make us get the broom and sweep the broken glass. Not a dignified look for the twin birthday girls.

Val's friends began to make their entrance one by one. They were all boisterous and good looking. He collected them. They lived glittering on the surface of the world. A champagne bottle was uncorked with a precise pop and a loud cheer. They sucked the light out of others while they grew stronger with each glass, their wives fading into the background.

Toby was the first of our friends to arrive and we flitted around him until he held his hands over his eyes and protested that he was dizzy. He had been invited to the party, but not to the sleep-over. Now that we were fourteen Chloe was adamant about that. He pretended he didn't care, but we could see he did. It marked the fact that we were getting older and there were different things involved than just running barefoot and smoking tea in the haystacks. More people arrived, the three girlfriends for the slumber party: Bonnie, Karen and Jen. Karen and Jen were sisters who looked nothing alike. One of them was red-headed and freckled while the other had dark hair and dark skin. Their father had light hair and pale smooth skin. Bonnie was a bossy, only child who hated Toby.

When Chloe came down the stairs, Toby froze and pretended to be so overwhelmed that he dropped to the floor.

She swatted in his direction. 'Stand up. Honestly.'

But we could see she was pleased by his reaction.

One of Val's friends, the tallest one called Tommy, with a bruised looking nose and flyaway white hair, hugged Val with one arm and imitated the noise of a trumpet. He ran to the middle of the lawn where he turned a cartwheel. It was not a good cartwheel, his legs were bent and he landed awkwardly. The group cheered and several others tried, but they were adults and had long forgotten the key to cartwheels.

'Dahlia,' Val called. 'Come show us your cartwheel.'

He singled out Dahlia. Why would he have singled out Dahlia, when both of us were the same? Something shifted and we were not *we*, we were Dahlia and Hetta, two separate people. Dahlia ran to the center of the lawn and whipped her body upside down in a straight-legged, stiff-armed cartwheel. She flew around in a circle doing several more in a row, and then for the finale, she dropped into a back bend. The group clapped and whistled. Chloe came and stood behind me. I could smell her perfume. She touched my shoulder and rested her hand there.

Val whispered to Dahlia and he lined up with her on the lawn and in one fluid motion, they sprung into simultaneous cartwheels, two trees, two sets of branches stretched to the sky. They finished and Dahlia clung to the front of Val, putting her feet on top of his and her arms around his waist. He launched into a cartwheel, Dahlia holding on and spinning with him — as if they were one.

I wondered if our lip prints looked different now. I shook off Chloe's arm and ran to the lawn and began a series of whip-fast cartwheels, ending with a frozen handstand, my legs stretching up, up, perfectly aligned. My heels clicked together and whipped down in perfect form. There was a big crash. I turned and saw I had knocked the barbecue, a bowl of marinade and several martinis onto the lawn. Everyone froze except Bird, who saw his opportunity and ran into the middle of the fracas, latching onto a dripping T-bone steak and tore off, dragging it across the lawn.

Val ran after him yelling, waving the barbecue prongs above his head. 'Goddamn dog, I'm going to kill you!'

He caught Bird and we heard a sharp yelp and a whimper and we went running across the lawn to protect our beloved dog. We screamed and cried at Val who stood there with the dripping steak in his hand while Bird cowered beneath him, head between his paws. The smell of the sweet brown-sugar marinade whirled around us. We cradled Bird in our arms. Val scowled, stalked back to the patio, rinsed off the steak, and threw it back on the barbecue, daring anyone to say anything.

Soon more martinis were made and everyone was laughing again. We stayed on the lawn cuddling Bird, who quickly forgot his trauma and scuttled away to chase a lizard. The food was brought out, we cut the cake together, opened presents: matching necklaces, a rhinestone collar for Bird, two wooden fans from China. We were we again...though I still felt the sting of the separation and the chasm was still there, small, but still there.

Chloe turned the lights out and we, the five birthday party girls, lay on the floor, spongy rugs underneath, encased in our sleeping bags. It was dark except for the outlines of shapes from the light of the street lamp outside. A murmur rose up to us from the few adults still left drinking on the lawn. Bonnie stood, her white night-gown glowing mysteriously, the light catching it as she moved. It was an adult nightgown with satin straps like a bra and we felt childish in our cotton print shifts with blue butterflies creeping along the hem.

'I have a game to play,' she said. 'Everyone in?'

We sat up and looked at her dark figure. She tossed her

hair over one shoulder and crossed her arms. Her face and hands contrasted darkly against the white.

'One person at a time. Karen, you first — lay here on my sleeping bag.'

Karen shuffled over to the sleeping bag and stretched out flat on her back, arms to her sides. We moved around her, two on one side, two on the other.

'The goal is to not laugh. We can touch her everywhere, lightly, a tickle with our fingertips, so she can barely feel it, starting on her head, going all the way down to her toes. Once she laughs, she's out.' Her dark outline pointed at Karen. 'Karen, naked. You have to take off your nightgown or you can't feel it.'

Karen sat up and tugged off her oversized T-shirt. She tossed it over our heads and lay back down, arms crossed over her chest. The light caught on the peaks of her skin, resting on her small breasts and hipbones. She giggled nervously.

'Silence. Arms straight at your sides — it feels good. No laughing or you're a loser,' Bonnie barked.

We skimmed our fingers over Karen, in her curly hair, over her ear lobes, down her cheeks to her chin, to her neck until she exploded into laughter and had to cover her mouth with her hand and turn onto her stomach.

'Next,' said our commander. She leaned across and tapped Dahlia on the arm.

Dahlia first again. She lay down and I heard her skin whispering against the nylon sleeping bag as she shifted. Dahlia didn't laugh, we've played this game before, just the two of us in bed. She breathed calmly, her eyes glistening as our fingers tap-tapped down her body, over her hard little nipples, around her belly button until we reached the tips of her toes. She sat up and grinned.

'Now Hetta,' Dahlia said.

'Not Hetta, she's the same as you. Someone different.'

I didn't want to play anymore. I lay down away from Bonnie and imagined what it would be like to not have a twin, to be alone in the world — just me, no *other's* eyes to seek or thoughts to compare. It wasn't possible to imagine. If Dahlia and I had not been born twins, we still would have found each other and we still would have looked alike, the way that old couples look alike or dogs look like their owners. They say that everyone has a twin somewhere. That's who she would have been, my twin on the other side of the world.

The game was a playoff between Bonnie and Dahlia. When I heard Dahlia laugh, I knew she lost on purpose and I knew she did it for me. The giggles stopped and Dahlia's hand edged over to mine before we drifted off to sleep.

We awoke to a horrible yelping coming from the front of the house. We ran to the window. It was dark outside with only the garden light illuminating a car halfway down the driveway, driver's door open, no engine running, no lights. The yelping went on and on, was silent for a moment, and then began again.

'Bird,' we whispered.

Chloe ran onto the scene in her red kimono, sleep-distressed hair tumbling around her shoulders in a cloud. Our car was parked in the driveway with both front doors wide open. Val kneeled in the driveway, in front of the open driver's door, with his hands held over his ears, hunched over. Tommy's white hair glowed in the night and it looked as though he was throwing up in the roses. His shirt was off and his white skin gleamed in the street-light. Chloe turned and looked up and saw us in the window.

'Stay there!' she yelled. 'Don't come downstairs.'

Her words freed us and we ran down the stairs. We huddled in the front doorway, afraid to go further into the night air, reeking of noise and pain. It was very early in the morning, the sky was turning a violent blue.

Val shouted, 'We weren't doing anything!' He threw his hands in the air and gestured behind the car, hugging himself.

'Why the hell were you in the car? You are too drunk to stand and you were going to drive?'

'I don't even have the keys!' he cried. 'It rolled. On its own it rolled back. My God, I swear, we were just talking... talking...'

Tommy stood up from the rose bushes and grabbed his shirt from inside the car, putting it on and slamming the door. He ran to his car parked on the street and opened the trunk, taking out a blanket. He turned quickly and dashed back behind our car where he stooped down. The howling stopped for a moment. Chloe went to Tommy and a moment later there was a yelp and he stood with something in his arms wrapped in the blanket. Bird...oh *Bird*...Chloe ran ahead of him and opened the back door. He hurried, shirt flapping open, leaned in and settled the blanket. Chloe slammed the door while he jogged to the driver's side and got in. The car started with a roar, tires screeching on the asphalt.

We ran down the driveway. 'Bird, Bird!'

Val collapsed on the lawn and Toby's mother, Coco, appeared, kneeling by his side, arms wrapped around him, red-nailed hands running though his hair. She saw Chloe moving toward her and released him, stepping back. Chloe kneeled by his side and we heard his great sobs. She took his face in her hands and made him look at her. He looked straight in her eyes and cried and we were scared, we had never seen an adult cry this way, unselfconsciously, with abandon, full-force. Chloe slapped him. He stopped making the noise and curled into a ball on the driveway. Toby's mother was standing on the edge of the grass. She gathered all the children around her.

'We are going to go to my house for a hot chocolate and then we will sleep in a bit until morning. Your dog has gone to the vet. Hold hands, let's go now.'

She started across the lawn. We clasped each other's hands and followed her like hollow dolls, trying to drown out the noise we heard and the sights we saw. She did not walk all the way down the driveway, past the mailboxes, the way she normally came in her car. She guided us through the garden, past the sweet peas growing to the sky, past the poisonous oleander bushes we were told never to even touch to our tongues, past the wooden fence tilted sideways in sections and into Toby's garden.

Toby's mother took us to the kitchen and gave us cookies from a metal tin decorated with pictures of little girls with scarves tied around their heads. She boiled water and made six hot chocolates. She made them correctly with marshmallows and extra powder mix. Toby didn't appear, he could sleep through a war. We gave hiccups of anguish every few moments. We dunked our cookies in the hot chocolate and talked about things other than what we just saw.

The kitchen door flew open without a knock and Chloe stomped in.

'Goddamn it, I didn't know where any of you went.' She glowered at Toby's mother who calmly sipped her hot chocolate. 'Let's go, girls. I've called your mothers, they'll be here any moment.'

We gulped our hot chocolate and gave Toby's mother a sheepish look before following Chloe out the door. She blew us kisses.

We walked back the same way, holding hands again. We sat on the side patio until we heard the sound of a car. Jen and Karen's mother was the first to arrive, in their Cadillac. She hugged Chloe, patted us on the back and hurried the girls into the big car as they started to cry. When Bonnie's mother arrived she didn't come near the house, she parked her station wagon at the curb and got out. She still wore her nightgown, one like Bonnie's, and she called out with a hoarse voice until she saw Bonnie running across the lawn at full speed.

Chloe took us inside and as we passed the living room we heard Val moaning.

She tucked us in bed and kissed our foreheads like she used to do when we were younger. We both got into Dahlia's bed and I thought about Val choosing Dahlia and my cartwheels and Val chasing Bird with the barbecue prongs.

'He did this to Bird,' I said.

She began to cry. Then I started to believe myself and I cried. We hugged each other and we worked ourselves into near hysteria, lungs heaving, eyes inflamed.

'He hates Bird.'

'We hate him,' Dahlia said.

Our tears slowed down and then I felt Dahlia's fingers moving over my body, light as feathers. Tracing streams through my hair, trails along my neck, whispers down my body until I wasn't sure if I was her or she was me and we were one again.

CHAPTER 7

PANAMA DUEX

By the morning, the lizard has moved far up the wall. Below it is a new pile of blue flakes. I sweep them up and go out to tip them over the balcony. They flutter down, sparkling like fairy dust, landing on the neighbor's pink geranium. It's the biggest one I've ever seen, more of a tree. The dust sticks to the little hairs on the geranium leaves and looks like day-glo aphids.

There is the rectangle of ocean visible from the sitting area. The apartment walls are painted deep blue and the kitchen a dark green. It probably looked fresh for a month or two, but the paint is bubbling off the walls and the entire apartment has a slight undercurrent of mildew. The iron balcony off the front has barely enough room for me to stand outside. I stare out at the rectangle of ocean.

Here I am in Panama, now what?

The morning air is light and the little blond hairs on my arm stand up to catch the breeze. In four or five hours I know the heat will be oppressive and make my skin damp and my hair lie flat. I look at the clock on the wall and see that it's five to seven. The café opens at eight and I want to be there early.

I walk down the street toward Roza's café. Seven-thirty in the morning and shopkeepers are outside sweeping, *panaderias* are open and the smell of fresh bread wafts through the neighborhood.

'Hey, beautiful lady, how about a donation for a poor man?'

It's the same bedraggled transvestite from yesterday, sitting on the curb, tossing pebbles into an unctuous puddle. I ignore him.

'Don't pretend you didn't hear me. I'm not nothing, you know.' His voice gets closer, he must be following me down the street. 'I've been to Paris — *Bonjour, Madame*.'

I walk a little faster. I can see Roza's café ahead, the big sign with the old-fashioned print: Queen's Café.

'I've stayed at Hotel Du Cap, *puta*.'

The café is open already. I enter and the door closes behind me. He stays outside talking through the window, his mouth moving, his finger jabbing in my direction. There are two young girls at one table and a man reading a newspaper at another. They are all watching me and the transvestite talking through the window with great interest. Roza is making coffee behind the counter. She tilts an eyebrow at me and I wave and head straight for the bathroom.

I dig into the bucket. I dig deeper. Nothing. No rag. I turn the bucket upside down. No money. Disappeared in one night. My hands begin to shake. I splash some water on my face and blink into the mirror. My eyes are wide and frightened. I go back into the café and Roza watches me.

'Lose something?' she raises her eyebrows.

I hear a snort from behind me and turn around to look at the man reading the paper. He has thick silver-grey hair that curls over his ears and he is staring intently at an article.

'I...no.'

'You sure?' she asks.

'No.'

I glance at the man. There is something familiar about him.

'Isn't this the Switzerland of the Americas?' My voice cracks and I have to sit down.

'Hey, calm down.' She lowers her voice. 'I have your money.'

She slides me a plastic bag and I can feel the bills inside. I rest my head on the table. Through the window I see the transvestite gesturing frantically at me. His shirt is wide open revealing a bony chest.

'Why me?' I ask her.

She smiles sympathetically. 'Fresh blood.'

'He wants a donation.'

'Of course he does, he's a junkie.' She cuts off a generous piece of date cake, puts it on a napkin and hands it to me. 'Give this to him, he probably hasn't eaten in days.'

I open the door and hand it to him. He sneers at me and snatches the cake from my hand, his upper lip curling in disdain for food and not drugs, sustenance instead of escape.

'How about a cappuccino?' he calls as I go through the door.

I turn to stare at him in disbelief.

'Extra sugar,' he says.

I walk into the café shaking my head at his audacity. 'Now he wants a cappuccino.'

'You wanna buy him one?'

Outside he is spreading a napkin on his lap and looking at me expectantly.

'Okay,' I say, 'and one for me.'

She makes the coffee, foams the milk and puts one in a coffee mug, the other in a big paper cup. I add lots of sugar to the paper cup and walk back out the door. The transvestite is settled on the curb and has saved his date cake to eat with his cappuccino. It is delicately balanced on one knee, napkin adjusted across both legs. He takes the cup and blows on it, sipping a bit of the foam, not thanking me.

'Thank you,' I prompt.

'How about a dollar?' he says.

I shake my head and go back inside. We watch him eat and drink with surprising delicacy.

'Ignacio was a beautiful boy,' Roza says. 'His lover was an older man, fantastically rich. And married. Took him all over the world, kept him in his guestroom for years. When he died of AIDs, his wife threw Ignacio out of the house and here he is.'

'Is that why this is called Queen's Café?'

She looks stunned and then starts pounding her knee and laughing, spilling her cappuccino. 'I never thought of it in relation to the trannies. But honey, it's got nothing to do with Ignatio or any of them.' She starts to laugh again.

'So?'

'I'm from Queens — Queens, New York.'

'Why are you here?'

'Why is either of us here?' She bats her eyes and gives me a grin. 'Don't look so worried, I'm not asking you to tell me anything.'

'Do you miss New York?'

'Every day. Casco Viejo is the closest I can find to my Queens. Don't care for the rest of Panama City.'

'What do you miss the most?'

'The violence.'

There is something violent about her. It comes from inside and I can hear it in the center of her voice, it came out in her laugh and even in the voraciousness of her curly hair.

'No violence here?'

'It's not the same.'

'I like your apartment.'

'So, you want to stay?'

'There is a little lizard on the wall.'

'It's a gecko.' She made the kissing, clicking noise I had been hearing all night.

'The lizard makes that noise?'

'Gecko. Yes. They're good luck.'

'I need some luck.' I think about the gecko and how glad I am that he is there. 'Can I stay one more night?'

'Only one more night?' She tilts an eyebrow.

I see behind her, suddenly in focus, a television showing the earthquake devastation. The sound is off, but I can see fires still burning and buildings collapsed into piles of bricks. Ambulances race through debris-strewn streets and people covered in blood are carried into hospitals. It comes to me, like a terrible aftershock, that I have no idea if Toby and Lorna have been injured, or worse. I remember seeing a phone in the apartment and I know I have to call, not to talk, just to listen. Just to hear they are alive.

My eyes refocus and I see Roza watching me. I realize my hands are covering my mouth. She nods her head as though a piece of the puzzle has dropped into place. Roza's eyes shift to my left and I turn. The man from the table is standing next to me, also watching me. I see that despite his silver hair, he's not that old, or rather he gives the impression of being youthful. Roza has an odd expression on her face, as if she is going to say something, but she doesn't open her mouth. He lays down a handful of cash on the counter and Roza rings it into the register. He blushes, or maybe he's sun-burnt. He has two bullet-blue eyes that twinkle at me in a shared sorrow.

The man never looks away from me and I find I cannot look away either. The intense blue of his eyes is lined in black against pure white and he has these black eyebrows that arch cynically, one of them permanently higher. He blinks, breaks our gaze, turns and strides out the door without a backward glance.

When I can speak, I ask Roza, 'Can I have my bill?'

She exhales. 'He just paid it.'

'What? Why?'

'He wanted to. He's the one.'

'The one?'

'He saved you from drowning.'

'He...' I think of my savior's hair changing color like silk and realized it was the silver hair. The man who I couldn't stop looking at is the one who pulled me out of the water and found my Zanzibar box. Do people automatically fall for their saviors? According to Japanese custom, I owe him my life. I run to the door and look up and down the street. He's gone.

I hurry back to the apartment with the money and go straight to the phone and pick it up. No dial tone. I jiggle the receiver around and press the receiver button. Nothing. I turn on the television and watch the California scenes. The stations are in Spanish so I have to imagine what the newscasters are saying. It's not hard.

I work on the money, using the palm of my hand to flatten it onto the tile floor of the bathroom. The other money, which is dry, I put under the mattress where it will hopefully compress back to its original size. If not, I will have to iron it.

I stay awake most of the night looking for our building in the rubble. *Our* is not the correct word anymore, it is *their* building. I have given up any right to call it our building. In the morning I head back to the café. I need a phone and news in a language I understand. I want to hear names of streets and buildings and neighborhoods. Ignacio appears from a side street as I approach the café.

'Cappuccino?' he asks hopefully.

I dart in the door and ignore him. Roza walks up and gives me a big kiss on my cheek.

'You've got a friend.'

I smile at her until I realize she is not talking about herself, she is talking about Ignacio who is standing in front of the window waving both arms at me.

I sigh. 'Two cappuccinos,' I say. 'And, please, I need to use a phone. The one in the apartment is dead.'

'Sure, honey, you can use the phone right here.' She points to one behind the counter. 'Long distance?'

'Yes.'

'There's an access code taped to the register.'

Roza prepares the cappuccinos and flicks on the news. CNN. I move closer to the television and she hands me the remote. I turn up the sound to hear the anchor talking about the collapse of the Bay Bridge and I realize there is no reason for anyone to think I am still alive.

'Know anyone there?' Roza asks.

'No...no one.' I keep my eyes glued to the news and avoid her eyes. I want to use the phone, but don't want anyone watching me and I see the stares of the locals when they think I am not aware of them. I assume gossip in Casco Viejo moves quickly.

There is an in-between time, after coffee and before beer, when the café is quiet. I sidle over to the counter and dial in the access code then my old phone number. It clicks through and rings. I duck behind the counter. It keeps ringing. I hang up before the answering machine can connect.

Where is he? He can't be working at a time like this. Anyway, he works at home and I can't believe he would be isolated in his office writing his weekly technology newspaper column with all this disaster around him. And me missing.

All day I watch the news with Roza and various locals. Every hour or so I go behind the counter and call again. One time I let the answering machine pick up and my own voice scares me into hanging up quickly.

I sit in front of the television all night, maybe I dozed off, but I can't remember. My eyes feel as though they have a handful of dust in them. I take a shower to try and wash off the gritty feeling and it works until I step out of the water.

As soon as the café is open, I leave the apartment.

When I walk in the door Roza points to the phone. 'Go ahead, I know you need to use it. And I want you to watch me make these cappuccinos since you seem to be becoming a regular and I have enough people to wait on.'

I take my place behind the counter and crouch down. Still no answer, but the answering machine seems to be off. I watch Roza grind the beans and pour the grounds into the silver cup before twisting it onto the machine. She pushes a button and after the machine makes a whirring noise, the coffee pours out. Easy, I can do that. I deliver the coffees to customers and make more. It's preferable to sitting around watching the same news short and avoiding the locals' stares. Although they are staring less today and greet me familiarly, almost in a friendly manner.

This time I wait until mid-morning to call again and when Toby answers I drop the phone and push the disconnect button. I slide sideways from my crouched position and sit on the floor, chest heaving. That was so stupid, now I know Toby is fine, but what about Lorna? I should have held onto the line until I could hear her. Of course Toby is answering the phone, he is waiting to hear about news regarding me. I don't want to call back again — it must give him as much of a shock as me, both of us silent waiting to hear what we don't want to hear. I don't want to torture him anymore, so I vow not to call again. I place the phone back on the counter and when I stand up the customers are staring at me. I smile nervously and make another coffee.

Every morning I return to the café. I can't help calling Toby. Now he has the answering machine back on, so I am careful to hang up before it connects. The customers look at me less and less as a curiosity and soon I am a permanent fixture. Roza asks me to keep on eye on things while she runs errands. I make coffee for the clients, serve them *empanadas* and clean off tables, the whole while keeping an eye on the news. In the morning I bring Ignacio his coffee with three sugars and he asks me for the dollar I never give him. My money is dry and ironed smoothly in the apartment and ready to be deposited in a bank.

The rain is hammering down so hard today that even Ignacio does not follow me on the street for his free morning cappuccino. Roza sits in front of the window watching the water pour down the glass. She shakes her head at my soaked clothing when I walk in and stand dripping.

'*Déjà vu.*'

I look down at my wet clothing. 'How about that hot pink sweatsuit?'

'How about that cash?'

I hold my breath as I figure out what to say.

'Hey don't look so worried. Just teasing you.'

'No, I...I need to find a good bank.'

She squints at me with one eye. 'A good bank or a not-so-good bank? Those are two different things.'

'To deposit some money and have a security box.'

'What kind of documents do you have?'

'I have a passport.'

'No bank letter of credit? So you want a bank that will take anything from anyone.'

'I...'

'One that will let anyone make a deposit, with only one ID, no bank letters and no proof of residence? One that will take your wad of cash, no questions asked?' She wipes the counter and throws the cloth into the sink. 'One that deals with drug dealers, arms dealers and all the riff raff that the canal attracts?'

'I...'

'Listen honey, gone are the days when you can dance into a bank with a bag of cash and a song. Twenty years gone.'

I stare at Roza. Twenty years gone? What about the Switzerland of the Americas? What about my IDs and money? Bury them? Hide them under the floor?

The doorbell in my house rings and I go downstairs to open the door. Manuel stands with a box in his hands, his sunglasses pushed up on his head. His eyes are sharp and black with thunderous brows above them. He struts in humming under his breath, looking at me as though I were the one intruding. His tight black T-shirt is tucked into his jeans and I notice a snake tattoo winding around the muscle of his upper arm. Latino men have an unmistakable

masculinity mixed with a streak of femininity, a softness in
their round cheeks and small, neat hands. He holds out the
box to me.

'This is for you.'

I take the box and look inside. Drinking glasses, of all
shapes and forms. '*Gracias.*'

I move into the kitchen and begin to take them out
and set them on the counter. There are dozens of them:
margarita glasses, martini glasses, whiskey glasses: some
clear, others with colored rims. He follows me into the
kitchen, I can smell the wave of aftershave, far too strong.

'I guess you think I am going to have a party.'

He grabs me by the shoulders and turns me to face him
and kisses me. I hadn't had anyone kiss me in that way in
a long time and I responded. I didn't mean to respond, I
wasn't attracted to him. The whole macho swagger repulsed
me, yet something in me, something more primal and needy,
returned the kiss. And more. My tongue roves his mouth,
my hips thrust toward him and then I smell something —
another odor under the aftershave, a sharp and pungent
reek. It's fear. He's afraid of me.

I draw away from him, but he grabs me and brings our
lips back together and tunnels his tongue in. I swing my
hand up to push him away and accidentally clip him across
the nose. He holds onto his nose and his eyes water, they
also change expression. Gone is the taunting machismo and
in its place is hatred.

He zeroes in on my nose and darts his fist out, I duck
and he is left standing there looking dumb, his eyes still
smarting. A violence surges behind his black eyes. I see that
he hates me for rejecting him, hates me for being taller
and hates me for being a woman. He hates the money that
he knows I have and the three-bedroom house with the

automatic garage door opener. He hates my thin skin and long neck.

I run for my balcony and stand on it ready to scream. He watches me stand there, grasping the railing with both hands.

'*Eres una puta de madre*. Bitch cunt.'

'I didn't mean to hurt you, it was a reaction.'

'Hurt me? *Chinga...* '

'I'm sorry, I didn't mean to kiss you.'

'And I felt sorry for you. Ugly barren American.'

He starts to walk toward me, teeth tight in his mouth, clenching and unclenching his fists.

'I'll scream. I'll scream from this balcony and Roza will hear me and come.' I was pretty sure Roza would not hear me.

He stops walking and sneers at me. 'Scared?'

'I don't trust you.'

'American bitches are all the same. *Pendeja* women who cannot make babies or cook a meal. What use are you?'

'I can cook.' I certainly wasn't going to tell him I had a child. 'Get out of my house.'

'My house,' he sneers.

'I am renting the apartment right now so it's my apartment. Remember?'

'Fucking American liars who come at a man like a whore.'

'I thought you were my friend, Roza's cousin.' Mentioning her name seems to have an effect on him.

'You will see, America's time is coming. They are falling like the Romans.'

He spits on the floor and strolls slowly to the door, leaving it open after he walks out. I am afraid to walk to the door. What if he is hiding just outside and grabs me when

I try to close it? I stand on my balcony and wait until I can see him below. He stops, facing me, and lights a cigarette, holding his middle finger up before he meanders down the street, shoulders squared.

I run to the door and lock the inner metal door. Even if he had a key, there would be no way to open the second door. Maybe this was why it was here. I don't think he will tell anyone what happened, it would be too big of a blow to his machismo. I run the water until it's scalding hot and I wash my face and hands and rinse out my mouth with the foul-tasting soap. I don't even want to put my toothbrush in my mouth.

With one of the dish towels soaked in soap and hot water, I wipe up his spittle, rubbing the towel on the floor with my foot and then throwing it in the trash. My hands are sore from the hot water, but I run more and add washing liquid until it foams over the edge of the sink and I start to scrub the glasses clean of him.

Soon there is a pyramid of them drying on the counter, glistening in the light. Maybe I will have a party, let's see, I can invite everyone I know: Roza, not her cousin, the trannie, the taxi driver and the skinny cat. I dry the glasses and open a cupboard to put them away. The cupboard is full of glasses. The exact same kind of glasses. Maybe he usually has better luck.

The ocean is rough with lots of tiny little whitecaps jumping up so that it looks as though the water is alive. Next to the seawall the water is clear and schools of miniscule fish feed among the rocks. I walk along the edge and the skinny cat appears, flopping on his back in front of my toes. I scratch his stomach and he responds with a rusty meow.

'Hola, gato,' I say to him.

My Spanish is improving with all that I hear in the
café. I'm not paying much attention to grammar, but after
a week of Roza's informal lessons, I can take a coffee order
as though I'm fluent. I continue around the curve of the
seawall and turn right down a narrow street and head into
the center of Casco Viejo. A line of bright dripping laundry
is being strung across the street by a round-backed woman.
She leans over the windowsill to peer at me. Old men sit on
milk crates in store fronts playing dominoes with chipped
yellowed pieces. They openly ogle me, the younger ones lick
their lips.

At a t-junction I see a newly refurbished building and
a sign: *Banco de Ciudad de Panama*. I decide to go inside
and see if Roza is right about the banks here. I don't see
any SUV's with blacked out windows and the sign looks
respectable enough, so I head inside.

The bank is cool and quiet inside with guards on either
side of the doorway, standing spread-legged in combat gear
holding AK-47s. If this bank is robbed it's not just the thief
going down, it's everyone in the bank. I look around for
drug dealers or arms runners and I see a woman with two
children, a very old man with a straw satchel and several
men in business suits. Do criminals wear business suits
these days? A young man, who moves so smoothly it seems
his black shiny shoes must have wheels, approaches me.

'*Puedes...*'

'*Si, quiero un*, ah, bank account.'

'Of course,' he replies in English.

The man grandly waves me to an empty desk and I have
a flash of paranoia that I am in a foreign bank surrounded
by machine guns with thousands in cash and five fake IDs
back in a rented apartment. I sit down stiffly and the man
hands me a form to fill out.

The first line asks for: *nombre*. My name. Which name? Blood rushes to my face. I am afraid of this man with his unctuous smile and empty desk. I feel lightheaded, shivering in the coldness of the bank and roaring air conditioner. I shake my head and stand, heading cautiously for the door, glancing at the guards who only look away with bored faces.

I go straight to my apartment. I open the door and notice a sour smell. I check the cupboards, under the sink and the garbage. Nothing anywhere. I sit on the sofa and stare out the window. Something is bothering me. I stand and walk around and it's then that I notice my Zanzibar box is missing. I walk through the apartment thinking maybe I left it in the bedroom or bathroom or hid it somewhere absentmindedly. It's not here. My brain can't take this in. I can't believe it is not somewhere in my sight. I run up and down the stairs checking everywhere it could fit, even the refrigerator. The stacks of my new underwear are gone too. The box is really not here. Fuck. My money and IDs.

The first suspect flits into my mind: Roza's cousin. Although it's been over a week, I hurt his pride and this could be his revenge on me. Then I think of Roza. Could all this have been a set-up? No one to trust.

I walk around the house, a wailing permeating my mind. I stop and it stops, I walk and it wails. The sound is coming from me. A roar escapes from my lungs and I pick up a glass from the kitchen counter and throw it against the blue wall. It shatters beautifully, precisely, the way it would in a film, with a crisp noise and splinters of light along the wall and glass tinkling down onto the terra cotta floor.

I pick up another and another. The glasses make unique sounds, they must be handmade, different thicknesses. Between each glass I shriek. The pile of glass is growing and

it lays translucent across the floor, the light catching flares
of blue and red, like a prism that was shaved into thin slices.
Several small shards lay on my feet. I pick one up and press it
along my arm until a line of blood begins to open. I examine
the blood and think about cutting more, but I find it does
nothing for me. No relief, no calm. I throw the piece away and
wash off my arm. It's not myself I want to hurt, it's whoever
stole my things and I realize I am through cutting myself, it
no longer helps me control my life and feel alive – I am alive.

I throw a few more glasses, but my enthusiasm is gone.
There is a knocking on the door and Roza is shouting my
name. I freeze and listen. There are several people out there.
They have the main door open, but I have locked the inside
metal door.

'Lucy...Lucy...'

Lucy? It takes me a moment to remember that this is the
ID I am using now. I told her Jillie was a nickname and she
rolled her eyes. Roza rolls her eyes a lot. I calmly walk to the
front door and face them. It is Roza and a man and two other
women. They fall silent.

'Yes?' I ask.

'What happened?'

'I've been robbed.'

'Mi pobre –'

Roza pushes the other three away, down the hallway. 'Can
you open the door, please, I can help you.'

Was Roza involved in this? I study her face and see so
much concern, her forehead is wrinkled like a walnut. Who
knows – regular people are brilliant actors, the best of liars,
myself at the top of the list.

'We will need to file a report with the police,' she says.

This is logical and gives me a glimmer of hope, and really,
I have nowhere else to turn, so I open the door and go into

the living room. She comes in and pauses near the kitchen, taking in the mess. She sits next to me on the couch and dials the police on her mobile, staring at the blood on my toe.

'What did they steal?'

'My box, my wooden box.'

I remember the money under the mattress and race up the stairs and lift it up. Empty. I walk back down the stairs slowly.

'They took your Zanzibar chest.'

'What? How did you know?'

'Oscar told me, he knew exactly what it was. What was in it?'

My mind conjures up an image of my box, an x-ray image where I can see the stack of hundred-dollar bills in the main drawer and the IDs in the side drawers. My lips open and close and no sound comes out.

The police arrive in record time. At least I think they arrive fast. Possibly it has been hours. I am numb and helpless and can't foresee a future in my future. The thought occurs that I could surrender to the police and tell them everything. Tell them I am on the lam, tell them I faked my death and abandoned my husband and child and killed off my twin and they could put me behind bars and I would feel protected, safe. They would take care of me and feed me. However, I have seen too many movies and I know it would not be that way behind bars in Panama.

The police ask me many questions and I lie. I lie about everything. I have no choice, the truth is not possible. Their smooth faces show nothing, no sympathy, no hope. Two dark masks poised in front of me, thick short hair shining in the light, not even a spot of sweat under their arms. They do not write down anything I say and I feel they know I am lying.

They leave and I sit on the couch staring at the rectangle of ocean. Roza sweeps the glass and mops up the shards. Her phone rings. She comes around the front of the sofa and sits on the coffee table in front of me. She takes me by the shoulders.

'The police want to see us.'

I mentally prepare to be arrested.

The police station is in an old building that looks like someone's dilapidated house. In the entryway is a reception desk with no one behind it and nothing on it. There are several doors leading out of the room, they are all closed. There are no chairs. We hover around the desk for a while, talking loud to attract attraction. Finally Roza walks over to the doors and tries them one by one. All locked.

'Follow me,' she says and walks back out the front door.

We walk around the side of the building and at the back we find three policemen sitting and laughing underneath an arbor of bright red bougainvillea. They look Roza up and down, taking in her full body, with only a minimal glance at me.

The youngest one, still with the round cheeks of a teenager, reddens and says, 'Roza?'

'Si.'

He guides us through a back door and up some winding concrete stairs into a large room filled with twenty or thirty old-fashioned school desks. The wooden kind with the seat and desk attached. I notice that children from all over the globe carve penises into their desks. There is nowhere else to sit, so we sit in two of the desks like two children punished for not doing our homework.

'So...how did you know who it was?' Roza asks me.

'Know who was what?'

'The police said you told them. Who stole your box.'

'I didn't.'

There is a scuffle at the door and a man is brought in, between two policemen with big bellies. The man has his head hung low and he looks familiar. He is clean shaven with a nick above one of his high cheekbones. When I see his over-plucked eyebrows I realize it's Ignacio. Unrecognizable, smooth-faced with a crisp white shirt and shiny shoes. I see remnants of the handsome boy he must have been. They prop him up in front of us. His skin is light compared to the policemen and they look at him through narrowed eyes. He raises his head and scowls at us.

'Don't pity me.'

'Pity? Ha! *Eres un pendejo, no tienes huevos...*' Roza lets go with a string of curses.

The policemen look impressed.

'We fed him cake.' I say. 'And cappuccino.'

'He stole the key from your cousin,' the biggest pot bellied policeman says to Roza. 'That's how he got in. Walked right in the house, lifted the key off the hook, stole the goods and put the key back on the hook.'

I think about the cousin, what had happened between us and if it would have any bearing on the theft. The policemen are burly and macho and somehow I think my story will get turned around and I will look bad in the end.

'I didn't tell you that.'

'You told us someone stole your underwear.'

A fat tear leaks out of Ignacio's eye. He wrestles with the guards and spits on the floor. They haul him away.

'Did you find anything on him?' I ask.

He shouts out the door and the other policeman walks back in with a handful of clothing which he deposits in front of me on the desk. It is my new underwear and the enormous bra folded on the top, the one I tossed in the trash. Everyone gets an eyeful of it and Roza lifts a brow at me.

'Anything else?'

'Like what?'

'Money. IDs...an ID.'

He shakes his head sorrowfully. My breath comes in bursts and the edges of my vision starts to grey. It's all too much — too many years of planning and now nothing. How will I live? The blood runs from my face and I can feel the whiteness.

Roza places her hand on my shoulder and the policeman brings me a cup of water. I pour the water over my head and they exchange looks over my wet hair.

The policemen drive Roza and me back to Roza's café. I am numb. All I can think is: No money. No IDs.

Roza seats me at a table and gives me date cake and a foamy coffee. 'I feel responsible,' she says.

I stare at the date cake.

'Am I correct that you can't go to the embassy for a new passport?'

I nod. She rummages behind the bar and finds a small round bottle that she holds up to the light and looks at with satisfaction. She pours some into two shot glasses and hands me one.

'Tequila,' she says. 'Good tequila.'

I drink it down in one gulp. The liquid burns down my throat and into my stomach where it turns into pure heat. Seconds later it hits my head. I feel a release, a lightening. Roza swallows her shot and shivers with pleasure, her whole body moving. She stares at me, she seems to be trying to see inside my brain. I want to tell her there is nothing to see at this moment, nothing but emptiness and fog. She comes to a decision and grabs the bottle and the glasses, flips the sign in the window to closed and takes me by the arm, ushering me out the door and down the street.

The seawall is empty except for three men fishing. One of them glances over and waves at Roza. We sit swinging our legs and Roza pours another glass.

'I've got a son in the US. Good kid. Studying to be a veterinarian. He visits when he can. You have kids?'

'No.' I drink down my tequila and choke and my eyes water and then I'm crying on the seawall in front of Roza and the fishermen.

I think of Lorna in her tutu and how she wore it for three months straight and wanted to wear it to bed, except that I convinced her to take it off and sleep with it next to her pillow. I think of Toby as a boy when we first met him and showed him our webbed toes. Why is it that all my best memories of Toby are when he was young? I remember the way his jeans hung on his hips and the way he moved when he walked, shoulders back, chest out, a boy's swagger.

Roza wraps both of her arms around me. I lean into her, thankful that someone cares enough to hug me. For such a tough woman, she has a lot of softness in her.

'I want to leave.'

'Don't think badly of Panama. There is so much here: coral reefs, coffee plantations, the Kuna Islands.'

'I need to be somewhere I can understand people.'

'Was it really better in the US, or wherever you came from? Somehow I don't think so, or you wouldn't be here.' She holds me at arm's length and looks at me. 'Where do you want to go?'

Where do I want to go? Not back to California where the sun is always shining, but the people are not. Not to Europe where the history matters more than the person.

New York. New York is halfway between it all. The world's melting pot. I remember how it was to be there when I changed my identity to Dahlia's. The perfect place to blend and disappear and become my new self.

'New York,' I say.

'I don't think New York is an easy place to understand the people, but no matter, it is an easy place to disappear. New Yorkers don't care where you're from, believe me, I'm one of them. And if someone asks where you're from, tell them Nebraska or Kansas, that'll shut them up real quick. You have any money?'

I shake my head. 'Only what I had on me.'

'In the future, forget about carrying cash around. It's outdated, bulky and easy to spot. Keep it in diamonds. Simple to transfer and sell.'

'You're talking to an average person who knows nothing of banks in Panama or diamonds as cash. In fact, I don't know what I do know about.'

'You know about something...you may not know what it is, but you know about something.'

I think about what Roza said. I'm pretty sure I don't know about anything, but I like the fact that she thinks I know about something. Roza ruffles my hair as if I'm a child and pours two more glasses of tequila. We clink them together and I realize we have become friends. My first friend as myself, not Dahlia. I smile into my tequila.

'Diamonds,' she says. 'You buy the smallest, highest clarity and you wear them. Like gypsies wear their gold.'

Instead of large breasts I could cross the border wearing an ostentatious necklace with large drops hanging from my ears and several carats on my fingers.

'I could get mugged.'

'You disguise them. The key in all this is to hide them

in something a thief won't take. Heels of shoes, belt buckle, hollow plastic bracelets, hair clips. Most important is that you wear decoys so they focus on those. You can even sew them into the hem of your jacket or trousers or bra. But get rid of that bra. I don't know how you slid through customs, they must have taken pity on you.'

There is a note from the police on the door of Roza's café. We go inside, blinking at the bright lights. She makes a phone call, her eyes sliding back and forth across the room, resting briefly on me between movements.

Roza puts the phone down and stands in front of me, hands on hips, bottom lip thrust out. 'You didn't tell me.'

'Tell you what?'

'About my cousin. My thieving, assailant cousin.'

'Ah, he —'

'He told me you attacked him.'

'What? No...' He told Roza and the police that I came on to him? I can imagine the jokes about the foreigner and the analyzation of my underwear.

'Of course I knew immediately what happened.' She touches my shoulder.

'You believe me?'

'I don't want to hear any details, I only wish you had said something. I'm really sorry that this has happened. I feel responsible.'

'I'm afraid it's possible I led him on a little. That mixed with the Latino machismo made him very angry.'

'Ah, the Latino machismo. Don't knock it. The men never stop looking at you like a woman. I remember my mother telling me that in the US, at the age of fifty, she had become invisible to men. Not here, thanks to the good ole Latino libido.'

'Guess I could have used a little less Latino libido the other night.'

Roza finds a thick padlock under the counter and hands it to me. We leave the café and walk back to my apartment where she shows me how to loop it around the metal door for extra security.

'We are the only two with a key to this, so if anything is stolen, you can throw me in jail. Or yourself.'

'What does it matter? What do I have left to steal?'

Roza looks at me from the corner of her eyes. 'I like that you're not a tattle tale. shows a lot about you.' She sits down and leans forward, resting her elbows on the table. 'And I appreciate you didn't press changes against him.'

'He's your cousin.'

'Thank you. Anyway, he'll be in jail for some time. The police told me he's wanted for another break-in and I have no doubt he's guilty. I know he's trouble, but I needed help with my business so I hired him. Not the café, another business I have.'

We fix each other with our tequila bleary eyes.

'And now, he's locked up and that leaves me with no one to help.'

'I'm sorry.'

'I wonder...'

'What?'

'If...tomorrow I could use a little help.'

'Of course. Tell me what I can do.'

'I have to go out to the islands for a transaction.'

'Sure, I can take care of the café.'

'No, I'd like you to come with me.'

'But I know nothing about your business.'

'You don't need to know anything. There is a ship coming through the canal and I need to meet it before it goes through. Tomorrow evening. Obviously I'll pay you. And you'll get to visit the Kuna.'

'A ship in the canal? Kuna?'

'Kuna Indians. They own the San Blas islands. Never heard of them?'

I shake my head. Then I remember the old man on the airplane looking at me with wide eyes – '*Real Indians...The Kuna.*'

'I can see you don't want to go. Think about it. I leave midmorning. Despite the money in the bra and the fact that you're running away from something...I do trust you.'

I sit on the floor all night near the blue wall and peel sheets of paint off with my fingertips. Dahlia would go with Roza to the islands, but I am petrified. Not petrified as in scared, petrified as in frozen, unable to move. My muscles are hardening, turning to stone. The gecko appears and watches me with his black bulb eyes, his eyes flicker as the paint strips fall onto the ground.

Later, tiny little moths blow in through the balcony doors. Dark grey-brown with imprints of wood markings on their wings. They don't land on the wood, they land on one of the white walls, not one of the colored ones, where instead of blending, they stick out and say to their predators, '*Eat me.*' I catch one and move it next to the gecko. He cranes his neck and watches me. He scratches his underside like a dog and eyes the moth. He acts as if he is going to leave the moth there, but he can't resist and turns around to face it. He still watches at me. As though the moth is a trick, a diversion.

A bell rings and I jolt upright from the floor, next to the pile of blue flakes. There are lights flashing outside on the

street. The sky is rosy with dawn and I peer out the window
at a police car with the top lights on and no one inside. The
bell rings again. I find the light switch and the key to the
padlock and open the door to Roza. Her hair is a cloud of
curls around her sleepy face. She steps inside followed by
the young policeman with the robust moustache carrying
my Zanzibar box, cautiously, like a crown jewel. He hands it
to me and I hug it to my body.

Roza smiles at me and motions for the policeman to
leave and she follows behind him. At the door she stops
and faces me.

'I am leaving in an hour. Think about it. If you change
your mind, come by the café in an hour.'

I run my fingers over the smooth carvings and open the
lid. I inhale the scent and set the box down on the table,
giving it a hopeful little shake. Something shifts in the front
drawer. I open the drawer and find an envelope with my
rental contract and the rental money refunded. Then I open
the rest of the drawers. Empty. I open each one separately,
peering into the deepest corners. Maybe one of the IDs
got stuck and was still there. Empty, empty and empty. My
finger snags on something metal in the box. I close one eye
and try to see inside. Dark. I stick my finger back in and feel
a smooth round ball. I try to grab it with my fingers but it is
embedded in the wood. I push it back and forth and when
I put pressure directly on it, another hidden drawer springs
out from the back, one I hadn't seen.

Inside I find a lump of newspaper tied with twine. I
unwrap the twine, there is a lot twisted around and around.
The newspaper is brittle and I can't read a word, it's written
in a language I don't recognize. Inside there is a black swatch
of velvet that falls open and a light blue stone tumbles out
into my lap.

A gem. It is clear, beautiful, simply cut, an aquamarine maybe. Or tourmaline. Or sapphire. Or glass. Must be glass. For a split second I think it is Chloe's stone, the blue one I put in my mouth so long ago. The one I hid in the tree the night Dahlia died. It's egg-shaped and fits perfectly into the palm of my hand. The blue shines, light emitting from within, as if it will glow in the dark. It feels warm, alive. I wish I could swallow it, protect it, keep it safe inside me away from anything harmful.

At the same time, the stone feels strong, as though it will protect me. A gift from gods I do not have faith in. I sit for a long time staring at the stone. This stone is my stone.

I don't believe in fate and I don't believe in destiny, yet as I sit here and hold this stone in my hand, a talisman for the nonbeliever, I know that I will go to the islands with Roza.

CHAPTER 8

CHLOE TALKS

Bird's death marked the end of our family. Val disappeared and I sent Hetta and Dahlia to New York to stay with my sister Celia until the end of the summer. The twins began their own journeys...and I realized then I was truly alone. Val would call and leave messages on the answering machine, but never spoke to me directly. He realized his audience was gone forever and where there was no audience, there would be no performance. All of the twins' lives I covered for him, telling them he was away on business or had client dinners, but they were too old for that and I was too tired and bored of his antics. And the way the girls looked at him that night...well, he exposed a weakness that the young were not willing to ignore.

My mother warned me that life was like this, that I would find myself alone. She warned me that I should be prepared to raise my children by myself. She said every woman should be told this before they get pregnant. And, damn it, she was right about it all.

When the girls first left for New York, I wandered through the house. The silence was far louder than the twins' voices and Bird's yapping. I lay on their beds – red for Dahlia, blue for Hetta – and stared up at the ceilings we had looked at for fourteen years. I saw the dragons and pirates and whales that we had always seen, but then above Hetta's bed I saw a great winged phoenix. How could I have missed something so clear to me now? When I spoke to her on the phone I asked if she had seen it and there was a sigh and then silence on the other end.

I have come to realize that I prefer being by myself rather than with people. What is it Sartre said? Hell is other people. I never irritate or disappoint myself and I laugh at the absurd thoughts that pop into my head. I can read what I want, when I want. I devour books at all hours. I am an autodidact, partly because of my guilt from never attending college and partly because I refused to be an uneducated, dim-witted eighteen year old mother of twins.

Most people don't spend time alone. I don't mean time alone in front of the television or time alone in the shower. I mean long periods of time alone contemplating. Not meditating — meditating is the opposite of contemplation. I mean alone thinking, not doing.

There's a lot to think about it when you take the time. I review my life and where exactly it swerved into the oncoming lane. Some days I think it was all the way back before I was pregnant with the twins. Back when all I cared about was the next party and which boy I would let touch me that night. Sex was sex in the pre-AIDS days, back when the biggest threat was herpes or getting caught with a hickey on my neck...or getting pregnant.

When I lost my virginity I remember thinking, this is it? This is what everyone is making such a fuss about: the censors and Moral Majority and my own mother? I tried it out with a few different boys and found them to be impatient or rough or the kind of kissers that are all slick tongue. Then I met Val. I remember he wore a rich aqua shirt that contrasted with his dark foreign skin and Slavic eyes. I knew Romanians weren't Slavs, but I liked to tease him and hear him defend a country he hated. All those countries over there hate each other and don't want to be compared to their neighbors. Val was giving and sweet and above all, experienced.

I wish I could say that I married young to escape a horrible life at home...but I didn't. I married young to escape the pressure, the assumption of my future. The expectation of my greatness.

My mother raised me to be a smart girl. It was ingrained in me that things were different for women of my generation. I didn't have to get married. I could have a job, explore the world, have drinks with girlfriends in dark bars. Live before I settled down.

My mother had high hopes for me. I was to live the life she never could. She worked jobs she hated to save money for my college. What else could I do, but fall hopelessly in love with a swarthy Romanian and immediately get pregnant at the age of eighteen? When I told my mother I was pregnant, she said it was the end of my life. When I told her it was twins, she burst into tears.

I wondered why marriage was invented: it seems so unnatural to be with someone longer than is needed for the first growth of your children. Everyone talks about love as though it is a tangible thing. People can't even agree on what it means. Stendhal studied it for years and where did it get him in the end? Preferring desire to consummation, yet suffering from rampant syphilis. The feelings I have for my children far surpassed any feelings I ever had for another human. Marriage forces us to be confronted with our partner's faults. You think you are getting into it for one reason and it turns out to be something totally different. It must have been religious leaders who invented such a thing in order to keep their flocks in line.

One night, many years ago, I was out searching for Bird. He had this trick of running down the street to a neighbor's house and jumping into their swimming pool. The sky was a treacherous blue, the color right before it turns inky black. As I crossed the dew-swamped grass, my toes tingled with the chill, and I imagined just walking past the stupid dog in the pool, alongside the dented mailboxes and out onto the road. I made it past the pool and nearly to the mailboxes when the splashing of the water reminded me of the twins. I turned around. I wonder if abandoning your life and starting anew is a common dream. I've always been too ashamed to ask anyone.

I sat at the counter trimming the stem of one of my bearded irises when a mammoth dragonfly flew in the window and perched on my knee. It had fluorescent purple wings and an emerald-green head. What would it be like to be born with skin those colors? I must have talked to that insect for nearly an hour before it finally whirled its wings and took flight, zigzagging its way back outside.

As a kid, I was convinced I could talk to animals.

I talked to the dragonfly about how I wanted to recreate the exact purple-black color of my iris on one of my living room walls. Bring a little of the garden inside. He seemed to like that idea and flitted his wings once. I told him that I wished one of the twins liked to garden. It would be nice to have a daughter to work in the garden with and discuss why the camellia buds had fallen off or how to stop the gopher from chewing its way through my agapanthus roots. I mentioned that the wooden floors needed sanding now that the twins were older and more careful. We didn't talk about anything major really. I didn't tell him about Val.

The dragonfly flapped its wings every so often, never turning its beady bulb eyes from my face. It was pleasant, the two of us sitting there, no rush, the soft breeze blowing through the room, the sunlight beaming through the window and warming my body.

Celia thinks the twins' individual identity needs to be nurtured. I told her to nurture away and I hope those girls are ready for Celia. When we were kids she was the adventurous one, like Dahlia, and I was more like Hetta. I wonder how my life would be if I had been more like Celia and if I hadn't been pregnant and enamored with the dashing Val and his great white teeth. Val had the ability to make me feel unique. The masthead of his ship, the Anais to his Henry. He loves women and it took me far too long to discover he loves *all* women. Celia has lived her life her own way – no husband, no kids, painting when and where she wants – and I am sure she never thinks about abandoning her life.

The sun becomes too bright. I feel lethargic and my brain is bringing up half-words and discombobulated thoughts. There is a pressure in my head that I know will increase. Light is beginning to look star shaped and sounds are amplified. Migraine. I close the shades in the kitchen and take two pills. It's hard to know what to do with a migraine hovering in my head. One of the worst things I could do would be to watch television as the flickering of the screen sets off the pain in epic waves. I decide to bake some cookies.

The ticking of the clock in the kitchen echoes in my ears as if it is a jackhammer against metal. I put my finger on the minute hand and hold it until it stops. I cream the butter

and sugar and extra vanilla together and the scraping of the
spoon on the bowl hurts my head. The pain is suspended
in the back of my skull because of the pills, lurking, waiting
for a gap, a breach to open so it can plunge into the rest
of my brain. I mix in the eggs one by one, stirring slowly
and carefully. Flour next, baking soda, pinch of salt, even
the sharp white of salt is too much and *wham* it finds the
opening and hits with full force.

How can there be so much pain, so much pressure that
my skull does not crack open? Burst with the violence of a
volcano? I whimper and walk cautiously to the couch where
I press a pillow over my eyes. I lay there trapped in my world
of pain.

A floorboard creaks and I hear the whisper of cloth.
'Chloe? I saw your blinds down, so I knew.'

Toby's soft voice hammers into my head. His voice is
amplified one hundred times. I whimper.

'I'll help you to your room.'

I hold up a hand and as soon as his hand touches my
skin, there is a jolt through my body that radiates in a sharp
jolt straight between my legs. My God...a migraine orgasm.
He pulls me up and we walk slowly to the stairway. I hold
my head between my hands and push all of my fingers, as
hard as I can, into my skull. One step at a time. Breathing
slowly, I make my way to my bedroom and lower myself onto
the bed. Toby closes my blackout shades. Dark except for
one slit I can never block. He hangs something from the
top and it becomes totally dark. Even so, I wrap a black scarf
around my eyes. He leaves, I don't know for how long, I am
shivering and crying. I bolt out of bed and make it to the
toilet before I vomit and fall onto the floor. Tears leak out
of the sides of my eyes and I press my pulsing head on the
cold tile floor.

In the morning I have the usual migraine hangover. Still sensitive to light, sound and smell with a bonus of amazing visual clarity. I feel I could solve complex molecular formulas in record time. I open the shades, taking care to avert my eyes from direct light. I throw on my robe and splash cold water on my face without bending over, any extra blood in my head could bring the pain creeping back. There is a voice outside the house calling my name. Toby walks up the lawn, holding up a bakery bag that I know has bagels and vegetable cream cheese. He knows the food I need after a migraine night.

I put on a slash of lipstick and head downstairs. He is already in the kitchen laying out the bagels and cream cheese. He has opened the curtains so that some light comes through, yet not too much to shock my eyes. I am so thankful to have someone around who knows what I need.

'You are a honey.' I look at him slouching against the counter. 'I'm sorry about Bird. I never told you that.'

He nods. 'Bird was a good dog. And that was a bad way to die.'

I make some strong coffee, good to keep the blood vessels dilated, and get a knife to cut open the bagels and toast them. My head fills with the earthiness of the coffee and I relax...such a peaceful morning. Sparkles of dew litter the garden and it looks magical. The knife slips, my body not particularly coordinated on the day after such pain. It cuts into my finger with the point of the blade and opens a small deep incision.

Toby hears my sharp intake of breath and moves to my side, taking my hand to see the cut which is now boiling over with beads of red blood. I am surprised at the height of him, he soars above me. When did that happen? He looks at me as if he too is surprised and I notice he is unshaven... he shaves?

He puts his lips to my finger and sucks the blood off, looking at the cut to see how big it is. The memory of his touch last night sends a shiver through my skin.

'I'll get the disinfectant,' he says.

He looks at me with concern and I see the stain of my bright blood on his bottom lip. He turns and bounds up the stairs. I sit in a chair, disconcerted, alone in the dark kitchen with my finger and the spot where he pressed those lips of his. He is gone a while, I don't know how long. It seems I would be content to sit in the kitchen and look at my finger for hours. There is a reflection of myself in the window with tousled hair, puffy eyes and reddened lips. The image wavers as Toby reappears behind me with alcohol, anti-bacterial cream, Band-Aids and a wrap for a sprained ankle.

He wets a washrag and gently takes my hand, washing it with warm water and soap. He pours a little alcohol over it and looks at me to see if I react to the sting. I don't. He blots the wound dry, blowing on it to get rid of all the moisture and squeezes out a bit of the cream dabbing it on the cut. He winces the way I should. He turns again to see my face and presses his lips to the crook of my elbow. He slides the robe up my arm and kisses the skin, leaving his lips pressed to me for what seems to be a long time. The sensation makes the hairs on my arm stand up and I see them, little blond hairs upright and at attention. My whole body is waiting. I don't move, I can't move. My mind is saying to me, this is Toby, little Toby, the twins' friend, but my mind does not connect with my body and I stay right where I am.

He takes the sides of my robe, one in each hand and opens them as if he were a magician parting the curtains. He kneels before me, in between my legs and runs his fingers, exploring, titillating everywhere, looking at me from under

that heavy black hair that falls into his eyes. He touches me
curiously and he is mouthing something I can barely hear.

'...vulva, clitoris.' He kisses me.

'Why are you..?'

'I looked them up at the library.' He continues. 'Labia...'
He kisses me again.

It dawns on me that this is the first time he has ever seen
these things in the flesh...so to speak. He is reverent and
gentle and it makes me want to weep. I can't weep, if I weep
my headache could come back. I close my eyes. His breath is
loud, as if it were coming from my own lungs and out of my
mouth. I hear the unzip of his jeans and the madness of all
this is pushed into the back of my mind as I slide onto the
floor. He enters me and I am full of him as I grasp his soft
hair in my fingers and smell the freshness of his skin.

I breathe slowly so the blood does not pump into my
brain too quickly. When I open my eyes Toby stands before
me looking shy and pleased with himself. He smiles, his
smile is honest and pure.

As you get older you don't trust moments. Or maybe
you don't trust the people you have the moments with.
There are so many memories and emotions the other
person could be feeling, how could it ever be mutual? That
person could have already had that moment with someone
else and is merely reliving it, rather than being there in the
moment with you. When you're young your emotions and
memories are limited and it's easier to believe in another
person. Easier to fall for someone.

I smile back at Toby, but what I am remembering is the
lipstick I put on this morning and his mother's long red
claws running through Val's hair...and the duplicity of my
smile saddens me.

CHAPTER 9

THE KUNA

We fly from Panama City on the smallest plane I've ever set foot in, six seats besides the pilot. We sit across from two tourists, a couple with sun-darkened skin and unwashed hair. Our knees are inside each other's legs. We avoid eye contact. Roza catches my eye and we have to laugh at the forced intimacy.

In moments we move from skyscrapers to canopied jungle. The airplane flies above the canal, thick green jungle on either side. Up here in the sky the openness of my life spreads before me and I squint, seeing the rays shooting off the sun, through the jungle, out to the sea, straight along the canal — the directions of my past and future.

I like to think about random events and how one event can send your life in a totally new direction. If Dahlia hadn't stepped in front of that truck, if Bird hadn't been run over, if Toby hadn't touched my tongue at the funeral. This trip with Roza is one of those events where my life is swerving into the unknown.

I touch the stone that I have slotted into my bra. A small cut into the lining and it fit in perfectly. I can feel the blue through the material. If I hadn't found the stone, I wouldn't have decided to go with Roza to the islands and

I would be back in the apartment, peeling blue paint from the wall.

The airplane banks sharply, dropping down to the bright water and we glide toward an island. As the airplane edges lower and lower, I can see a long white beach to the left and in front of me is an airport carved out of a tangle of mangrove trees growing right up and into the water's edge. There are no roads leading to the airstrip. I crack my head on the window trying to peer out to see if we are going to land in the water or airstrip. We bump down and clatter over the potholes before coming to a stop. My heart is pounding, but I feel euphoric and Roza catches my eye, smiling.

Half a dozen people come out from under a thatched roof shelter. They are all dark brown and very short. The long-haired tourist couple get into a wooden boat with four of them and glide off into the water. The other two lift our bags onto their shoulders and wade into the water where they stand and gaze out to the empty sea. I look at Roza quizzically.

'Have a seat. The Kuna are on Kuna time.'

We sit on a log and wave the mosquitoes away. The heat is thick and smothering. The two Kuna men wait patiently.

'They own these islands, the Kuna. Smuggler's paradise.'

'Are you smuggling?'

'Picking up a delivery.'

Roza shakes her curls and tilts her chin up. The pilot smiles and waves and with a roar of his engine the airplane winds up and rattles back down the runway, ascending at the last moment possible, soaring precariously above the treetops.

I see the boat before I hear it. A dark speck moving toward us. Then the sound catches up and follows the boat as it motors in between the two men. We wade into the water, warm as a bath, with swirls of brown silt spouting up through my toes.

The boat is narrow, made from a single hollowed-out tree trunk with a motor attached to the back and seats across it. The Kuna perch at opposite ends of the boat while we sit on the seats in the middle.

The engine revs and we skim off over the water, the boat feeling wobbly and unstable. I clench the rough edges and notice a small leak near my foot, water spurting in a mini-fountain. Roza sees my white knuckles and the leak.

'Don't rock the boat.' She laughs and winks.

I feel the heat of the blue stone next to my misplaced heart and I laugh too, beginning to embrace the danger knowing that if I died it wouldn't matter, I was already dead. I laugh out loud again. The water is remarkably clear and I see flashes of red that are brilliant starfishes and purple tinges that are jellyfish. We pass pale sand islands full of trees and fragrant white flowers whose scent drifts to me over the placid water.

The boat pulls into a tiny island. The most perfect island with two cane huts and exactly nine palm trees. Hammocks are strung in the shade and the sand is blindingly white, even with sunglasses. We sit in the shade of one of the *palapas* and one of the Kuna sharpens his machete against a stone. Instantly the perfect island becomes a perfect setting for a horror movie. Roza seems unaware of the sinister change. She sits with her eyes closed, humming a tune.

Now that there is no wind from the moving boat, the midday heat is oppressive. I walk to the water, my feet making soft indents in the sand, and stare at its crystal stillness. I kick off my sandals and walk into the blue until my skirt and then my shirt are wet and I am immersed.

I swim out into the ocean until the island shrinks. So peaceful surrounded by the azure water and brilliant sky. Below my treading feet I can see the sandy floor. The whine of a high-speed motor echoes over the water. I can't tell the direction of the boat until the sleek black hull is almost on top of me and I see the whites of four eyes peering down at me as they veer away.

Back on the island Roza is inside the hut, sitting at a table, with a high-tech digital scale and a pile of broken bits of frosted glass in front of her. Behind her stands a very tall, thin black man and a paunchy white man. A Kuna woman sits across from the table. She has a single black line painted from between her eyes straight down to the tip of her nose, which is pierced with a thick gold hoop. Her forearms and calves are tightly wrapped in yellow, orange and black beads forming geometric patterns. She is wearing three different unmatching bright prints, yet she looks exotic instead of mismatched.

Roza picks up a piece of glass and I see that it is a stone with a silvery, milky surface. She places it in the scale and the Kuna woman measures it, then records the information in a book. They both hold the stones between their fingers with reverence and I wonder if they are drugs. Crack? I've never seen crack before. Would Roza smuggle crack? Have I gone from mother to drug smuggler within one week?

Roza motions for me to sit next to her. I pull out a cane chair and sit, dripping into the sand. She glances up and catches the expression on my face. She puts her hand on my arm, and with her other hand, puts a finger up in front of her lips.

'Shh.'

I glance at the serious faces around the table and lean closer to look at the stones. They look like quartz or any old stone you would pick up off the ground: uneven, murky. The men standing behind the table watch me closely. There is an outline of a gun butt under the shirt of the white man.

'Please make sure the measurements I call out are the measurements recorded.' Roza says to me.

'I —'

'I'll explain later.'

She looks into my eyes and I see a tinge of fear. I also see she has put her trust in me and I know I will not let her down. I nod and look at the chart on the table.

After a silent boat ride, with all of us in the boat, we arrive at a village and pull into a wooden dock. The village consists of cane walled houses with hard packed dirt floors. All of the Kuna are short, the tallest men are about five foot tall. We sit in the shade of a *palapa* and wait for the chief who is busy with some other foreigners, some other smugglers.

Despite the Kuna's' height, there are three basketball courts. They are playing in the mid-afternoon sun, some barefoot and others in flip-flops. The basket is lowered slightly. The ball bounces out of bounds and hurls straight for Roza's head. I catch it and throw it back in the correct fashion, the way they showed us in gym class. The Kuna look impressed. They converse in their language for a moment and then one of them yells over to Roza in Spanish.

'They heard you are American and they want to watch you shoot a basket,' Roza says.

'Not all Americans play basketball.'

'Doesn't matter.'

'And I was never any good.'

'I think it's a good idea if you play. I told them you played on a team in California.'

'You what?'

'No one knows you. Good for our public relations.'

'This is ridiculous.'

They stand scattered around the court, looking at me expectantly. Roza gives me the thumbs up. I step onto the pavement and one of them tosses me the ball. Here I am in Panama playing basketball with Kuna Indians. I am a head taller than most of the men and this gives me an Amazon status that pressures me to do something spectacular. I stand at the foul line and bounce the ball a few times. My gym teacher used to tell us to clear our minds before shooting. I look out at the piece of tranquil blue water that I can see, line up the basket and shoot, a little jump in the air, arm straightened out. It's a good shot, rims the basket twice and goes in. I am amazed and hold my arms up, Rocky style. They cheer, but stop suddenly.

They are staring at the basketball court near my feet. I look down and see, on the ground, my blue stone, glittering and twinkling in the sun, it obviously slipped out of my bra. I snatch it up and the players press around me. Rapid talking breaks into shouting.

Roza elbows her way into the group to see what is happening. They crowd closer and a couple of them try to pry the stone from my fingers, but I won't give it to them. This is my talisman, my stone from my box. I put the stone in my mouth and hold it under my tongue, safe. The Kuna woman from the island pushes her way through the players and stands in front of me, not looking at me, speaking rapidly to Roza.

Roza says, 'Give her the stone.'

'It's mine.' I consider swallowing it.

'These people rule themselves. They have their own laws. Do you understand what I am saying?'

I look at the angry scowls and crowd of dark faces, the

gold nose rings and facial tattoos and think of cannibalism and sacrifices.

'She is a respected medicine woman, please hand her the stone or we will be in serious trouble.'

'Medicine woman? You mean witch doctor?'

I spit out the stone and wipe it on my skirt, holding it out to the woman in the palm of my hand. She gazes at it in her hand and then squints one eye up at me. She holds the stone up to the sun to see through it and gasps. The others push forward and several of them force my hands behind me and tie them. I am driven along the street like a cow until I reach a grass hut with iron bars across the door. They shove me inside and Roza stumbles behind me. She frowns at me.

'I'm sorry, I found it in my box after the police returned it. I didn't want to leave it behind, not after the theft.'

'They think it's a diamond.'

'It's blue.'

'They still think it's a diamond and that we were holding out from them. Now we will have to wait for the chief to take control.'

'So...you're smuggling diamonds. I'm not sure if I am relieved or not, I thought it was drugs. Cocaine or something.'

'Do I look like a drug runner to you?' she asks, one hand on her hip.

'I don't know what a drug runner looks like.'

'Anyway, the Columbians have a monopoly on that. A lucrative business, but unfortunately for the Kuna, they are paid in kind...in cocaine... for use of their islands and water space and they end up using themselves. I didn't tell you we were picking up diamonds because I was afraid you would say no.'

'You know what those rocks are financing.'

She looks at me directly. 'They are not blood diamonds.'

'Where was that ship coming from, the one that brought the diamonds?'

'Africa, the delivery was from Angola.'

'For God's sake, they are blood diamonds.'

'There is no more war in Angola.'

'And why do you think these are not blood diamonds?'

'Because I know the man who sent them to me. And I trust this man with my life. I *have* trusted him with my life. He is my husband, he is a bad husband, but he has never lied to me.'

'And he sent you these diamonds.'

'He's from Angola. He left me when he went back to fight and now he has connections with independent miners. It's the Wild West over there, complete with a corrupt sheriff controlling everything. After the war, the government nationalized all the mines and now there is a law that the miners must sell the diamonds to them for a miniscule fraction of their value. If I buy the diamonds from De Beers, there are huge taxes, up to forty percent. If I buy them directly from the miners, everyone makes more money. They're able to buy equipment, dig deeper wells for clean water and build hospitals.

'These diamonds are as clean as they come. Thousands of diamonds are being smuggled into Brazil and Botswana, because of the high prices, and then given clean certificates. At least I know where mine come from: the miners themselves and not fucking De Beers.'

Roza sees the skepticism on my face.

'Research it yourself when we return. If you show me I'm wrong, I'll throw the diamonds in the canal. When the miners go to sell their stones, there is no bargaining and if they protest about the low price, they are tossed out of the office with no money *and* no stones.'

'We could be put in jail for this.'

'I haven't figured out what your deal is, but I don't think you yourself are exactly in the clear. Believe me, the Angolan government is stealing from the people. Their diamond income has tripled over the past few years and there's nothing to show for it. No clean drinking water, no schools, no hospitals...They pay them the lowest per-carat prices in Africa. This is how I know these are not blood diamonds — who would smuggle their stones into Angola to sell them for such a low price?'

We are escorted to the chief's hut. He sits inside, a pale man with skin the color of a night worm. He wears sunglasses and has white-blond hair and rashes down both arms. He is sitting in a big chair, but it takes a moment for me to realize it's not a big chair, it's a normal-sized chair which looks enormous with him sitting on it. The chair is black carved wood, inlaid with a lighter wood and upholstered in torn green velvet. The dark interior of the hut, combined with the dark wood and green upholstery, make him glow.

We are given two straw mats to sit on at the base of his feet, very close to his chair. Behind him is a large yellow and orange swastika flag. He laughs when he sees me examining the flag and then Roza laughs, a little nervously. I am afraid.

'He sees you looking at their flag. The swastika is an ancient symbol of the Kuna's, the Nazis high jacked it.'

The witch doctor walks in and hands the chief my stone. The colors of the flag are the same as the beads wrapped around her arms and legs. She stands to one side of him and stares at me with unbridled animosity, her body so rigid that she is standing on her toes.

Roza continues. 'It symbolized the creation of the world, of the rainbow, sun, moon and stars. In 1942 they added a gold ring around the center to separate themselves from the Nazis. They said no German will ever wear a ring in his nose.' She snorts. 'They were wrong about that.'

The chief takes off his sunglasses to look at the stone and I see that under his white eyebrows his pupils are red. Maroon. An albino. I remember that Albinos eyes are red because there is no pigment in them and the color is actually the blood vessels showing through from the back of the eye. I try to look deep into his eyes to see if I can make out the vessels, but all I can see is dark red. He ignores my inspection and holds out the stone to the witch doctor who spits on it. He rubs it clean, his eyes flicking back and forth over the stone. He shrugs and hands it to me.

'No is diamond,' he says.

We all visibly relax. The witch doctor drops down off her toes. I clench the stone in my hand until it warms. The chief speaks to the witch doctor and then she talks to Roza and then Roza talks to me.

'He says you are a good basketball player.'

'No, no, it was pure luck. And shorter baskets.'

The witch doctor frowns and snaps at Roza. Roza looks at me and shakes her head slightly.

'She says the baskets are not lower. They are regulation height.'

I know they are not, but I apologize and agree with her. Suddenly she smiles and her gold teeth glint in the dark room. The chief claps his hands and Roza hands him the tally from the island along with the bag of stones. He weighs them in his hands and nods. We stand and shake his hand, American style and turn to leave.

When we step outside, I ask in an undertone, 'With all these diamonds, why do the Kuna live in grass huts?'

The chief bellows in Spanish from inside the hut and Roza translates.

'He says that if they build houses of bricks, then everyone

will have to buy air conditioners. And if everyone buys air conditioners, they will have to have electricity.'

'How could he hear that?'

He bellows out again.

'He says he is a moon child.'

The dugout drops us off at the same beaten airstrip. We sit under the thatch roof with two Kuna women and four sacks of coconuts. One of the women is also an albino. I have never seen two albinos in one day. Roza whispers that it is a recessive gene in the Kuna. Her whisper drops until I can barely hear it. She says they cannot see very well, so their hearing is exceptional and you have to be careful what you say around them. She adds that they used to kill the albino babies, but now they are more than likely to become shaman.

I finger the tiny leather pouch around my neck that the witch doctor has given me for the stone. She said the pouch will never break, but that the stone is powerful and I need to be careful. She painted red lipstick circles on my cheeks before I left. Roza has colorful beads wrapped around both legs, cutting off her circulation.

'Why did you bring me with you?'

'I've been doing business with the Kuna for years...and it's not that I don't trust them, but I never know how they will react. One time an old lady thought I insulted her. I didn't. I ran into her when it started to pour rain and I had to go in front of the elders and explain myself. I apologized and offered to buy her five chickens, the council agreed and all was forgiven. It's all about the apology here, not whether you were wrong or wronged.'

'I think you were testing me.'

Roza laughs and does not deny it. She flicks the stone around my neck. 'You need to talk to Oscar about your stone. It may be valuable.'

'Oscar.'

She gives me a warped smile. 'My mentor. My boss.'

I smile. I'd like to talk to Oscar. I'd like to hear his gravelly voice again.

'We'll call him on the phone.'

'Is he here?'

'I never know. He may be here.'

'He lives here?'

'He banks here. We'll call from my house when we are back in Panama City.'

Roza's house is wide, light and modern, but not tasteful. Chrome and glass tables, zebra wall paper, a white ceramic stallion head on top of a white piano next to white lilies in a black vase. Roza looks small and dark in her white house. We sit down and she hands me a glass of wine. White wine. We toast.

'My name is not Roza,' she says.

'What?'

'And your name is not Lucy. Or even Jillie.'

I stare at her.

'You're running from something and you better be smart about it.' She sizes me up and says, 'The second part of my business is done in New York. And you said you wanted to melt into the New York melting pot.'

She leans forward and smiles at me.

'You want me to smuggle diamonds to New York?'

'I am involved in the diamond...trade. It's your decision, I only wanted you to listen to my idea.'

'Idea? I don't know what I am listening to. What do you do with the diamonds?'

'Sell them. I told you the other night that they are safer than cash. If someone has money they don't want to declare, they deposit it somewhere, say in an offshore account. Then they transfer their money to a country, say Panama, where the accounts are private. There are very few crimes that can give outside governments any right to the account holder information. Then in Panama, the money is withdrawn within one year of deposit and changed to rough diamonds straight from the miners. No record. The rough diamonds can then be taken into the US or the UK and changed for cash. You can lose five to ten percent or more on the exchange, but you will have clean money.'

Roza pours more wine and continues.

'We have a perfect record for non-blood diamonds and those money washers with a conscience come to us.'

'Money washers with a conscience?'

'Just because you are a criminal doesn't mean you don't have morals.'

I stare at Roza. Her transformation from café owner to diamond smuggler has changed the way she looks. She is tough with a strength I hadn't been aware of. We are both fugitives and I like this.

She says, 'I know that because of the theft, you are not in a good position. Ignacio owed his dealer over twenty-five thousand and I've heard that he paid it back. That was a good chunk of change you lost. I have a proposition for you.'

'How will this help me?'

'There are a lot of women involved in this trade.'

'Why?'

'Think about it — women are built to smuggle diamonds.'

I think about how many diamonds you could get into a large brassiere. Roza shakes her head and I see from her expression that she is talking about somewhere else.

'Not here?' I point to my chest.

She places her hands on her breasts. 'Not here,' she

agrees. 'Think of a big penis inside, full of diamonds. That's a lot of diamonds.'

'No,' I say quickly, 'I'm not going to do that.'

'You don't have to. We have a better way of moving the diamonds. I can pay you and I need you to go to New York. I will get you a Panamanian passport. I'm sorry, it's the best I can do quickly. Later I'll find a better one, maybe Canadian. It's tough since 9/11.'

'I don't think I want to hear this, but how do you get the diamonds in?'

'Denim jacket.'

'Denim jacket?'

'You'll see – and you'll be well paid. It'll give you some of your money back, not all of it, but a good amount. We'll pay you in diamonds that you can sell.'

I picture myself in New York trying to buy a cappuccino with a handful of stones. 'I don't know...'

'Think about it.' She picks up her phone, it's white, and dials and hands it to me. 'Talk to Oscar about your blue stone. He'll help you.'

The phone rings and rings. 'Oscar here.' His voice still makes me feel warm.

'This is, ah...'

'Hello, have I lost you?'

'No, this is...' My eyes flick to Roza. 'Jillie Martin. Hello...hello.? I can't hear you very well.'

'I'm on an airplane.'

'It sounds as though you're in the cockpit.'

'I am... And?'

'And what?'

'You called me.'

'Roza called you. It's about a stone. I'm...the one you saved. In the water.'

'The little mermaid. Well, are you buying or selling?'

What do I want to do with my stone? I can't sell it, not now. My life would become uncentered, it would teeter to one side and there I would be, holding on by my fingertips again.

'Hello?'

'I'm not sure.'

'Well, what is this stone you are not sure about?'

'I don't know. It's blue.'

'How big?'

'Good size.'

'Ladybug? Cockroach?'

'More of a cockroach, an oval.'

'Hmm, okay, Jillie. I need to see it. Come see me in New York. Get the number from Roza and call me when you're there.' Click.

'Oh for God sake. He said to get his New York number from you.' I hand the phone to Roza. 'Now why would he think I would be in New York?'

She shrugs and won't meet my eyes. 'Everyone ends up there at some point.'

And so, I've slipped into a new life, complete with a friend and a job and an identity. But I am not Jillie Martin and my friend is not Roza and I am now a diamond smuggler.

CHAPTER 10

ROZA TALKS

I've never believed in love at first sight. *Por Dios*, what bullshit — who can love someone they've never spoken to? How many people open their mouths and nothing worth a damn cent comes out? And how would you know what they think about God or if they wash often enough? Or their mental state? There are enough of them out there with minds lighter than a feather or with so many holes, they can't hold a thought. Love at first sight has got nothing to do with love, it's all about wanting to hop in the sack with someone and screwing all night long. That kinda love lasts until one of you figures out that the other is nothing like what you thought. Then you're left with empty blue eyes or strong arms you don't want to touch.

But from behind her shoulder, I could see Oscar's face. I had known that face for years, worked with that face, talked to that face, hated that face and loved that face. I had never seen that face change the way it did when she walked into the café. I never knew his face was capable of such a movement.

At first I thought she might be one of those born-agains. Never trusted those people. Why didn't they have their faith all along? What catastrophe happened that brought them to

God? That's no way to find God — God is inside you, not borne of calamity or illness.

As soon as she spoke, I could see that she wasn't one of them. And I could see Oscar staring at her back, his eyes shining over her shoulder.

He loved her, hard ol' Oscar. *Amor veradero.* I saw it. I didn't think he knew it until I spoke to him the next day and the first thing he said was, 'Keep an eye on her.' Then I knew he knew. He had bought a lot of property in Panama. No one was buying it in Casco Viejo in those days and when she asked about a apartment, he winked those blue eyes at me.

My mother used to say I was born on the street. I think she meant I could take care of myself. Or it could have been my foul mouth. My mother claims my first spoken word was damn. Not ma or pa or da — damn. Her breast milk was drying up and I couldn't get that last suck, so I bit down hard on the nipple and looked up at her and screeched, *damn.* Damn.

Some of us choose the easy way in life. We marry partners our parents approve of, we take jobs that get us by, we raise our children in the churches we were born into. There are others who make wild decisions based on high emotions, they trek along mountain ridges and swim with sharks. In the end, those easy choices are what kill us inside. Those easy choices make life as hard as it could be.

Sane love has no place in my life — give me a grand passion that borders on insanity. Fuck soundly, flash your breasts, make rash statements, slap someone...give me violence — silence is for the dead and we'll be there soon enough.

My husband never should have married me. He never should have married anyone. He tried to settle down and be with me and raise a child. All along I knew he was thinking about revolutions and how to save a country and what sort of man could remain true to a cause. He's the kind of man who gets involved in big issues in small ways. He sees clearly within his own vision.

Unfortunately, he made a terrible husband. I could sense the longing in him, the itch. At first it was a ghost of a feeling that hovered around our house, over our heads, but it grew stronger and I felt it on my skin and whenever I looked at him, I could see it in the way he moved or spoke. I told him to get the hell out and he went.

I met him when he sailed into the local yacht club and docked. It was one of those scorching hot days where the air burns the inside of your nose raw. I sat on the dock with my big mutt dog – a real *perro de calle*, half boxer and half St. Bernard, named Che. Even then I was attracted to revolutionaries. Dogs in general are man magnets, and Che was a big mangy thing that only attracted men who appreciated the odd side of life. Che lay panting in the shade of the pilings while I sat near the edge of the water wistfully thinking about jumping in.

He stopped and looked at Che and started laughing like hell. Agostino was olive-black and his white teeth, so small and perfect between his thick lips, shone in the sun. He sat down and started talking to my dog.

'You and me, dog, we got some hair issues.'

They did look alike with scraggly dreadlocked hair, strong jaws and big noses with nostrils the size of eyeballs. Agostino was very thin with sailing muscles, not the kind from a gym. His cheeks were pockmarked and he looked dangerous, or maybe like an adventurer.

He licked his lips and out came this bubble-gum pink tongue, like a snake about to bite my nose. So perhaps I was as bad as Oscar, falling for that pink tongue that made me wonder about his insides and between his toes and his belly button. Were they the same bubble-gum pink?

That afternoon we adventured straight to a nearby table and through five cups of coffee before we started on the beer and we didn't stop until we were married. When I kissed him he tasted of bubble gum and I explored every pink bit of him, down to his tiny puckered asshole.

Every day was bliss with that man. I will never divorce him, I love him too much and I know he loves me no matter where he is or what he does. Ours is not a situational love. I am old enough not to care, only that he is mine in my mind. These kinds of men are not meant to be rooted to one place, yet they're the only ones worth loving.

Oscar saved my life and my husband gave me one.

I met Oscar when I tried to sell him a stolen emerald. I hadn't stolen it, but I had a deal for a percentage of the sale. He told me that if I had any brains in my head, I would immediately return that stone to its owner. Or I could keep it and the owner would hunt me down and string me up. He arranged the return of the stone and hired me.

I have never met a perfectly moral person. There are degrees of morality. A steady churchgoer can be rotten to the core and someone who lives in the grey area of the law can be the kindest, least hypocritical person. What I trust is the eyes. If you can't look into someone's eyes and be taken immediately to the center of their character, then it will be a twisted path to discover his true core.

Oscar's not a woman hater, far from it, but I've watched women try to weasel their way into his heart and money and

I've seen him slam the door with gusto. He loves married women the most — they're safe. I never knew his wife, she killed herself long before I met him. Her daughter was only five weeks old. She must have had postnatal depression before it even existed. One late martini night Oscar told me how his wife wouldn't hold the baby, or look at her perfect fingernails or her wispy eyebrows. She just sat in a rocking chair staring out the window, watching the sparrows build their nests.

I've watched Oscar raise his daughter and try to shield her from reality. This has created a spoiled suspicious woman who can play him with a glance. He is helpless in her presence.

Both Agostino and I worked for Oscar. He was a good mentor, a fair boss and always trustworthy, which makes him a star in his profession. After the civil war in Angola broke out, Agostino returned to his country to fight with the US-funded rebels. At first he was fighting off the communists, but soon he was fighting against the government. We started selling diamonds from the local men who were starving and had no water to drink in their villages. They risked their lives for these stones.

The rebel leader lost a supervised election and refused to give up, continuing his fight until decades later, when he was assassinated. Now the government takes all the diamonds and the rebels have retreated to the hills maintaining some control of mines.

Shortly after Agostino had returned to Angola, Oscar received a shipment of stones from Africa. I found out from the mule that they had come from Sierra Leone and when I told him I didn't want them, he threatened me and I tossed those goddamn diamonds straight out the window. He took out a contract on my life. Oscar got me out of the US and down to Panama where he bought me a new name and set me up running the Panama side of the business.

If the government is not hunting you and you don't pay taxes, it's easy as pie to disappear...because no one cares.

CHAPTER 11

APPENDIX RECOVERY

Sister Mary's lecture on Mesopotamia was hideously boring...Sumerian language...the wheel... the girl in front of me picked at a scab on the back of her calf until a drop of blood traveled its way down her leg and was sucked up by her white sock.

As Sister Mary droned on, I stared out the window and tried to ignore the pain growing in my stomach. I thought back to what I ate last. Macaroni and cheese, chocolate milk and a peanut butter cookie. A perfectly normal lunch was twisting my stomach and the ache in the middle of it was growing astronomically. I leaned forward on my desk to hold my stomach and then felt nauseous and rushed out of the room, running for the bathroom.

I made it to the toilet and even after I threw up, the pain was still excruciating. I sat on the lid of the toilet and drew my legs up in a fetal position. That helped a bit. The door to the bathroom opened and someone came in, walking to the window and tossing it open loudly. I heard the strike of a match. One of the smokers who Dahlia had been hanging around.

I jumped off the toilet seat and opened it just in time to throw up again.

'Oh shit, who's hiding in here?'

'Not hiding, barfing.'

The door swung open cautiously and a girl with dark lined eyes peered in. Bianca. She wore her skirt rolled up at the waist to make it shorter, her bare white legs looked blue in the fluorescent bathroom light.

Ever since we returned from Celia's, after Bird's death, Dahlia had been different. In the morning, as Dahlia walked ahead of me on the way to our classes, she was sashaying more than walking, her skirt whipping from side to side. She'd never walked like that before. Chloe, too, seemed changed, happier than I'd ever seen her. Maybe it was Val's absence. Her migraines had all but vanished. If whistling is any indication of happiness, she was at the top of the happiness meter. Only I was the same.

'Dahlia,' Bianca said to me with relief.

I threw up again.

'Jesus, are you drunk?'

I looked up at her, eyes tearing, nose streaming.

Bianca stepped back. 'You look horrible.'

'Nurse,' I croaked.

The nurse was not in her office. Bianca seated me and ran off only to return with the news that the nurse had to deal with an emergency. I was shivering and when Bianca touched my forehead, she yelped and made a cool press with a paper towel and water from the faucet.

'What are you two doing out of class?'

We both jumped and turned to see Sister Claudia looming over us. I grabbed my stomach.

'She's...Dahlia's sick.'

'Not Dahlia, Hetta.'

Bianca folded her arms and squinted, annoyed. Sister Claudia peered at me suspiciously. She put her hand on

my forehead and handed me a thermometer. I dutifully put
it in my mouth. She dismissed Bianca with a flick of her
wrist and tapped out the minute with the tip of her black
round-toed nun's shoe. When she read the thermometer
she frowned at me as though I had managed to influence
the mercury.

'Your sister's already at the hospital.'

When we were younger and we went to Celia's for a
visit, I crept into her sitting room and stood below her
cuckoo clock. I wanted to catch the bird when it popped
out and save it from a life of cuckooing inside the clock. It
was a few minutes before eleven in the morning and I held
my breath, ready to free the bird, when I heard footsteps. I
ducked behind the sofa and when I heard the bird sing its
song, I peered over the edge to see Dahlia snapping off the
bird with a squawk.

So the fact that Dahlia was already at the hospital did
not surprise me. She was always first. Sister Claudia bustled
me out the door, I walked behind her holding my stomach
and trying to keep up.

'Please, what's wrong with us?'

'Honestly I don't know. She left five minutes before you
came to the nurse's station. Nurse drove her there.'

Sister Claudia drove like a maniac and at first I thought
it was out of concern for my health, but then I realized that
she believed stop signs and speed limits did not apply to a
woman of her religious order. She constantly crossed herself
whenever she broke the law, dangerously taking one hand
off the wheel, seeking forgiveness for her sins. When we
arrived at the hospital I dry heaved once more in the bushes
as Sister Claudia went in through the sliding doors.

The school nurse appeared alongside a hospital nurse
and they brought me inside, down a hallway and into a room

where it is all white and too bright. They sat me on a white-papered lounge and the hospital nurse stuck a thermometer in my ear.

'Where is the pain?' she asked.

I touched my stomach and moved my hand to the left and down. It felt as if a balloon had been blown up inside me and when I pressed on the area, it hurt even more. She slid up my sleeve and took my blood pressure. Then she pricked me with a needle and flexed my wrist as I watched as she filled five vials with my deep red blood. Her eyes moved down to where my hands rested.

'There?' She looked confused. 'On the left side?'

I nodded and leaned sideways, curling up on the lounge. It relieved the pain about ten percent and ten percent made a difference. She walked out and left me to my pain.

A man and a woman appeared, two doctors judging by their white coats. They asked me the same questions, poked me in the stomach and moved my legs around. The woman, who had red nails and dyed blond hair, jabbed another needle in my arm and left it there, attached to a clear bag that dripped into me. The man, who had those big ears that stick out and endear people to him, studied the chart at the end of my bed and watched me carefully.

'God, this hurts.' I tried to sit up. 'Can I see Dahlia?'

'You should worry about yourself. Please try to keep still.'

'I want Dahlia.' I started to weep.

'Dahlia is fine.'

'You can see we are twins, don't you think we have the same problem?'

'It's very possible. But we have to be sure before we operate. We'll run a sonogram and we will be able...'

His voice faded out and felt as though I was going to faint...but I didn't...I could see her and the other doctor, but I couldn't hear them. They jumped up and ran to me and I closed my eyes and concentrated on breathing and containing the pain...a cold gel was squirted onto my stomach, then a light pressure and voices, many voices...and I was wheeled to a room where mercifully the pain receded and I felt myself drift...

'Hetta. Hetta, I can see you moving. Answer me. Over here, to your right.'

I opened my eyes to the glaring whiteness of a hospital room and turned my head to see Dahlia in the bed next to me, her face wobbling in and out of focus.

'How do you feel?'

'Bad,' I said.

'No kidding. You are not going to believe this. You know how our feet are mirror webbed? And the moles on our stomachs?'

'So?'

'Your fucking heart is on the wrong side of your body.'

'What?' My voice came out hoarse and weedy.

'Our insides are mirrored. It's called inverse —'

'Situs inversus,' said the doctor with the big ears.

He read from a chart at the base of my bed. I tried to move my hand up to the right side of my body where apparently my heart had lain ticking all these years, but my hand was heavy, it might as well have been a one-ton stone. My thoughts wouldn't stay in my head and all I could focus on were those ears sticking out like wings. I found it hard to grasp a misplaced heart.

I woke up every day and stared at the x-rays of my innards. Dahlia had hung them in the window at home so I could see them at all times, but honestly, I didn't want to look at them. Her recovery had been fast. Her organs were in the correct place: heart, spleen, stomach on the left, appendix, liver and gall bladder on the right. The doctors had stalled in fear of taking out an organ that wasn't there and by the time they operated on me, toxins had entered my blood and made me a very ill twin. Then they had to keep me in the hospital for a while so they could all talk about my rare condition and how brilliant they were to figure it out in time to save my life.

If I tried to sleep on my stomach, I would feel my misplaced heart beating so loudly, so wrongly, into the mattress that I couldn't sleep. I hated having my organs reversed. If I had felt like a freak with webbed toes, I felt like a double freak with situs inversus. I belonged in a circus, next to the fat lady with her coils of skin and the chicken eating geek who I was sure reeked of blood and inner disease. Tears bubbled in my eyes.

I lay in bed and practiced Dahlia's new movements. She had this way of standing, one foot forward, hip tilted, chin down. She had also mastered the raising of one eyebrow. After several days of practice, I found I could also raise and lower the same eyebrow. Yet somehow, my face didn't have the same insolent, sophisticated look as hers.

The front door opened downstairs and the sound of Dahlia's boots clomped across the wood floor. She went into the kitchen, the refrigerator door opened, she took out the milk, then I heard the rattle of the utensil drawer as she got out a spoon, the clank of the spoon knocking the sides of the glass when she stirred her chocolate milk.

I looked around my room at the ceramic horses from China, from Celia, with their broken legs glued on: red for her and blue for me. Our basket of shells from Hawaii, with two puka shell necklaces hooked around a piece of coral. A whole shelf of twin dolls given to us over the years. Our

twin red tutus sat on the top shelf in our closet encased in
clear plastic. Next to me on my bedside table was a photo
of Bird that Toby took: Bird was leaping in the air after a
grasshopper and it looked as though he was airborne, being
sucked back up into the sky.

Dahlia's footsteps left the kitchen and came up the
stairs slowly, so I knew she had made me a glass of chocolate
milk too.

'You forgot to put the milk back,' I said.

'You need to get out of this house.'

She handed me my glass and sat at the foot of my bed.
She took a deep drink and there were dots of undissolved
chocolate powder left on her upper lip. She licked them off
and crunched them between her teeth.

'Chloe's acting weird.'

'So?'

'She keeps following me and acting like she's trying to
catch me off guard.'

'Maybe she thinks you're bothering me.'

'I think it's Toby.'

'What does that mean?'

'Like she doesn't want him around anymore.'

'That's dumb.'

'I'm serious. She follows me every time I go in the barn
and she said she doesn't want me to go there anymore.'

I stared at her. 'You have straw in your hair.'

Dahlia ran her fingers through her hair, picking out the
pieces. 'Toby tells me to leave her alone, so now when I see
her, I hide.'

She drained the rest of her milk. 'Come downstairs, I
have something for us to try.'

I floated down the stairs behind her, through the kitchen
and into the laundry room, pain medication pumping

through my blood. She tossed in a load of laundry, pushed the start button and sat on the top of the washing machine, patting the area next to her for me to sit. It was warm in the laundry room and smelled of soap and dryer sheets. We sat on the washer, back to back, as the water spilled into the machine with a steady hiss. The washer began to agitate the clothes and we were jostled around a bit.

'Why are we sitting on the washing machine?' I asked.

'Bonnie says we'll have an orgasm.'

We sat for several moments to see if anything happened.

'I don't know...maybe it has to be spin cycle.'

Dahlia whacked her foot against the side of the washer. 'I can't go to college as a virgin.'

'I am.'

'Well, I'm not...Don't look so upset.'

'You always have to do everything first.'

'Okay, we'll race.'

'This is a serious thing.'

'You sound like that damn Sister Claudia.'

'Don't be in such a hurry.'

'What do you want me to do, wait for you? Did you think we were going to do this together? At the same time? That's sick.'

'It makes you an adult. It makes you one of them.'

'I'm tired of being one of us.'

My breath went out of my lungs and I couldn't breathe. I wouldn't look at her. I slid off the washing machine, turned on the dryer and climbed on top to see if maybe Bonnie had confused the two. My hair fell over my face and I peered out at Dahlia as she chewed on a hangnail. How was it that Dahlia had started moving her face so differently from mine? I had tried on her school uniform, it was the exact same one as mine, yet it looked so different on her.

And Dahlia had the good name. Dahlia. Hetta was ugly. And most important, Dahlia's heart was in the right place.

We heard a voice through the back door. Toby called us. Dahlia jumped off the washer and undressed, pulling on a nightgown and handing me a shirt and jeans.

'It's Toby, let's do a switch.'

We threw on the clothing and arranged ourselves casually next to the washing machine.

Toby stuck his head in the room. He had a stethoscope around his neck and was smiling so hard I thought his lips might split. He was smiling at Dahlia in my nightgown.

'At last, the twins back together, it's just not the same with only one.'

I beamed at him. Dahlia as Hetta frowned. How was it that our twinness had changed into competiveness?

'How about it? Let's find that lost heart.'

He waggled the stethoscope. And for a moment I wasn't sure what was happening: I got our identities mixed up as I saw Toby head for Dahlia as me, stethoscope in one hand. He inserted the earpieces in his ears and placed the metal disk on the right side of her chest. Dahlia's eyes met mine over the top of Toby's head and we stared at each other. He listened, pursed his lips and moved the disk to the left side.

'What the hell? The doctors are wrong,' he said. 'I thought this was going to be the coolest thing in the world. Only twenty-five percent of twins have mirroring and usually it's just fingerprints or something minor, but to have the internal organs...' He stopped and listened again. He narrowed his eyes. 'You switched. Damn you two.'

He threw the stethoscope on the floor and glared at us. Toby had actually thought it was cool. I smiled, proud of my situs inversus. The power of suggestion again. My misplaced heart had become interesting, not freakish. Something I had and Dahlia didn't. Something close to my misplaced heart realigned, and I smiled.

Toby grabbed Dahlia around the neck and pretended to throttle her. She laughed a little too hysterically. He dropped his hands, picked up the stethoscope and headed for me. Dahlia grabbed his arm and pulled him toward her.

'Let's show her the California choke.'

He stopped and looked back at her. She tossed her hair back and bared her throat to him.

'We've got something new. A natural high. No drugs. You'll like it.'

He walked over to Dahlia, my heart forgotten, and stood in front of her. She leaned against the wall and took deep gulping breaths, more and more, quickly. She nodded and his hands went around her neck, pinching it. I could see the indentations in her skin, her face flushed, grew fuller and she crumpled to the ground. Toby caught her, she jerked once, coughed and opened her eyes, momentarily lost, then grinned straight at me. Toby smiled at her proudly.

'Try it.'

'What was that?' I asked.

'It's a double rush.'

'You strangled her.'

'She's not hurt. I'd never hurt her, you moron.'

'You try it,' Dahlia said. 'It's the choking game, the Flatline Game. They call it Airplaning, American dream, California Knockout. You try it.'

I stood where Dahlia had been standing and took deep sharp breathes, exposing my throat to Toby. He looked me in the eyes and touched my throat, his hands felt cool. I felt the beating of my pulse against his fingertips and then blackness leaked in from the corners of my eyes, the world shrinking to a black spot as peace fell over me in a great flash...I opened my eyes, my chest heaving up and down and I was on the ground, looking straight up. There was a boy leaning over me, big green eyes, straight black hair that fell over one of his eyes.

Behind him I recognized myself, or rather I recognized my twin, Dahlia. She stood away from us, clasping her hands together so that her knuckles were red. She looked at me with concern, but also with something else, something that worried me, something I didn't understand. I always understood my twin. I tried to sit up, but I was dizzy again.

Toby, it was Toby, took my hand and held it tight. Dahlia came closer and I saw her eyes dart back and forth between me and Toby. They focused on my hand in his. Toby and I pulled our hands away at the same time.

'Wow,' I said quickly, 'that was two different rushes, one when I passed out and another when I woke up. It's like waking out of a peaceful dream, waking up and not knowing where I am or who I am.'

'Jesus. You really had us scared,' Toby said. 'You weren't supposed to go out for that long.'

'And your eyes were wide open,' Dahlia said, 'freaky.'

'I want to do it again.'

Toby helped me up and I stood on legs that felt like pins and needles. I stomped on the floor a bit to get rid of the tingles. I felt good, as if everything was balanced and smooth. I reached for Dahlia and we hugged. Toby leaned against the far wall, arms crossed, a tiny smile glowing on his face. The sound of Chloe's car door slamming nudged Toby into action. He dashed to the window, threw it open, springing out in one leap like Superman and vanishing into the bright daylight.

CHAPTER 12

MANHATTAN AND THE LION-MAN

My flight out of Panama leaves early, wheels rolling down the tarmac fifteen minutes before scheduled departure time. We arrive in Manhattan early, something about strong tailwinds. I have no luggage and whisk through customs in minutes with only a momentary panic about my new Panamanian passport — now I am Pilar Vega — and then I grin to myself and embrace the adrenaline rush. I don't care if they arrest me, what can they do? Throw me in jail? It's not as if I've murdered someone, at least not physically. I look into the customs officers' eyes and dare them to expose me, handcuff me, take me to a back room with a one-way mirror and play good cop/bad cop. They don't.

The arrivals area is deserted as no one is expecting the plane for another thirty minutes. No sign of Roza's contact this early, so I walk to the bathroom and when I look in the mirror I am relieved to see it is still only me and not Dahlia. I stare at my short dyed hair. I lean closer to try to find the wife of Toby and the mother of Lorna. I can't find that woman from San Francisco.

I wander around the waiting room a bit and find myself drifting toward the train signs. I follow the arrows until find myself standing in front of the open doors. I glance around to see if Roza's contact might be watching me, but no one looks in my direction and so I step into the train. Once again I get a flash of random freedom, my life shooting of in odd directions. When the flashing green dot on the subway map stops at Chinatown, I push my way through the passengers out onto the platform.

Chinatown is swarming. Highest population density in Manhattan. Does that increase or decrease my chances of being recognized? Hordes of people bump shoulders, cough into each other's faces, hack on the sidewalks and shuffle around vendors with tin windup ducks and frogs that actually swim in water. There is no directional movement, purely random.

I get caught up in the Chinese movement and buy myself a red satin dragon overcoat and a pair of flat black shoes which I immediately put on. Next door to the shop is a soup kitchen with a line of people stretching halfway down the block. These people are not druggies or bums, mostly they are women, middle-aged women standing with their faces turned down to the pavement. A thin line of pain runs down my body and centers in the pit of my stomach. Could this be me? The weight of my denim jacket reminds me that I am carrying enough diamonds to buy not only the soup kitchen but the bar next door.

Winnie's. It's on the bottom level of a five-story brick building with beautiful wrought iron balconies. There is a black door and a window that has been blocked from the inside. A cold drink to soften the reality of New York. The door is partially open, I peer inside. Half a dozen people are scattered along the bar.

No one looks up as I enter, but they slide their eyes sideways. I sit on a barstool and set my Zanzibar box on the floor with a thunk. An old lady turns and stares indignantly. She is dressed in a trim dark suit and pumps. Her hair is arranged in tight curls. Red lipstick shines out from the gloom of the bar. I smile slightly and turn to my other side. There is a man sitting there, studiously ignoring me. He looks rough, in a good way, with shoulder-length brown hair that curls rather than waves and a scruffy beard long enough that I know it wouldn't hurt my cheeks.

The bartender is a young Asian girl with several piercings. The one above her eyebrow looks infected.

'I'd like a Cuba Libre,' I say.

'It's new.'

'It's a rum and coke.'

'I know what it is.' She points to her swollen eyebrow. 'I mean this is new, that's why it looks kinda nasty.'

'A little peroxide and it should be fine.'

'That's what my fucking mother said.'

'Listen to your mother.'

'My mother doesn't know jack shit.'

'That's right,' the old lady to my right says. She kicks my stool. 'Where you come from?'

Jesus, so much for Roza's theory that New Yorkers didn't ask anyone where they were from. 'Kansas,' I say.

She snorts, turns and faces the bartender.

I kick her bar stool. 'Where you from?'

'Here,' she says, 'all of us are from here. Right?' She talks loudly and looks down the bar.

The bartender speaks first. 'I'm from Brooklyn.'

A black man down the bar says, 'I'm from New Orleans.'

A woman with a black eye, or smeared mascara, says, 'I'm from Korea.'

'Fuck you all.' The old lady stares at me again. 'You'd be an okay little thing if you'd dress a little better and sit up straight.' She raises her eyebrows, which are penciled in unevenly.

I automatically sit up. And look down at the red Chinese dragon coat. The satin glows in the dim bar, even the black rubber shoes stand out.

'Aw, leave her alone. She's a born-again Chinese.' This is uttered from the lion-man sitting next to me. He doesn't look at me or anyone else when he speaks, he just rustles his newspaper and keeps on reading.

Several guffaws from the bar. The old lady rummages in her purse and pulls out a lipstick and applies it, squinting at the mirror across the bar from her. She tosses it into her purse. 'If I were young I sure wouldn't be sitting here in this bar.'

She slides off her barstool and minces past my neighbor, hissing, 'Damn fool,' at his back.

The lion-man rolls his eyes and tosses down the paper.

'Her tragedy is that she used to be beautiful,' he says before walking behind the bar and disappearing through a doorway.

The bartender rolls her eyes. 'Don't bother about her. She's just worried about her son.'

'Son?'

'The big guy next to you.'

'Why's she worried?'

'He liked you.'

'He called me a born-again Chinese.'

'Exactly.'

I finish my drink and order another. I am aware that I am becoming relaxed, too relaxed and that soon I will want to sit in this dark bar where I feel safe until it closes. And then where will I go? I have no desire to contact Oscar. I feel as though I need some time to float around New York and adjust to my new existence, minus Dahlia.

'Can you help me?' I ask the bartender. 'I need an apartment or room or somewhere to stay.'

She nods her head in the direction of the door where the lion-man disappeared. 'Ask him.'

'I...don't think so...'

'Scared?' She smirks.

'A hotel?'

She shrugs. 'Can't help you there, not from the area.'

It is dark outside and the wind has picked up. I stayed too long in Winnie's Bar. I set my box on the ground between my feet and look both ways down the street. To the left, a slump-shouldered guy lounges on the street corner, hands in pockets, neck twitching. To the right a group of kids sits on the steps of a house with loud music booming from a ghetto blaster with blown-out speakers.

I roll back and forth on my feet and will myself to move in a direction, either up or down the street. My body doesn't obey. Leaves rush by and a small whirlwind of dust and cigarette butts shoots up in front of me.

The soup kitchen is closing, I wonder if they have beds. A worn out man with a dangerously thin comb-over shuffles through the door and slams it closed. Behind the door I notice a little nook with a painted Buddha on the wall.

Stores all around are closed. The walking teddy bears and mirrored sunglasses are packed away, the battery-operated action figures and red-fringed lanterns carried inside. No one looks at me. I don't exist in their world.

A wave of loneliness overwhelms me, hits me so hard that I stumble back, trip over my box and find myself on the sidewalk next to the Buddha drawing. I pull my box over and squeeze into the nook, with my back to the Buddha. I sit in the nook and shake and shiver with guilt and still no one sees me.

I am awakened by a hand on my head and I open my eyes to find a face six inches away from mine, eyes scrunched with concern. I shrink back and knock my head on the hard wall behind me.

'Thank the Lord. I thought you were another goner.'

He straightens up and I see that it is the worn out man with the bad comb-over from the night before.

'That Buddha attracts them.'

He touches his hair self-consciously and suddenly I am embarrassed to have been caught sleeping on the street. He sees my expression and holds out a hand to pull me up.

'I see you're one of the early volunteers. We don't get too many of you eager beavers.'

He winks at me and unlocks the soup kitchen door. He ushers me inside and turns on the lights. I don't resist. I am curious to see what a soup kitchen looks like, it may be somewhere I will be dining in the near future. It's a big white room with high ceilings set up canteen style, stark yet stylish, the tables are black and the chairs are red. He points to a door across the room.

'Bathrooms and showers in there.' He nudges me toward them. 'Clean up. Have a splash.'

He heads into a massive kitchen and I walk to the bathrooms, which are also clean and white. A stack of towels rests on top of a metal trolley. I turn on the shower and wait for it to warm up. My eyes feel scratchy and when I look in the mirror, my face looks dirty as if it has taken on the mask of a homeless person already. I shower and scrub at my face and when I get out I press my face into the towel and inhale the fresh detergent. The morning feels bright and new, it's the nights that drag me down.

When I emerge from the bathroom, the room has moved into action. There are people moving in all directions,

carrying boxes and containers and bags of meat. The man
with the bad comb-over waves at me from the kitchen and
I head to him. He starts talking as soon as I am in earshot.

'No drink or drugs allowed.'

'I don't have any.'

He stops moving and surveys me. 'Actually, I don't
care what you do, I'm talking about the guests. I call them
guests because accepting charity for these ladies is difficult.
Against their culture and they are quite shy on top of it.
Most of them would never dream of doing drugs, but there
are always a few.'

He walks me over to the counter and motions to a large
basin full of moldy potatoes. He ties an apron around my
waist and hands me a paring knife. I am standing in front of
the biggest pile of spuds I have ever seen.

'You are a godsend, my dear. What's your name?'

I don't answer him, I can't think of what to call myself.
He starts to walk off and I call after him. 'Pilar. Pilar Vega.'

'Welcome.'

I look down at the pile in front of me and shake my
head at his audacity. I glance around the room. No one has
noticed that I have been hustled off the streets and put to
work. Or maybe that's how everyone ends up working in the
soup kitchen. One of the cooks catches my eye and waves
her ladle at me. I flourish the knife in her direction and she
grins, showing two missing front teeth. Her smile is kind
and it sets me to work on the pile of spuds.

Despite the monotonous work I enjoy the bustle, the
cooking and chopping and jostling as people come to the
sink filling various receptacles with water. I focus on the
potato peeling, there is a certain satisfaction watching
the mound grow smaller. My rhythm is interrupted as I
slowly become aware of a presence in the room. It is as if

the volume on a stereo is slowly, slowly being turned up. I look around me and see nothing, until I notice him rapidly unloading a box of tomatoes and I drop my knife in the sink with a clatter. The lion-man. I'm sure he has seen me and has decided to ignore me.

I work hard and I finish the potatoes faster than I thought possible. Next the man with the comb-over brings me a box of lettuce, slightly brown, that I need to pick through. About noon, the place fills up with noise. Outside the line forms.

We start to serve the food. I work at the end of the line near the bread buns. I sneak one and put it in my pocket. When no one is looking, I break it into pieces and stuff it into my mouth. One of the women in line catches my movement and I flush.

Most of the people eating are women. They are simply dressed and talk in low voices. When the tables are full, the doors are closed. There are still people waiting outside, but they are mostly men with beards and dirty clothes. Most of the women stare down at the table in front of them, eating quickly.

As soon as the kitchen is empty, all of us remaining sit down to eat. I am so hungry my hands shake. Vegetable soup with miniscule beef chunks never tasted so good. I finish and look up. He's watching me without watching me. I walk over to him and stand in front of him until he raises his head and looks at me. A surge of adrenaline charges through my body.

'Little China doll,' he says.

When I was with Toby I never noticed other men. Now it's as if something has opened up and it's not mental, it's purely physical. My body is reacting before my mind.

'The bartender said you... well, I need a place to rent.'

He looks at me as if he wants to devour me. 'I may know of something,' he says.

I shiver. His clothes look expensive, but the kind of grungy expensive that only thin-moneyed frames can carry off. His collar is out of shape and his cuffs frayed. I look away and out the doorway. What would happen if I went to Celia's? Would she slam the door in my face? Call the police? I look back at him. He is watching me with a half smile, lips twisted.

'But, I don't...you're looking at me...'

'You don't trust me?'

'I don't know you.'

'I never lie.'

I give him a dubious look.

'Ask anyone here.'

I walk over to the worn out man. 'Excuse me.'

He turns to look at me.

'Do you know him?' I turn and point at the lion-man.

'Sure do.'

'Is he...okay?'

'He's not gonna slit your throat, if that's what you mean.' He walks away.

I sigh and walk back to him. 'Okay, where's the apartment?'

'Very near.'

'Can I see it?'

He washes his hands, dries them and walks past me. I inhale the air he leaves behind and slowly follow him. He walks out of the soup kitchen and unlocks a door next to Winnie's Bar.

I look up. 'The apartment is in the same building as the bar?'

'It's above the bar. So?' He looks me up and down.

We go upstairs. The stairs are lightly scuffed, yet in perfect repair. He opens the door and ushers me in. The apartment is magnificent. Big windows and lots of them. All open, loft style. Waxed hardwood floors. Not much furniture. High ceilings, a leather hammock hanging in the corner of the room. The bed is in a corner and I try not to look at it too long.

'I don't think I can afford this.'

'No, this is my place. Yours is in the attic. But we have to wait for the keys. Drink?'

'You have some tea or coffee?'

He opens a cupboard and takes out a bottle of tequila, Patron. He sets out a salt shaker, slices a lime and hands me a shot glass.

We do two shots each, no talking, lots of looking. He reaches into a cupboard and brings down a sugar bowl, tapping out a small mound onto the counter. He then takes a gleaming butcher knife and my heart starts pounding for another reason. The man said he wouldn't slit my throat, but what about cutting my eyes out? I move back to the doorway and watch him dice the sugar into two lines and snort it into his nostrils. Cocaine. He offers me some and I shake my head. I think I need to keep my wits around this man. He motions for me to come closer and I take slow steps toward him until I am in front of him. He lifts me up by the waist onto the kitchen counter, our lips grinding, he is swallowing me whole and then we are horizontal on the kitchen table, vertical on the windowsill, horizontal again on the bed.

I don't think about Toby until I think that I'm not thinking about him and then I think about him. I shove the lion-man away and run into the bathroom. I don't do anything in the bathroom. I close my eyes and clear my mind and imagine the feeling I used to get when we played the choking game. The clearness of everything afterwards.

I wake up sometime later. It is silent in the apartment. I open the bathroom door and step outside. He is stretched out on the couch with both hands over his chest coffin style. His shirt is off and I see the rise and fall of his ribs. His eyes open and he looks at me and opens up his arms. I slowly walk over and fold myself into them and feel two tears drip down my cheeks onto his chest. We sleep like this all night.

In the morning, there is no sign of the lion-man, no note, nothing. I don't even know his name and this makes me chortle to myself like an old crone. I wander around his house and look at everything. No photos, no mail, almost nothing on the walls, only one framed poster in the kitchen of an old theatre production. I lean closer to peer at the actors and I think that one of the women is the old lady, his mother.

The lion-man has left, on my thigh, four small bruises lined up like little stars. Fingerprints of the night. I line up my fingers next to the bruises and my heart starts to beat more loudly.

By now I am sure the word has gotten back to Roza that I am missing. She wrote down Oscar's number inside a matchbook. I open it and stare at her bold writing. I want to deliver his diamonds and I want to have him see my stone. I have high hopes that it is an aquamarine or topaz or...a sapphire. Maybe a crown jewel worth a kingdom. But even more than the jewels, I want to hear his voice. I dial his number and as soon as it rings, I hang up.

I wander into the kitchen and look in a cupboard: wheat flakes, rye bread, peanut butter, all new and spotless. Even a honey drip has been wiped from around the edge of the jar, I can see the outline of the mark. The man is a clean freak. I walk back and stare at the phone. I dial the number again and let it ring until someone picks up.

'Oscar here.' The same low voice, husky Scottish accent.

I hold onto the phone and listen. I hear him listening on the other end. He hears me listening. We sit like this for a few moments before I press the off button – there is a loud click and then nothing.

CHAPTER 13

LION-MAN TALKS

When I'm alone with a woman, I find a thousand things to love about her. It's only when she's out in the every day world that all her scars and faults are revealed before my ever-critical eyes.

Yet I want to fuck'em all. I think about sex all the time now that I can't do it. My desire for women never changes. I love their soft skin and stiff mascara-coated lashes. I love how the same perfume can smell different on each one, their body chemistry changing the scent. I love tight jeans that crawl up their ass-cracks and I love baggy jeans that hang off the tops of their butts. I love the sluttiness of stilettos and the athleticness of flats. I love big cleavage and small girl-boobs under white T-shirts. I love how they seem so innocent yet in a split second they turn into tigers, fangs bared — ready to gouge out an opponent's eyes with their red-tipped nails.

I am, possibly, a misogynist. Not that I think women don't have a place in business or that they belong in the kitchen, but it's their principles and morals I can't stand. Women are their own worst enemies. Silly cunts who would shove their best friend over a cliff to screw some guy they met ten minutes ago. Listening to women verbally attack one another is akin to cannibalism. Gives me the creeps.

When my mother took a dislike to Pilar, who sat next to her on the barstool, I immediately had to like her. My mother and I have this kinda fucked-up relationship. Women always want something from me. Money, sex, a baby, a ring, cash: always something. Pilar's the first one who seems to want nothing. And I give her nothing. She's a strange one, never mentions family or friends, debts or jobs. Doesn't pout or play games, in fact if anything, she made me feel too obvious in my own games. And it's not about the sex with her, sadly my addiction has taken me past that point.

Most women insert themselves in your life, fake interest in your hobbies, watch football, learn racquet ball, even tag along on the fishing trips. They'll befriend your friends, ditch their own, push away their family to take on yours — anything to be part of your world. At first I thought this was what Pilar was up to, but I was wrong.

She does things that other men would fall in love with. She plays with her earlobe, twiddling it between two fingers as if she were massaging a sex organ. When she washes her hair and wraps it up into a towel, she walks out of the bathroom like an Indian princess. These are things men fall in love with.

I don't think I'm in love with her, but I don't know how I would know. Maybe it will take her to leave for me to know. Maybe when she's gone I'll cruise the streets for years searching for her. At thirty-seven, it seems I must be immune the possibility of love. Things are different when you're older, different symptoms of different illnesses. Isn't that what love really is? An illness?

People think that I haven't married because my parents have such an awesome relationship and I haven't been able to match it. While it's true that they're still in love, it's not a love I would want. Truth of it is that I've had a firsthand look at a lifelong relationship and what it turns into and I don't want anything to do with it. Loss of passion, false affection. Tolerance, compromise. And no variety. Marriage should have nothing to do with sex, that should be found outside the relationship.

My father was a famous conductor and as a kid I was always dumped with a nanny when my father, along with my mother for moral support, went on tour with an orchestra. My mother wouldn't have considered staying at home and to bring me along — who wants a third wheel?

They made a half-assed effort to be interested in my life, but all their conversations circled around to music and tours and lead violins. I learned to play the piano, thinking it would catch their attention. They clapped their hands and said, 'Encore, encore,' but then they packed for their fucking tour in Berlin.

My mother's a piece-a-work. Her lifelong discontent comes from the inner vision she has of herself. I'm sure it hit her like a freight train in the brain, when the thought occurred to her that she'd missed her moment and it was my father who was the star. Once that thought wormed its way into her brain, she put up a mental barrier the size of the Great Wall of China. Every day she puts on her best pearls and reddest lipstick thinking that today might be her lucky day. She won't look at recent photos of herself, claims the digital cameras of today don't catch the true spirit of a person.

My father is an enabler. He lets her believe in her inner world and introduces her to theatre people and movie producers as if she's the next goddamn Marilyn Monroe or Helen Hayes. She bats her lashes at them and speaks slowly, letting her lower lip hang slightly open. Some producer must have told her it looked hot back when she was nineteen. Now it looks as though she has had a stroke and is about to drool.

In high school, basketball was my game. Junior year the coach said I would be scouted right out of senior year. The single mindedness of the game hooked me – the way pros have to be, if they want to be the best. My whole life was about a ball and a basket. I looked at girls, dreamt about fucking them, but didn't touch them. Always hanging around practice, watching and giggling. Cheerleaders were the worst, with their possessive attitude and their show-off splits. They loved to spin and give the audience a look at their young pussies.

Basketball was pure – all about concentration, dribbling down the court, setting up the hook and checking out the swish as it sliced through the net. I always knew what was waiting for me at the end of the court. The other team wasn't human to me, only moving objects I had to avoid. I knew their moves before they knew them themselves.

My team made it to the top, the nationals, with me as captain. Neither of my parents bothered to come to the championship game. We won and I quit and began my life of parental torment. Best way to piss them off was to have a revolving door of unacceptable women. I should move on and start my own life away from them, but then I'd have to find a job and work. And I'm old enough to admit I'm lazy and a coward. The soup kitchen suits me fine.

At first the soup kitchen was a way to poke at my mother for all the rude comments she made about the filth of a

homeless woman's hair or the stench of a beggar's feet. I
grew so tired of asking her how they were supposed to keep
clean with no home, let alone a shower or bath.

She grew up in Washington Heights back when it was
a high-flying place to live. She watched it slide into the
muck. She watched crack appear and saw the neighborhood
change, ripped apart by a white, chemically-produced rock.

My grandparents were rich Jewish land-owners —
translation: *slumlords*. They disowned her when, at the age
of twenty-five, she married my father, an atheist Romanian
immigrant with a bald head. As the supreme dig, when my
grandfather died, he willed her this house in Chinatown.
He told her that if she was so drawn to the Chinks and
Wops and Wetbacks, she could live among them. For sure
he never thought that one day his dig would backfire and
the value of this house blow away the value of his own
Washington Heights home.

After the World Trade Center bombings, the economy
in Chinatown tanked. No tourists and the sweatshops
couldn't deliver the garments because of security. Three-
quarters of the jobs went down the drain those first weeks
after the attacks. That was the start of the soup kitchen.

From the beginning my mother hated the soup kitchen
and I realized how much I loved it. The energy and noise
and soft spoken Mandarin. There were a few smelly bums
who showed up, but most of the people were out of jobs
and most of them were women — very young or very old.
Some of the bums simply liked the life of no attachments,
no mortgages or taxes. Those were the ones I identified
with. They had a nasty sense of humor and I'm sure that if I
hadn't been born with dough, I would've been one of them.

Money gives you freedom to do what you want when
you want. It also kills any life you might've had if you were

forced to make your own way. No doubt that my shallow outlook on life is related to my happiness, but why get all introspective about this and ruin things?

Never thought of myself as an addictive personality. Addictive personalities smoke or slam down cup after cup of coffee or drink vodka early in the morning. Used to admire addicts, at least they wanted something badly and it seems I never really wanted anything. Until now. Until cocaine.

Years later, when I asked my parents why they didn't show up at the basketball finals, they looked at me, honestly confused. Didn't even remember their son had been a goddamn basketball champ.

I wonder if I've fucked too many women. Maybe this is why I can't fuck. Or fall in love. Almost makes me wish I had rationed myself. *Ha.* Key word, almost. I wonder about short men and their sex lives: How do they view life compared to their tall competition? How differently do I view the world, me at six foot five, who has never met a woman near my height? Women crawl up my body like cats on a tree. Short men are attracted to positions of power and fame to boost their little egos. Maybe it's not money that ruined me, but my height.

I've always been a lunger. There are two kinds of guys: Smooth ones who start with the fingertip on the arm or a tickle on the knee, then the arm around the shoulders moving onto the chin between two fingers and slowly turning the face for a kiss. Then there are the lungers. That's *moi.* Can't take that slow stuff. Didn't even want to have sex sometimes because of all the effort – all that undressing. Taking off the shirt – does it slide over the head or unbutton down the front or maybe unbutton down the back? Unzip the pants and get them down. Don't forget the shoes – if you forget the shoes and they get caught in the hems of the pants, it all goes awkward. There's the bra — front snap or back? Underwear — yank them down, all the way, not caught on a toe, or the legs won't open wide enough. Too many things to think about...and that's not including the foreplay. Attention to the lips, the neck, the breasts, slowly moving the hand down, don't linger on the stomach, most women don't like it, down to the tip of the hair, so smooth, down further, opening the lips, touching the inner tongue, wiggling it around til they are wet and open. I want them naked and ready without all the undressing and touching. So much effort. I don't pretend to know if I've given them an orgasm.

Virgins are boring as hell — why would anyone want a virgin? They just lie there and wait for something to happen and then they shriek with pain. Give me an experienced hooker any day. All these New York women think they're hot shit taking pole dancing lessons from strippers — a better investment would be a fucking class from a hooker.

When I saw Pilar standing over the sink in the soup kitchen, it was as if someone had punched me in the gut. Her knuckles were red from the cold water, thin arms flexed as she plucked the eyes out of the green-shaded potatoes. She puckered her lips and blew upward to remove a piece of hair stuck in front of her eyes.

I looked away. She had invaded my private space. My soup kitchen. I was furious that she could trigger such a reaction in me. How dare she jolt me out of my jaded New York world? My stomach ached. I leaned over to relieve the pain and took several breaths. I clenched the tomato in my fist and red pulp ran down my arm. My heart slowed and I retreated back into the safety of my own self-centered soup kitchen.

I ignored her and started unpacking the boxes, leftover frozen peas and turkey donated from the hospital, overripe tomatoes from an importer down the street, perfect for bolognaise, bruised apples for strudel. I hummed a tune. I knew the moment she looked up and saw me. Her knife clattered, metal on metal, into the sink.

I finished what I had to do without looking in her direction and got ready to take off for a quick snort — goddamn, I needed one. I listened to her footsteps as she marched up to me and stood, hands on hips. I couldn't speak. Two red spots appeared on her cheeks.

'Little China doll,' I whispered finally.

CHAPTER 14

MY SISTER DAHLIA

I walked into the bathroom and Dahlia stood nude before the mirror with two egg-shaped tears running down her cheeks. She was rubbing cocoa butter into her skin, the room smelled rich and chocolaty. We had no modesty, why would we when it was one body doubled? Our scars were the same, almost invisible, small red lines from the pinhole surgery that cut out our appendixes. Mirrored. Her nose was red and she sniffed and pointed to the mirror, looking down at herself.

'This is it. This is as beautiful as we will ever be.'

I looked at her body, it was beautiful. Her body, my body, they were young and strong and our skin had a gleam to it, like polished metal.

'It's all going to waste. Who sees it?'

'Me.'

'You,' she wailed, 'who cares? You have one just like it. I keep waiting for my life to start. When's it going to start?' Then she smiled at herself in the mirror. 'I even picked out the boy.'

'No.'

'I'm seventeen and done with waiting. No one will know. I won't look any different.'

'Your eyes will be different.'

'What, you think I will have blue eyes all of a sudden? Or round ones? I'll be the same Dahlia, with the same grey eyes.'

'Something will change in you and there's no way back.'

'Good. Adults try to hide sex from us. Here everything's about pre-sex. How you look or smell. In Europe they show real sex in movies. What's wrong with people here?'

'Maybe try a blow job?' I suggested.

'I won't lose my virginity with a blow job. Just my innocence.'

I stood in front of the mirror and began breathing in and out. 'Do that to me again.'

'Hetta, you're doing this too much. I don't want to do this to you anymore.'

'Better than drugs, isn't that what you said?'

'No more.'

'Come on, it's our drug. Ours.'

'There was a kid who died the other day from it, his mother found him in his closet with a belt around his neck.'

'I don't need a belt, I've got you.'

She stood in front of me and I breathed faster, she put her hands around my neck gently and squeezed. I had learned to elongate the high. Carry on the drift, ride it like a wave. I could shut out the world and live in the center of nothingness. I pinpointed the hole and focused. I became blind and deaf and the world spun opposite to a tornado, an inward spiral of calm and numbness. The dark spots spread and her face receded, her dear twin face.

I opened my eyes slowly and saw that I was on the floor. I sat up and shook out my arms. Dahlia was getting dressed, pulling on her skirt and shoes.

'It's Toby, isn't it?' Even as I asked, I knew. I'd known that our threesome had become a twosome as I lay in bed recovering from my toxins. After that first time Toby put his hands around my neck, I saw his concern for me was overshadowed by her concern for him.

She smoothed her hair and looked me in the eyes. 'Dahlia, not Toby. He's like one of us.'

'He's Toby, he's not one of us. There are only two of us. Not three. I know he wants to.'

'Of course he wants to, every boy wants to.'

'And I'm not going to ask him to fuck us both.' Dahlia says.

'For God's sake, did he tell you it was you he wanted to have sex with you in particular, or just that he wants to have sex?'

'He says he loves me...maybe I'll marry him.'

'He loves both of us.'

'We are not the same. It's me he wants. *Me.*'

'To be sure, test him.' I say. If Dahlia lost her virginity to Toby, I would lose both of them forever.

'I don't need to test him.'

'Pretend to be me...wear my clothes and see if he kisses you. Then you'll know. You alone with him, as me.'

'He won't.'

'It's the only way you'll be sure.'

Dinner was early in the evening as Chloe had a meeting after dinner. We didn't ask her where she went, she never told us. Dahlia watched me closely all evening. I knew she was thinking about Toby and what I had said and how much validity was in it. Her eyes studied me as I slowly cut my steak and brought it to my mouth. The meat was perfect, lightly salted and seared in an old iron pan. The beans were steamed, the greenness vivid next to the red blood of the steak. Fresh-baked bread from the old cleaning lady. We never cut our bread but tore it barbarically with our hands, like the French, Chloe said.

I remembered everything from that dinner. The noise of the crickets outside. A fly trapped between the glass and the sheer white curtain. A neighbor cutting his grass and the mower droning in the background. Chloe showering upstairs, the sound of the water running melodically through the pipes.

We went outside and I sat on the porch, drowsing. It was still light outside and the aroma of the fresh-cut grass wafted along the light breeze. I heard the squeak of the old swing start up way under the oak trees.

The front door opened, Chloe came out and I could smell her shower oil mixed with a light perfume. She set down her book, another thick Russian novel and kissed me on the top of my head.

I heard a sharp intake of her breath. I looked up to see what was wrong. She was watching Dahlia on the swing. In front of Dahlia was Toby, leaning against a tree, chewing on a grass blade, also watching her swinging. He took tiny bites out of the wheat stalk and spit them into the air, never taking his eyes off Dahlia, who swung higher and higher until I saw the red V of her underwear, the red ones with yellow polka dots. We did not share our underwear and we bought them in different colors. Mine were always blue and Dahlia's always red. I knew that from where Toby was standing, he could look straight up her dress.

'She's going to do it with him.'

'What?' Her voice was low, raw.

'Nothing.'

'What did you say?' Her eyes were wide.

'Forget it. Leave me alone.'

Chloe grabbed my shoulders and shook me, my head wobbling. She stopped, breathing hard. 'Goddamn it.'

I ran from her and joined Dahlia on the swing. We got our rhythm going, making the same underwear V, two long stretches of legs in polka-dot undies. Somehow I felt mine looked different, maybe grey instead of white or the elastic had stretched and broken into little wormlike pieces. Toby watched both of us, he was in heaven. Chloe was still on the porch her face twitching between us. I jumped off the swing, not timing it right so the swing tossed me off awkwardly and I slipped into a puddle. Toby was next to me in a second, his hand on my leg, looking at my scuffed knee. Dahlia was left on the swing, gyrating unevenly, hanging on so she didn't fly off into the garden. She scowled at Toby kneeling in front me, holding my leg so gently in his hand. Her eyes were fierce.

Toby sprawled away from me, flat onto the ground. Chloe had shoved him over and she stood above him, hands on her hips. He stared at her and melted back.

'Get into the house, girls, I want to talk to you. Now.'

She turned and stomped back to the house. We shrugged at Toby and followed her. She was waiting just inside the door and slammed it hard as soon as we were past the doorframe.

'You girls are not acting like ladies. Tomorrow you are out of here...to Celia's for the rest of the summer.'

'You think we're ladies at Celia's?' Dahlia said.

Her cheeks flushed a bright red. 'Go pack your clothes.'

That night we climbed through the bathroom window and ran over the lawn to Toby's house. We tossed acorns at his window until he saw us and came down. We skipped wildly into the forest, arms akimbo, noses in the air sniffing the hot earth cooling in the night. We would test Toby. We buzzed around him, flitting and poking and laughing like a couple of magic fairies. But I saw a new watchfulness in

Dahlia's teasing. We darted down the path and behind a tree to change our clothes. *Quick, quick.*

Before we slipped out again she grabbed my arm, hard. 'You will always follow me. One twin is born first and that was me. It's your fate.' Then she spun and ran away. My white skirt looked different on her, it swirled gracefully around her legs.

As planned, I feigned a headache and left them alone in the woods. I walked back along the path, the breeze bringing goose bumps to my skin. The smell of cocoa butter clung to Dahlia's shirt. I put on my headphones and listened to a band called Pink Martini from Portland, Oregon. Dahlia called it old lady music. They played these old fashioned songs, most of them in another language, but it was the words on some of them that cracked me up. My favorite was called *Dosvedanya Mio Bambimo.* The lead singer wrote it about a guy she met at a party who was half Russian and half Italian.

By the time I reached the house, I had several mosquito bites and I knew Dahlia wouldn't be out long, she hated mosquitoes as much as I did. I rubbed a little lavender oil on the bites and made an X across them with my fingernail to stop the itching.

I sprawled on my bed to finish *The Old Man and the Sea* and tried not to think about Dahlia as me, with Toby, but images kept repeating in my head. I threw the book against the door and stomped around the room restlessly. Hemingway was so simple, I didn't understand what the big deal was about him. It seemed any kid could write what he wrote. It was just some story about an old guy in a boat who never even got his damn fish. I understood it. I got the symbolism between the old man and the fish, but so what? It was too obvious. For God sake, hit me over the head with a hammer.

Was it my misplaced heart that had allowed this to happen? It was suddenly dark outside and I had a panic attack — things were not going to turn out the way I had hoped. My blood raced. The hairs on my arm jumped and I thought Dahlia must have lost her virginity right at that moment. Without me, with my second best friend, and my love. That's what it had come to. Was that fate?

The wailing of a siren broke through my music, red lights slashed across the white walls of my room. I ran to the window and looked out as a fire engine stopped along the road followed by an ambulance and several police cars. I ripped out my earplugs and listened to the sirens.

I got a bad feeling in my misplaced heart. I tore down the stairs and over the lawn and into the flashing lights.

I saw a white canvas plimsole in front of me on the road. I saw a big truck and a man leaning against the hood with his head down in his hands. I saw police standing on the road stopping all the cars. I saw Toby's mother with her arms around Toby who was standing straight as a post, in the middle of the road. I saw Chloe throw herself on the ground next to two paramedics who were covering a body with a reflective blanket and putting a mask over the mouth.

I slowed down. My legs were wobbly and wouldn't support me. I walked by the policemen, who told me to stop and waved their arms at approaching cars. I walked by the truck driver who was sobbing and saying, '...like a deer in the headlights, looked straight in my eyes and kept running...' I walked toward the paramedics who were loading the figure onto a stretcher. Chloe kissed the body and when I reached the back of the ambulance, the blanket slid off and I saw that the body was me — there was my white skirt, now soaked bright red and my hikikomori T-shirt and I screamed and screamed and screamed until someone jabbed me with something sharp and it all went black.

CHAPTER 15

THE LION-MAN AND THE SOUP KITCHEN

I don't call Oscar again. As much as I want to dial those numbers and listen — just listen — I don't. I have flickers of guilt, I am sure Roza is worried sick about her diamonds... and also about me. But I can't make my fingers dial that number again. I find myself staring at the phone for long periods of time. I realize that I am in some sort of shock over what I have done, *all* of it, yet I am powerless to do anything about it.

The lion-man, Peter, doesn't touch me after the first time. The bed has become mine and when I look at him asleep on the couch, I see the lines and unhealthy reddened cheeks. Sometimes I smooth the hollowed-out space beneath his eyes with a fingertip. Not in a sexual way. We seem to have reached a truce without ever fighting.

My Zanzibar box stays in the apartment upstairs, but I have yet to sleep there. Or have a discussion about rent. Every morning I check the Internet for the list of the dead from the earthquake. When I don't see my name, I head to the soup kitchen where I wash and chop and serve all day.

After the disaster in Panama, life with Peter is so comfortable. Predictable. We talk about everything. Or rather Peter talks. He's a good talker when he's in a bar. He mostly converses in monologues and never about me. He talks a lot about basketball and terrorists and North Korea. If his monologue becomes too difficult to follow, I order another drink or maybe do a line until I understand the gist of his words.

We eat dinners in the local restaurants where the staff have known Peter since he was a child. They bring Bejing duck, Kung Pao beef, lo mein, and the freshest dim sum in Chinatown. Peter doesn't eat a lot, he picks at his food and I eat for both of us. We don't say much in the restaurants. The waiters must think we are horribly unhappy, but we're not. After dinner we go to the bar downstairs from his apartment or one across the street.

I sit in front of the computer and search the death list in San Francisco. It's the same every morning: my shoulders tense, pain speeds along my spine, my hands tremble. But today, there it is. There is Dahlia's name. My eyes see the letters, but they continue reading down the list until the end. Then they start at the top again and this time they stop and read it: *Dahlia T. Carter.* Moved from the missing list to the dead list. Officially dead.

I am dead to Toby and Lorna and my friends and Val and Celia and the mother's from Lorna's school and the nice lady at the grocery store with the goiter. Dead. They will have a funeral for me. With crying and flowers. Black dresses and soggy tissues. Val will arrange a service, inappropriately religious, that he will convince himself I would have wanted.

I slide onto the floor and hug my knees. I start to hiccup and this pisses me off so I choke and scream, not caring that Peter's mother is probably listening from downstairs, one eyebrow raised, lipsticked mouth turning up at the corners.

I am thoroughly disgusted with myself. There is nothing I can do about the funeral. I am dead. Suddenly I want to go home. I miss Toby and Lorna. I want to see their two sleek heads together and hear Toby call me Lambchop. I miss my bearded irises and the Golden Gate Bridge and even packing Lorna's lunch. I want it all back.

What if I appeared and had a story about being lost? Amnesia or something? It happens. Or a kidnapping? But I know the truth would come out and everyone would hate me. It would be national news. I would be put in jail. Then Lorna would have a mother in jail rather than a dead one.

Peter has done this before. I found remnants of previous girlfriends in his closet: black T-shirts, tight designer jeans — such a mixture of sizes that I can see the clothes are from quite a few women. This is not about me and him. He likes me, but beyond that I am simply filling his time as he is mine. He didn't even bother to clear his old girlfriends out of his closet. What will he add to his collection from me?

Taking a new name has helped me transition into a different life. Just as taking Dahlia turned me into Dahlia, taking Pilar has turned me into Pilar. The greatest obstacle I face daily is to not deliberate over my previous life and because I am not willing to face any other options at this moment, I stay.

Last night Peter told me the reason his mother hates me. I didn't even know she hated me. He said she hates me because I'm not pretty enough. I pretended I didn't care, but I do. I feel vacant, drained and ugly. I'd felt lonely through my marriage, but this is a different kind of loneliness. With Toby at least I had the bond of marriage and our past to hold us together. Peter just seems content to have me here, like some kind of pet.

I look around the room. I've let Roza down by not contacting Oscar and bringing him his diamonds. And possibly endangering my life and hers. A man smuggling diamonds has a certain amount of shadiness and menace ingrained in his character.

I have to get the diamonds to Oscar today. Now. I take a quick shower, throw on some clothes and try to put on a little mascara, but I find my hand shaking so badly that most of it lands on my eyelid and I have to rub like hell to remove it. I give up and locate Oscar's number. It takes me a while to find the ugly denim jacket and I panic for a while until I remember I locked it in one of Peter's suitcases. Then I have to find the key which is another half an hour until I locate it at the back of one of the kitchen drawers and then I remember, only after it is in my hand, hiding it there. It would be easy to call Oscar from Peter's phone, but the small amount of logic left in my brain tells me this is a bad idea.

Outside it is windy and difficult to find a phone booth with a phone intact. I drift around Chinatown smelling the roast duck and watching the counterfeit-watch sellers troll for victims, sweeping their arms expansively at their collections in see-through cabinets. Next to the seafood stalls, an old man with unnaturally perfect teeth bites into a sticky bun that stretches into a narrow thread before snapping back against his lips.

Two blocks away I spot a phone booth that seems to have a phone. I squeeze into it without touching the doors. I don't like to touch any part of it. I don't trust the sort of people who use pay phones, they could have a plethora of odd diseases: TB, diphtheria, whooping cough, fleas. It smells of urine inside. I used to wonder who those people were on the payphones, after all, everyone from my cleaning lady to the garbage man has a mobile phone these days. Now I've become one of those payphone people.

I insert some of the coins and dial his number. After an inordinate number of rings, a man answers.

'Whitman here.'

'Oscar? Oscar Whitman?'

'Yeees,' he says cautiously.

'This is Lucy.'

'Lucy? I don't know any Lucys.'

I recognize his voice, low, husky with a Scottish accent.

'I spoke to you in Panama. Roza's friend. Lucy with the blue stone.'

'Blue stone, yes...your name wasn't Lucy in Panama.'

Pause.

'Lucy's sort of a nickname.'

'Okay, Lucy, I've been expecting you.'

'Yes, I know, there were some things I had to—'

'Never mind. When can you be here?'

'Today?'

He gives me his address and I squeeze out of the phone booth.

The address brings me to a high-rise building on Lexington. The exterior is simple, but I can see that behind the doorman's chest, which is blocking my entrance, the interior has sleek lines and black inlaid marble outlining the elevators and floor perimeter. The doorman takes my name, calls up and ushers me to the elevator.

There are no floor buttons in the elevator, simply up and down arrows above the door. The elevator doors close and it begins to move up, on its own. The interior is wall-to-wall mirrors. I look awful. Clothes mal-aligned, hair hanging limply. I adjust my skirt seams so they land right on my hip bones and smooth my wrinkled shirt. There's nothing I can do about my scuffed plimsoles.

I lick the palm of my hand and slick back my hair. In my purse I find a lipstick and as I am applying a thick coat, the door shushes open. The elevator opens straight into a house and a man stands watching me press the tube along my bottom lip. He is holding a martini glass in one hand.

He studies me. He has two of the liveliest blue eyes I've ever seen. They jump out at me and joke with me, as if we are two kids playing a joke on our parents. Only Dahlia ever gave me such a look of camaraderie. The last time I saw him he saved my life. Then he paid for my cappuccinos and I couldn't stop looking in his eyes and I'm doing it again. There is a noise from inside that causes him to start and we break our gaze. He motions for me to enter.

The apartment is elegant and cool, the direct opposite of how I feel in my Chinatown shoes and denim jacket. I thrust out my hand, but forget which name I told him, so I don't speak and neither does he. He takes my hand and pulls me into the room, the elevator doors clicking closed behind me. His hand envelops mine and I look down at it, pulling away from him when the heat becomes too much.

'Lucy,' he says.

I think maybe he is trying to trick me into divulging another name. I spin in a half circle and say, 'I told you, I have several nicknames.'

I stroll around the room. It has all the prerequisites of elegance: a highly polished Bosendorfer grand, floor-length silk curtains, ornate marble fireplace...yet there is a playfulness to it all. In one corner is a horse from a merry-go-round. An old wooden one still attached to the red and white striped pole. It's painted aqua with flowing blue ribbons as reins and a saddle made of little carved roses. The tail is a bit threadbare, but still plumes upward with panache. I would like nothing more than to vault onto its back and ride away.

The room is large enough to skip in, so I do a little skip. A grandfather clock stands next to the fireplace. Instead of the usual somber number plate, there is a vivid yellow sun with twelve orange tentacles representing the numbers. I look back at Oscar. He is watching me with a lopsided grin on his face and I realize that even with the playful furnishings, it is him that gives the room its mischievous feel.

'We were beginning to think Roza had lost her sense of judgment.'

The voice comes from the other side of the room where I see another man sitting quietly, watching me. He is wearing black and sitting in a dark throne chair. His lips curl up at the sides when he sees I've noticed him, but it's not a smile.

'Lucy, this is Dale.'

Dale rises and holds out his hand. A wiry man, his hand is bony and trembles, the palm is moist and soft like a rotten vegetable. He sits back down and crosses his legs, gyrating his foot up and down.

'Dale is my daughter's husband.' He does not say Dale is my son-in-law. He gestures. 'Please, have a seat. Join me for a cocktail?'

'Yes, thank you.'

He looks pleased and pushes a nearly silent bell. A woman dressed in a black and white maid's outfit appears and stands patiently inside the doorway.

'Two martinis,' he says.

She turns quickly on her rubber-soled shoes and with a squeak, leaves the room. Oscar opens a drawer and takes out a jeweler's monocle. Dale squirms in his chair and clears his throat. Oscar peers at him and then rings the bell again. The maid reappears.

'Three,' he says.

I take the blue stone out of my purse and warm it in the palm of my hand. It has come to mean more than a beautiful blue stone should mean. And it's blue, Hetta blue, not Dahlia red. It's part of my new life and I can sell it or keep it or throw it away or smash it. My life is anchored around it, it gives me hope that one day my life will be as calm and sane as the lucent blue color.

'Roza told me about you.'

'Roza.' Dale agitates his foot faster.

'She has been a good friend.' I say.

Oscar nods. 'She has a big heart.'

I think about Roza and her cousin's apartment and her trust in me. I see that Oscar is waiting for a response from me. 'Yes.'

'Too big,' Dale says with a sneer.

Oscar focuses on Dale and frowns. He catches me also frowning at Dale and winks conspiratorially. The maid returns with a tray of three martinis. I hand him the blue stone at the same time the maid hands him a martini. He looks at both of them, not knowing which to take first. I can see straight into his mind. He wants the martini. Dale is like a fresh mosquito bite and the martini will be relief from the itch. If he doesn't take the martini, it will be like scratching the itch and turning it into a full blown red bump. On the other hand, the stone has sparked his interest, he can't wait to touch it, but if he takes it, he misses out on the relief of the martini.

This internal debate passes quickly and he takes both of them at the same time, simultaneously having a drink from the martini while holding the stone up in the other hand, one eye squinting at it. He sighs and visibly relaxes, sitting down at a desk and turning on a green shaded light while rolling the stone onto a stretched piece of black velvet.

I take off my jacket and it clunks heavily when I set it down on his desk. He takes a knife from his pencil holder and slices off half a dozen of the stones and hands them to me.

'Better late than never.' He sweeps the jacket into the desk's center drawer without looking at it.

A woman breezes into the room. She is wearing a long white caftan and also holds a martini glass in her hand. Only martinis in this household. An overpowering floral perfume permeates the room. She looks straight at me.

'And this is my daughter, Francis.'

Francis is older than her husband and has had some work done on her face. Her skin is smooth and tight, but it is too thin and wrinkles in stiff lines rather than soft creases. She doesn't really look any younger, just thin skinned and freakishly smooth.

'Francis, this is Lucy.'

Oscar delicately wipes my fingerprints off the stone and holds it up to the light. He turns it in circles, looking at all angles. Francis purses her lips and takes a sip of her martini. She narrows her eyes at me and points a red long-nailed finger in my direction.

'I know you,' she says.

My heart starts to thrash and I feel a flush stain my face. 'Bathroom, please?'

She raises her eyebrows.

'First door on the right,' Oscar says.

I bolt out of the room, telling myself to walk slowly, but I can't. I run through the bathroom door and lock it and place my back against it and sink to the floor. I have no idea who she is, but she knows me. What will happen? Will she tell the police that I am alive? Will I have to face Toby? My only choice is to disappear again. I'll walk out the door and find someone else to sell my diamonds to. I stand up and open the door.

I go straight to the elevator and push the button. I lean my ear against the steel and the mechanism starts to hum. The blue stone. He still has my blue stone. I walk back toward the room. They are arguing. It is Dale's voice I hear, whiny and petulant.

'That little put down of yours is indicative of the way you feel about me.'

Then Oscar, speaking slowly. 'Whatever are you talking about?'

'Not offering me a martini, while you order one for that...cheap tart.'

The last two words are harshly whispered. I stop walking and look down at myself. Cheap tart? Fuck him. I'll show him cheap tart. I sashay into the room, pick up my martini and down the rest in one gulp. Then I head straight for Oscar. I lean over the desk, close to him.

'How do you like my stone?'

'Unusual.' He crinkles his blue eyes. 'Like its owner. It could be valuable, but I'd have to run tests on it. Where is it from?'

'I found it.'

'On the street?'

I sit sideways across the desk, one leg bent up on it, the other, dangling below in the shadows of the desk. I smile engagingly at Oscar as he tips over the stone with his fingertip. 'In a box.'

'Any papers?'

'No papers. But it was wrapped in a piece of cloth. Silk.'

His eyes wrinkle at me like a naughty boy. 'Silk?'

'A torn piece of silk.' I lean closer over the desk. 'Black silk.'

'She's lying,' says Dale from his corner chair.

Oscar's eyes glow out of the darkness above the desk. I hear the distinct swish of the elevator doors opening.

'Why would I —' I was about to say lie, but I couldn't get it out. Lie? Me lie? My life is a lie. I chuckle and then chortle and then really laugh, tears running down my face. I start to hiccup. The word lie sets me off and rushes at me, all the lies I've been telling forever swirl around me and tickle my head. I grab the stone off the black velvet and run out of the room and into the elevator, all the while feeling the amused imprint of Oscar's eyes on my back. The elevator doors swoosh closed.

Outside, I gaze way, way up at the penthouse and wave, just in case he is looking down, before sprinting down the street, rubber soles slapping the concrete.

CHAPTER 16

THE NEW DAHLIA

I am Dahlia.

'It's not unusual, survivor guilt, when there is the loss of twin,' Dr. Morton said and clicked his pen in and out. In and out.

Clearly I made him nervous. Perhaps it was because this was our third session and I hadn't said a word or looked him in the eye. He talked and talked and served me homemade cookies. The first time I came it was chocolate chip cookies and when I bit into the chocolate and smelled the cocoa, I vomited on his carpet and the tips of his shoes. Now he serves me soda crackers.

I didn't sleep the night Dahlia died. I sat on the windowsill, forehead pressed to the glass, staring at the road until early morning. When I thought I could see the first glow of the sun, I went into the safe in Val's office and stole our stones, the red one and the blue one, the ones Chloe told us would be ours when we were twenty-one. But we would never be twenty-one. We would always be seventeen. They felt chilled in my palm. I put the stones in my mouth, one on each side, between the cheek and the gum.

I tiptoed into the kitchen and found a couple of sharp knives, an ice pick and a meat tenderizer. The front door

creaked when I went outside and padded across the damp
lawn. The swings moved gently in the breeze. It seemed
I could see our shadows below the trees, leaning on the
swings, hair drifting across our faces. I stepped up to the
first swing and took hold of the rope, it was smooth where
our hands had held onto it. I began to saw the rope, the
bread knife with the serrated edge worked best. First one
side, then the next. One swing down. Then the second one
fell to the ground in a clink.

The sun was lighting the sky on the eastern edge a
thick blue. I placed the tools in the crotch of the tree and
hoisted myself up to the branch where we used to sit, soul
to soul – each of us at an end of the branch, feet touching,
toes grasping. The rough bark scraped my skin and I was
surprised to find I was nude. I kept my mouth tight against
my teeth, careful not to swallow the stones.

I knew where the middle of the branch was, as there
was a small branch jutting out where we would hide bags
of sunflower seeds from the birds, and this is where I began
to dig. It was hard work and my wrist ached. I used the
ice pick to chisel out the chunks, hitting it with the meat
tenderizer. When I had a small hole burrowed out, I shoved
the stones in. They nestled snugly. I climbed over to the
trunk and tugged off a piece of the spongy moss that grew
on the south side of the tree. I stuffed it into the hole on top
of the stones. It would grow over the top and no one would
ever know they were there.

I didn't go to her funeral. I almost had my own funeral.
Toby found me hanging from the clothing rack in the hall
closet. He snuck into the house and heard a banging noise
from the closet. My shoes staccatoing against the wooden
door as my brain spasomed from lack of oxygen. What

better way to join Dahlia in heavenly blackness than our own choking game?

But then I realized that Dahlia was still alive. I was her. I was Dahlia.

Now there were the two of us together in one body, it wasn't so different from before. Taking her name wasn't really a lie. After all my sister was half of me, a single zygote split. Two from one. I threw out Pink Martini, my blue underwear, and smashed my two china horses. Toby was sure Hetta had died, he had seen her run into the road with his own eyes. Chloe was so overwhelmed with grief that she would never think her twins had switched identities one last time. Val was gone.

I also knew I could fool the psychiatrist, he never knew us when we were two. He was tall and thin with a reddish beard and wrinkly eyelids. He smiled with his wrinkles but not his eyes. Every once in a while I would get a sour whiff, from him or his office.

Several times at a session he would ask me if I had felt any physical pain when my twin died. I found out later that he was writing a paper on the mental connection between twins. Using me as a case study...all the names have been changed to protect the innocent.

I seemed to get stuck staring at a spot quite often. I'd be looking at a particular area, rather than a thing, yet my eyes wouldn't register what was in front of me. It's not like I was blind, but I couldn't move, my whole body was frozen, eyes wide open, no blinking.

Such a big piece of her stayed behind despite her body leaving, her bones being buried. The piece that stayed with me was enormous, bigger than a house, too big for my one body. I liked to think of her with me and not trapped below her gravestone.

Chloe began sanding the floors of the house. By hand. It created a lot of dust and floating particles in the air and I continually coughed. Her prize garden died, the gladiolas and roses eaten by aphids and spider rot and black mold.

I stopped looking in mirrors. When I looked in a mirror, all I could think was that I was seeing my mirror image, my twin. When someone looks in a mirror, they never truly see themselves, they see a two-dimensional mirror image of themselves, reversed. No one, except identical non-mirror image twins are able to see a true copy of themselves. If someone were to meet themselves walking down the street, would they recognize themselves? I didn't want anyone looking at me, even though they weren't seeing Dahlia, they thought they were. There were so many reflections to avoid: mirrors, framed photos, windows, sunglasses.

And the number two. I couldn't stop thinking about the number two. I hated it, I feared it. I didn't want to have two of anything again. I knew everything came in twos: arms, legs, eyes — but I wanted three from then on whenever I could. I decided that Picasso was my favorite artist, he might draw figures with two eyes, but they were so fucked up that they became two unique ones, not like identical twins or identical eyes. Three became the magic number.

I wouldn't see Toby. He tried to visit me, he threw pebbles at my window and called on the phone. He wrote me a letter that I tore into bits and flushed down the toilet. Chloe said that she tried to keep him away from the house, but I saw her outside talking to him. She tugged on her hair a lot and looked down and chewed her sawdusty nails.

It got to where I couldn't stay in the house anymore and I couldn't go outside, outside is where I would find that look of pity. I didn't want pity, I wanted forgiveness. Pity was the worst emotion, pity meant that fate had dealt me a blow worse than the others. Pity meant that they were better off than me.

I decided to leave. I emptied Chloe's wallet and got a ride into town with the maid. I took a change of underwear and three books. That was all. *Le Petite Prince*, *Franny and Zooey*, and *The Painted Bird*. Even though I'd read them all more than once, I could always read them again and if I took something I hadn't read, I might have ended up with a book I hated. And then I would only have had two.

The maid dropped me off in the center of town and I walked to the Greyhound bus depot. I'd never been on a bus before. Derelicts lounged in the trash-strewn parking lot. They stared at me out of the corner of their eyes and passed a bottle of clear liquid to each other.

The bus ride to New York was almost exactly three days — two days, twenty-three hours and twenty minutes. I didn't want it to be two days. Two again. Why couldn't they stretch it to make it three days? At the first long stop in Salt Lake City, when we started to board, I told the driver I was sick to my stomach and I needed to run to the bathroom in the restaurant. He threw me a disgusted look, but I could see he didn't want me to throw up on his bus.

I walked into the bathroom and leaned against the sink, back to the mirror. I waited exactly fifteen minutes, splashed water on my face and went to the bus. The driver eyed me suspiciously, maybe I looked too triumphant to be ill.

I sat down and looked at my watch. I had taken a step to correct the time, my goal was to push it over into three days. No more twos. I sank into a deep, restful sleep. I woke up at 3:40 a.m. in Laramie, Wyoming. The bus schedule read that we were supposed to arrive at 3:45 am. Not only did the damn driver make up the time, we were early. I had to cause a longer delay.

When we stopped in Kansas City in the early evening, I ran across the street to a stationery store and bought a metal letter opener. I walked down the street and cut back through the parking lot so no one saw me approach the bus. I stabbed one of the back tires with the letter opener. I tried to force it in, between the treads. The tire was tough and I couldn't make any progress. I needed a hammer or something. By the time I found a brick, it was too late, people were milling about the bus. I hid the brick under my arm and got on.

At 1:10 a.m. we stopped in St. Louis, Missouri. I got out and loitered at the back of the bus. No one looked at me. I forced the letter opener back into the tire tread and whacked it a few times. The brick clinked loudly against the letter opener, so I took off a sock and wrapped it around the end of the metal part. It worked, the metal slid in, but no air came out. I tugged with all my strength to pull it out, but it was lodged in the rubber sticking out about three inches. I saw people walking toward the bus. I ran behind the parking lot and sat on a curb, away from the bus, and put on my sock. The shiny metal end of the letter opener glinted in the fluorescent parking lights.

The bus stopped again in Indianapolis, right on time. The sun was up and the city nearly deserted. I got off the bus and stretched and casually walked around it. I stretched, bent down and touched my toes next to the tire. No sign of the letter opener or a puncture. The tire swallowed it. We would be arriving in New York in less than twenty-four hours.

I read *Franny and Zooey*. I reached the part where Franny is reading the little book about the pilgrim and his adventures and his incessant chanting and how you don't need to have faith when you start out with the chanting and then she faints and gets hooked on the chanting. I got it. I got why she did it.

I slid into sleep and awoke as we were pulling into New Jersey. I drank two cups of weak coffee and ate a stale sweet roll with hard raisins. I was ready with my last attempt. I felt I would go mad if I weren't able to delay the bus. The driver honked his horn and I motioned for me to get on the bus. I stepped on, sat and gazed out the window. When we were almost on the entryway ramp, I stood up.

'Rat!' I screamed. 'Rat under the seats!' I screamed with all my lung power.

Sheer terror jolted through the bus. Panic, shrieking, everyone stood up...and the bus stopped. The passengers shoved their way out of the bus and the driver made his way from seat to seat looking for the rat. He finished and shook his head.

'Who called rat?'

No one answered, but an old lady pointed at me. The driver looked at me with exasperation and I could tell he wanted to yell at me. He swallowed, took a deep breath and smiled through gritted teeth.

'You're crazy, miss. Pure *loca*. False alarm, everyone back on the bus.'

Everyone shuffled back on the bus, giving me sideways glances.

When I walked past him, he said, under his breath, 'If you so much as say one single word, I will leave you on the interstate.'

I didn't care, I was happy. I did it, we'd be late, we'd be three days to Manhattan. Not two, three.

It was early evening when the bus arrived at Port
Authority. I was triumphant. I left the bus station and walked
around in a daze. It had just rained and the city smelled of oil
and decay. I turned the corner and found a barrage of erotic
neon billboards, flashing and pumping, reflected onto a
flooded street in front of me: red glistening lips mouthing an
ice cream, a gangster clothing model with pumped up breasts
wavered onto the street.

Yellow striped sawhorses with red lights blocked off
traffic. The whole sight was bewildering and I had to pause
and take in all the brilliance and reflections and noise...the
earringed babies, the johns adjusting their crotches for crabs
or anticipated glory. Whiffs of congealed fast food and soft
drinks passed by my nose. It was too much for the moment. I
turned my back on it and found I was facing a simply façaded
church that looked too normal in all the chaos. The organ
music drew me in.

The interior was gilded with a massive altar surrounded
by cherubs. It competed with the chaos outside. A man with
a microphone stood at the front shouting to about thirty
people interspersed throughout the pews. I sat in the back
and watched. The pastor was tall and worked himself into
a frenzy, sweat splashed his face reddened. He was too good
looking for a religious man and it seemed as if I were watching
an actor play the part of a pastor. A gaggle of young women
sat near the front fanning themselves.

The service ended and the congregation filed by me.
Grizzled old men, young harlots, slick pimps with big gold
crosses around their necks. They all had a scar or a limp or a
bruise on their cheek.

I followed them out through the door where they hung
around, drinking cups of coffee which an old lady, in a racy
leopard print dress, handed out. The pastor continued his

discourse in front of the church. Groups of tourists drifted by, pointing at the spectacle of Times Square, gawking and snapping photos. Across the street, a couple of old men had set up three boxes to form a table and two seats and they played chess, ignoring the turmoil around them. A group of kids with a boom box and a couple slats of cardboard were rapping in a circle. Several more old ladies appeared next to the one in the racy dress. They stood in a tight circle gossiping.

There was a moment of stillness, a stillness that was false for this part of New York. The old men stopped playing chess, ears turned, hands frozen above the pawns. They stared across the street at the church where I stood. I looked at the church. Nothing unusual, old ladies and street people drinking coffee. The old ladies had stopped gossiping.

A baby shrieked. People's heads turned, searching for the injured child or woman. An eerie silence fell, except for the shrieking again and again. But there was no baby, or woman. A seagull floated in the middle of the flooded street. A white dove with a broken wing struggled in the flooded street, swimming frantically in circles. The dove cried. The gull shrieked and attacked, feathers puffing into the air. It ripped off a piece of the dove's flesh, extending its neck and swallowing it. Everyone watched the spectacle silently. A mother covered her child's eyes.

The gull attacked again. The dove swam in its fated circle, injured wing dragging in the water. Two lovers buried their heads in each other's hair. The pastor stopped proselytizing and stood with his mouth slightly open watching the spectacle. Shouldn't this man of God have jumped into the murky water? I remained with my toes on the edge of the pool and glared at the pastor. It was happening in front of his church. A white dove, a holy symbol. Shouldn't he provide a good example by saving this bird from being eaten alive?

A second seagull landed and came in for a jab. The dove's wing flapped against the water futilely. I took a step toward the dove...but if I pulled it out of the water, what would I do with a mutilated bird? I'd have to kill it. I took out *Franny and Zooey* and hurled it at the seagull. I hated all seagulls. The book landed several feet from the gull and allowed the dove to swim away briefly. I tossed *Le Petite Prince* Frisbee style and it flew over the gull's head. He took flight and people cheered.

The seagull returned and began to rip out shreds of skin with each peck. The dove was weak. People looked away, ashamed. A dark red circle spread out from the dove. No one met anyone's eyes.

One of the pimps laughed, his laughter reverberating like a sob. I clasped my bag to my chest and ran down the street. I waved frantically for a taxi until one pulled over. He backed up and looked me up and down before he rolled down the window and spoke.

'You drunk?'

'No, no.'

He looked a few seconds more and unlocked the door. I stepped in and he adjusted his mirror to examine me again.

'No vomiting in my car.'

'I promise.' I handed him a slip of paper with Celia's address on it. 'Please take me to this address, I'm not drunk.'

He dropped me off in front of her well-kept brownstone. I stood outside and pressed my hands against my ears, the shrieks of the gull still echoing in my head. A young disheveled man opened the door and peered out at me. Big light-brown eyes, hooked Roman nose. I inhaled and choked and began to cry.

'Sweetheart.' He held up his hands. 'Stop.'

I gasped, 'Celia.'

He took me gingerly by the arm and ushered me into the house. He seemed as frightened as I felt. Through my tears I saw that he had a scar that ran from an earlobe to the outward tip of one eye, it looked red and new. I decided that this was the man who would deflower me.

We walked down a narrow hallway and through a large kitchen filled with stacked pots of paint and messy brushes. An open back door led outside. I had only seen Celia twice since our visit after Bird died. She stood in front of a massive canvas, twice her height, in the back of the garden. She wore some sort of full length red robe that hung open in the front. I knew she was an artist. I also knew her wealthy husband died many years ago in a car accident and had made her a wealthy widow. She stood when she saw me and I cried harder. She ran across the grass, robe fluttering and pulled me into a huge hug. She smelled of freshly sanded cedar wood.

'Trevor? What happened? Talk to me.'

The young man twisted his fingers, long and paint-specked. 'I found her on the street.'

She hugged me until I said, 'I just saw a seagull eat a dove. Alive.'

'Scavengers,' she hissed in my ear.

'They were in a flooded street.'

'Doves can't swim,' the young man said sadly. 'They don't have webbed feet like seagulls.'

'Those damn birds will eat anything. Even themselves. Cannibals.' Celia pushed back my hair and gazed at me.

'In Argentina they land on the backs of whales, pecking through their skin and eating the blubber,' the man added.

'The seagull pecked and pecked at this dove and ripped out its flesh while it was alive. Still cooing. In front of a church. With the pastor standing there watching. Shouldn't he have saved the dove? I mean, they're symbols of souls and he's a soul saver...'

'Never count on a religious man.'

I took a deep breath. 'I want to have my feet unwebbed.'

Both of them stood back and looked at me. The man rubbed a finger along his scar. Celia flapped her hand at him and he walked away. Celia reached for me again and hugged me. 'Oh honey,' she said, 'oh honey.'

The surgery took a little over two hours. They had to cut the web and take a graft from my inner leg. Unfuse a few blood vessels and nerves. No longer a freak on the outside, only the inside. I took this quiet time to fully integrate myself as Dahlia. The hospital was pure white, a peaceful white and I hated seagulls more than ever, but I was not as traumatized about the dove. And I thought a lot about how the pastor was such a coward.

I used my new name all the time, *Dahlia, Dahlia, Dahlia,* as if my self were unformed and newly tender. I introduced myself to people who didn't care. I forced myself on unsmiling New Yorkers. Dahlia grew stronger inside me.

Celia said that if I passed my high school exams she would sponsor a trip to Europe for me, with Trevor as my chaperone. He tutored me diligently as he had never been across the Atlantic. I studied and read and thought of ways to seduce Trevor in Paris. Dahlia would have approved.

CHAPTER 17

CONUNDRUM MAN

It is one of those dusty Manhattan mornings that make my head feel full of cobwebs. Peter has left the apartment already. I walk into the kitchen and find only the dregs of coffee in the pot and an empty bag of coffee beans. On the living room table I see that he has left two fat lines cut on top of the old framed movie poster in lieu of no coffee.

I turn on the shower and wait for the hot water. I have taken so quickly to my new life, abandoned my family so easily. I wonder if it has nothing to do with Dahlia, this decision to leave San Francisco. Maybe it wasn't the permanent betrayal to all who knew me, the exhaustion of being Dahlia all that time. Maybe it was simply the quest for a new beginning. Doesn't everyone envision leaving their lives behind, venturing forth to an unknown city or country, different friends, a better relationship? Don't we wonder about taking all the knowledge we have and applying it to something fresh? The old always say, *if only I knew then, what I know now, when I was twenty...thirty...forty, boy would life be different, easier, more fun.*

After the shower I am still groggy so I drip out into the living room and bend over to snort one of the lines. Slight burn and the cobwebs are gone. I lean toward the next one and inhale just as I hear the front door open behind me. I see, in the reflection of the mirror over the couch, Peter's mother. She stares at my nude rear end and then the poster on the table.

'I...Peter...'

She ignores me, walks to the table, standing a foot away from my nakedness and picks up the poster. She wipes off the remaining granules of coke and methodically polishes the glass with her elbow. Today she is dressed in an immaculate old style Chanel suit and a great big pearl brooch. Her spectator pumps resound on the hardwood floors as she walks to the wall and hangs the poster, stepping back to check that it is level. She tips it to the left slightly and nods. When I see her next to the poster, I realize she is indeed the actress in the center with the jet black bob, 20s style and a plunging cowl neck dress.

I can't move. I have turned to stone, but inside me, my blood is boiling and my heart is banging at a terrific rate and I wonder what she will do if I have a heart attack. Would she leave me convulsing on the floor, clutching my chest, or would she walk slowly to the phone and calmly dial 911 and tell them in her clipped voice that her son's whore has fallen to the ground in the throes of a drug-induced seizure?

She turns on her heel and *clank-clank* walks out of the door, without ever looking me in the eyes. The door closes with a precise yank.

I cover my eyes with my hands. I walk to the mirror and look at myself. My eyes are rimmed from yesterday's mascara, or maybe the day before. My dyed hair is lifeless. Pre-earthquake I looked so fresh.

In Peter's closet I find a tight pair of black designer trousers and a white silk shirt. At the bottom of a drawer I find a shawl and a pair of high heeled boots, slightly too big until I add thick socks and I am once again transformed into a new person. I have been borrowing clothes from his closet for days and he has never said a word. Doesn't he notice I am wearing another woman's clothing, or does he simply not care?

I get my key and go upstairs to my unused attic room. The Zanzibar box sits right where I left it, in the middle of the bedroom floor. I've missed it. Reunited with my talisman. I kiss the outside and sniff the wood, the scent is comforting to me. I push the secret latch and make sure my diamonds are inside. A handful of opaque stones – my smuggler's salary. There they are, ready to be converted to cash.

I leave and try to tiptoe down the stairs. There is no one in the stairwell, yet it seems there is an eyeball, a judgmental, intrusive eyeball, observing me from the peephole of Peter's mother's door. This is the end of Peter and his mother. I am becoming adept at stepping into people's lives and then stepping out, taking on different identities. The disturbing thing is me. I don't like the me I am becoming.

Out of the house I walk rapidly down the street until I find a phone booth. I wiggle inside with my box and dial Oscar's number again. There is a huge wad of gum stuck to the ear piece that reeks of rank peppermint.

A woman answers.

'Hello, Oscar please.'

'He is indisposed at the moment.'

'Indisposed? I need to reach him.'

'Whom may I ask is calling?'

'Lucy. Lucy with the blue stone.'

There is a discussion off line. I start to sweat. If I don't sell a diamond or two, I have no money. I balance my box on the top of the phone and step outside to take a breath of clean air. The same kid, or one identical to him, hangs out on the street corner jiggling his shoulders to his boom box. He watches me from the corners of his eyes.

'Hello? Hello?'

I step back inside.

'Lucy?' It's his voice, that husky voice.

'Yes.'

'Still Lucy?' He laughs quietly. 'You've caught me on the run again, my dear. I'll be back in a few weeks.'

'Weeks?'

'Vaccination season on the farm.'

'I need to change...well, I need to see you.'

'My dear, how flattering.' A low laugh. 'Roza's coming up to the farm in a few days, why don't you surprise her? She's been asking about you.'

'Roza... Where is the farm?'

'Nova Scotia.'

'Scotland?'

'You Americans and your geography.'

'Isn't your accent Scottish?'

'It is, but my farm is in Cape Breton. Canada.'

'But...'

'Listen, meet me at Teterboro Airport. Jump in a taxi.'

'Teterboro Airport?'

'Take the Lincoln tunnel. And bring a passport. Any passport. Don't forget your stone and, just in case, grab a few things.' Another quiet laugh.

He hangs up.

'I only have a few things,' I say to the empty receiver.

The taxi drops me off in less than twenty minutes. The airport is surprisingly big with several dozen hangers that belong to unfamiliar airlines. How is it that an airport of this size existed so close to New York and I've never heard of it? It is open and modern, light, lots of metal and white paint and glass. Oscar is nowhere in sight. There is no information desk. There are no check-in counters.

'What kind of an airport is this?' I wonder out loud.

'Charter or private?' A woman hovering nearby answers. 'Can I help you?'

She is a big woman dressed in a tight white suit and red stilettos. She is comfortable in her curves the way most women her size are not, she knows her curves are the kind men love.

'I'm looking for Oscar.'

'Mr. Whitman?'

'Ah...yes. Oscar Whitman.'

She tip-taps off down a long white hallway without looking behind her. She turns her head sideways and calls over her shoulder, 'Follow me. He is expecting you.'

I follow her white clad ass that sashays with the aplomb of a hooker of the highest rank. I am not sure if I am meeting Oscar for a quick eyeball of the stone or if I will actually go with him to his farm to see Roza. I'd like to go to Nova Scotia. I mean, why not? I don't know what I'll do if I don't go.

We walk down the corridor and come to an unmarked door. She opens it and searches the room. I see that it is a tiny private theater with about a dozen black leather lounger seats facing a large movie screen. The door closes and she is off down the hallway again until we come to a room marked Private. Inside are two men hunched over what looks like an enormous elephant tusk. Neither of them looks up.

'He left,' one of them says.

She whirls around and walks back out the door. Back down the white corridor and out a double glass door that reads Do Not Enter. We are on the tarmac. The wind blows hard and I clutch my box to me. She strides off toward an airplane parked to the left. It is a strange looking plane, painted in strong primal colors with a pointed sleek shape. I never thought I would call a plane sexy, but there is no doubt, this one is.

Oscar sits in the far back corner behind a small desk with a laptop. He looks at me with a tilted head and opens his eyes wide. His hair has been cut short and the silver shines as though it's lit within. He looks younger than before, more relaxed, with a white open necked shirt and faded jeans.

He stands and walks toward me, holding out his hand. I set my box down and we shake hands. His hand is as alive as his eyes, like a bird in the palm of my hand. He stares at me and raises his eyebrows.

'Different clothes.'

'Chic.'

'Well...' I look down and feel self conscious.

'And what should I call you this time?'

'Pilar.'

He sits on one of the benches and pats the seat next to him. 'Have a seat...Pilar.'

I take a seat and look at him sideways as he continues to examine me.

'Identification please.' The woman in tight white is before me again. I hand her the passport Roza gave me and glance at him again to see if he is still looking at me. He is. He watches me to see if I intend on flying with him and I watch him to see if I am really invited along in his airplane. We eye each other until the woman breaks our silence.

'Drink?' she asks me.

'What do you have?'

She shrugs. 'Everything.'

I look at Oscar. 'What are you drinking?'

'Vodka.' He holds up a clear glass with clear liquid inside, a shard of lime peel and a few ice cubes.

'Can you make a Manhattan?' I ask, testing her.

She cocks an eyebrow at me.

'Okay, Manhattan on the rocks, two cherries please.'

She turns to walk off.

'Oh, and Chivas 21, if you have it.'

She purses her lips and throws Oscar a look before disappearing through a door.

'She doesn't approve of mixing such a whiskey.'

'I don't usually either, but I got carried away with giving instructions.'

'Don't try to out alpha that one.'

'Is she your...?'

He looks at me, a little taken aback. 'She is my assistant,' he says succinctly.

I feel as though I've crossed some line of British propriety. 'Do you want to look at the stone now?'

'That would be nice.' He is looking at me and the corners of his eyes are slightly wrinkled at the corners, so I know he is holding back a smile.

I hand him the Kuna pouch I wear around my neck. After the robbery in Panama, I don't take any chances that it might disappear. He opens the pouch and slides the stone into his palm. He turns it in circles and holds it up. His assistant appears and hands him a monocle and he examines the stone more closely, turning it sideways and looking at it straight down the center. I can't stop staring at his hair, I want to run my hand over it to see if it is like steel wire or soft like new grass.

'Fakes are brilliant these days. I really will need to run some tests to see what it is. Could be topaz, aquamarine, even a corundum.'

'It's a conundrum to me.' I laugh too loudly.

He smiles anyway and I like him for that. The engines fire up and I sit on the edge of my seat and look around the airplane. He reaches behind him and pulls out an airline seatbelt made from a strap of colorful kilim and motions for me to do the same.

'I...are we leaving now?'

'What would you like to do?'

'I...yes, I would like to go.'

'Fine, then please fasten your seatbelt.'

He watches me insert the metal buckle and relaxes in his seat, taking a deep drink of vodka. I relax too, I am going to the Nova Scotia. I silently thank Roza for trusting me and then I have a twinge of regret and I realize I miss Panama and Roza and the scraggly cat on the seawall. I miss them in a way that I do not miss my old life. My old life seems so far in the distance, as if it were a life lived by someone in a book I read or a movie I saw.

'Please, settle down, order some food, sleep...there is a library there.' He points at a wall near the front. 'Push that black button and the shelves will open. I have some work to do before we arrive. I've got a meeting first thing, then we can talk about the stone.'

He hands the stone back to me and I drop it safely into my pouch. His assistant appears again and hands me my drink. I take a sip.

'Lovely,' I say. 'Not too dry.'

She smiles for the fist time and gives me a slight bow, more of a cynical curtsy.

She pulls a divider from the wall so that Oscar is

ensconced in his own room. She does the same for me on the other side of the airplane. She reappears with a blanket, a pillow, ear plugs and a chilled eye cover made of plastic gel.

'Another drink?'

I look down at my drink and see that it is nearly gone. 'Yes, please.'

I'm in heaven. I am so happy to sleep. I can't remember the last time I really slept. Before Peter, maybe before Panama. The airplane glides into the air.

She wakes me up as we're taxiing down the runway and puts a cup of coffee on a tray in front of me, walking out without a word. I feel frightened. It all seemed fine a few hours ago, but with the remnants of two Manhattans and my life in upheaval, I feel my lungs clenching. Isn't this what I wanted? To be free of Dahlia and time to be my own person? I didn't realize it would be so terrifying without her.

Oscar sticks his head around the partition. 'Cape Breton Island, my dear.'

I don't answer. I feel my eyes stinging. He stands before me and I crumple into his arms. He smells fresh...did he shower on the jet? I run my hand over his head, his hair is petal soft, yet thick, like rope. His body is solid, I don't feel any bones, only muscle and I feel momentarily protected, safe from my life of bedlam. There is a movement and I see another head coming around the partition. Oscar's son-in-law. Dale. He is shocked to see me and even more shocked to see me in Oscar's arms. His eyes narrow. I back away from Oscar and wipe my eyes. He pats me on the back and ushers me toward the door. I do not mention Dale watching us.

Outside, Dale stands waiting to ambush us. 'This is not a good time for you to be bringing home a...dalliance.'

'My life...is of no concern...to you.' Oscar speaks slowly and clearly as if talking to a child. 'Get in the car.'

Dale quickly sidles into the back of a car with dark windows. There is an identical one next to it. Oscar turns to me and says, 'You must excuse his behavior, he was never properly trained.' He sighs and looks toward the car. 'My dogs are better behaved.'

I shrug and think about the word dalliance. Does this mean that Oscar often brings women home? Am I one of many? Does it matter if this is true?

'I would like to offer you a guest room in my home. Or, if you would be more comfortable, a room in a hotel. Unfortunately I must deal with an urgent matter at this moment.'

'Either will be fine.'

'Please, Edward will take you to my home and show you to a room. I would be happy to have you as a guest. I will try to join you for supper, but I cannot say for sure. The stone will have to wait.'

Oscar gets into the car with dark windows and I ride in the other car with Edward, a taciturn bald man with a deep furrow across his forehead. The green of Nova Scotia is different from Panama, it is an octave brighter with more yellow. Pristine puffs of sheep dot the hills. We pass by a black lake without a ripple.

Oscar's farmhouse is an old style mansion with a metal colored slate roof. Crawling roses, manicured bushes, gravel turnaround, hyper-green smooth lawns. There are at least a dozen chimneys sprouting from the roof. A rose garden in the front sends waves of perfume billowing through the air.

The entry door is massive and carved from a single piece
of wood with the handle low, at child's level. It is chilly
inside, the windows are lined with faded velvet curtains. I
am met by a pink-cheeked woman about my age with long
blond hair braided down her back. She holds out a large
freckled hand.

'Anabelle.'

'Pilar,' I say.

'Oscar said to make you feel at home.' She winks. 'I'll
see what we can do about that.'

She smiles a gap-toothed smile. Her brogue is nearly
incomprehensible. I like her. She leads me down a hallway
and into a large room with sofas and a fire roaring in an
open fireplace. Overstuffed furniture, a few straight-backed
chairs with embroidered seats, a boar's head mounted above
the doorway. A silvery fur throw is draped over the back of
a curved sofa. And two full suits of armor complete with
spears guard either sides of the fireplace.

'Your luggage?' she asks.

I hold out my box and she looks at it with interest.

'African, I believe,' she says.

'I was told it was from the east coast. Zanzibar.'

'Oscar will know.'

We walk around the house and she shows me the library,
the sitting room and a beautiful black tiled pool in a glass
greenhouse structure attached to the house. My bedroom
is upstairs with a large paned window that looks out onto
the front garden. We head outside and there are gardens,
more roses, fountains, horses grazing. There is a large pen
with three black dogs panting and wagging their tails. She
leaves me alone and I wander through the gardens. As the
sun goes down, the air becomes misty and chilly and I find
the library where there is a smaller fire. Beside the fire, on

a small table, there are cold cuts, a fresh cut of soft cheese, crusty wheat bread next to a slab of butter and a carafe of red wine lightly chilled.

I wander up to my bedroom and stand in the middle of the room listening to the pure silence in the house. It is too quiet to sleep. The lights are out downstairs and the brightness of the moon guides me as I walk down the stairs and into the glass greenhouse structure where I hear splashing. It is steamingly warm inside. A man is swimming laps in the dark pool, butterfly stroke. Oscar. The pool is bottomless and the white of his arms gleam as they break out of the water followed by his torso, droplets flying, his hair a glint of hard metal in the clearness of the pool. He is nude and his body has no wasted flesh, either in length or width. He swims lap after lap, turning quickly and tightly at the ends of the pool, body bulleting through the reflection on the water.

Maybe this feeling of protection has nothing to do with Oscar, except for the primordial fact of body type. A provider of food and shelter. A Neanderthal protector of women, made beautiful by the buoyancy of water.

Is it possible to fall in love by watching someone swim? Is it possible to fall in love by the sight of two arms reaching out of the water?

He pulls himself out of the water and turns and sits along the edge of the pool. He doesn't see me, but stares in front of him, breathing hard. A black collie trots over to him and shimmers around him gleaming like an eel.

'Roy,' he says in a soft voice.

He rubs his eyes and then notices me watching him. He does not try to cover himself. He gestures for me to go in the pool. I take off my clothes, all of them, it seems rude to leave on my underwear. I stand at the very edge of the pool, with my back to him and the water. I bend my knees, jump into the air, hooking my hands together above my head and arching my back. My hands hit the water first and I feel my body slicing down in a back dive. I surface and he claps. I do handstands, back flips and somersaults until I inhale water and cough and sputter. I haul myself out of the water and sit next to him. Heat radiates from him. It is warm in the enclosure and I can see the stars shining through the glass.

'I will send the stone to my lab. Roza will be here in a few days. Take walks, ride a horse, relax and then I will send you on your way.'

'What's a corundum?'

'Aluminum oxide, a ruby or a sapphire. A ruby is actually a red sapphire. They can be blue, green, red, yellow, even black.'

'So green is an emerald?'

'An emerald is a beryl. Like an aquamarine or a heliodor.'

'A heliodor is black?'

'No, can be yellow, orange, brown, red. They look like a topaz, but they're not. Hard to tell them apart. Why do you ask if it's black?'

'Heliodor...hell...black.'

He looks at me out of the corner of his eyes and cocks his head sideways as if I'm nuts. We talk about stones and clarity and the backstroke and breathing properly and flotation tanks and the Red Sea and the honesty of shepherding. Neither of us realizes the time until a light haze fills the sky and our voices bring Anabelle into the room with thick white bathrobes for both of us. She discreetly leaves. We wrap ourselves in the softness of the robes and sniff at the smell of coffee wafting into the room. Oscar pats my hair with a large warm paw. 'You're an odd bird,' he says. 'But you're all right.'

I look up at him. He squints those shocking blue eyes at me and suddenly we are lip locked. He lifts me in the air as I wrap my legs around his waist and I think, I'm a slut, I'm a goddamn mother and a wife and I'm a slut. I feel as though I've never lived before. Is this reality or a dream? How do I know? Is it possible to have two realities in one life?

His waist and shoulders are solid and he holds me as though I weigh nothing. I press myself against him and he moans and I wrap my arms tight around the back of his head. Our mouths are crushing each other, teeth grating, enamel scraping. He pulls my hair until my head goes back and we look at each other, breath hoarse, eyes wild.

He sets me down and looks at his watch. 'Bloody hell.' He stares at the time. 'Visiting hours. Damn, I have to go.'

My legs are shaking as I watch him hurry out the door. My lips are swollen, stinging. I go to bed and leave my door unlocked thinking he might come to me. He doesn't.

CHAPTER 18

RUN AWAY EAST

I felt mildly guilty for ditching Trevor in Barcelona without any discussion, but if I had told him of my plans, he would have been such a drama queen. I laughed when Trevor told me he was gay, no wonder Celia had trusted him as a chaperone to accompany me to Europe. Trevor had never had sex with a woman, but he said he was not adverse to trying. He said it would be a great honor for a gay man to 'pop a virgin's cherry.'

In the end I left Trevor the guidebook, sold my return ticket and took a train to every country surrounding Romania before entering it. Eastern Europe was a relief. No one cared about my background or family. I was careful not to mention my father's connection. And so, I settled in the one place Val loathed and disparaged.

Bucharest was big and tasted of bitter pollution. Gypsies roamed the street in their glorious rags, begging and intimidating. A quirky group of foreigners inhabited the city: Australians, Mexicans, Scots, even a few Malaysians. They ran bakeries and bars, sold cigarettes and opened dry cleaners.

There were massage parlors and hookers on every street. The Eastern European sex trade was booming. You could see the men who came to Romania for sex. They stayed out late drinking and whoring, emerging from their hotel rooms late in the afternoon to start the whole process over again. Their booze-reddened noses shone like beacons on the dusty concrete sidewalks.

The scars of communism ran deep, resulting in a distrust of neighbors and friends and colleagues. Romanians were somber people who dressed in somber colors. They went about their business, non-smiling, eyeing the circling street dogs and potholed streets. The sidewalks were so crammed with parked cars that pedestrians were forced to walk in the streets.

I rented an old apartment for next to nothing and found an antique store that sold English books. I couldn't stop reading dead writers: Plath, Hemingway, and I found another copy of the Salinger book I threw at the seagull in New York. I even started reading Chloe's old favorites, Kosinski, Camus, Solzynitsyn. I was becoming my mother. I imagined migraines that never materialized and I slept all the time. When you read and sleep a lot, you don't have to eat very much. You also don't need many shoes.

I preferred to sleep rather than to be awake. In my dreams, Bird leapt in the air, Dahlia turned cartwheels and Val stayed at home. It was a kitten that forced me out of my cocoon. A black kitten that sat under my balcony and stared at me every time I looked out the window. It didn't meow or make a noise, it simply looked at me as though it adored me, silently serenading me. When I opened my front door, it walked in, tail held high and sat in the middle of my living room. I saw then that one of its front paws was injured. Badly broken and infected. I gave it a bowl of milk, but all it wanted was a scratch on its head.

I took it to the veterinarian three blocks away and he said the cat was healthy, but its leg was not. By then I was attached to the tiny creature with its oversized ears and six white hairs on its stomach. The kitten, I called it Rat, went into surgery and emerged several hours later with only three legs. I held the tiny thing in my hands and every nerve in my body ached. A fat old man in the waiting room told me not to worry, cats were fine with only three legs. His name was Thassos and he hired me to correspond with clients for his booming fish import business.

Thassos was a crusty old Greek who imported fresh fish from Athens. He had a wife and two kids in Greece and two mistresses in Romania. They all knew about each other and lived quite happily, until one of the mistresses became pregnant. The passing of DNA was one step too far for his wife, so that was the end of the Greek harem. Now he was divorced and saddled with alimony, child support, and an infant. A Greek tragedy.

I took classes at the American University to fill my evenings. It was easier to fill my brain with thoughts than to let my mind drift to the past. So I thought about religion and when it became fused into one god instead of many gods. American Indians believed in many gods, it seemed so logical compared to one god. God of sun, god of rain, god of animals. It's still sort of the same, but now they're called saints — who demoted them? I would wonder.

And I thought about language. How did language develop simultaneously in different areas of the world? Grunts that turned into words that turned into sentences that turned into theories. I couldn't shut off my brain at night as I lay awake considering those things.

The expatriates in Romania were so busy creating new lives and reinventing the past that they didn't care about mine. I realized that people have such a strong urge to talk about themselves that a good listener can spend a lifetime not talking about herself.

I found myself sitting in churches despite my atheism. I liked the smell of the honey wax candles as I approached the entrances and the damp high ceilings inside. There were still quite a few churches that survived Ceausescu's annihilation of Bucharest to build his *people's palace.* He displaced forty thousand people, destroyed twenty-seven churches and monasteries and seven thousand homes to build his mega-ego-palace. There were no seats inside the churches. I would find somewhere to prop myself and watch the old ladies who came in to pray. They kissed the icons with wet lips and mumbled their worries to ancient saints painted in the wall murals.

They say after a trauma there can be a loss of memory. There was no loss of memory for me. I remember every detail, from the smell of cocoa butter on her shirt to the way she skipped down the path with Toby. What I didn't remember was me — who I had been before her death.

Sometimes whole days were taken up with avoiding reflections. I taped newspapers over all the mirrors in my house. Every once in a while I would think I had forgotten what I looked like, but when I looked in the mirror, it all came back and I would find the tape and cover the surface again.

After Dahlia died, I couldn't stop thinking about death. I thought about all the deaths I would have to experience in my life: my parents, Celia, Toby, Toby's mother, Sister Mary, neighbors, the fat guy at the gas pump. It seemed the rest of my life would be about death and grieving, unless I beat them to it. I learned how to choke myself. It was the closest I could be to Dahlia in her death. Until I realized that she lived inside me.

To seal the fate Dahlia had predicted – as the younger twin, I would always follow her – I had wrapped the belt around my neck and stepped off the shoe rack. Toby found me. He had been trying to see me since her death, hanging around the house, but I refused to see him. He might have spotted my transformation into Dahlia, just as he knew I would try to join her. When Dahlia had started moving her face differently and walking in her own way I either had to follow her or lose myself. I had become an expert at mimicking for a good reason.

They put me in the hospital with a sentry and gave me green ice cream and yogurt to eat until I could swallow again. That's when Dr. Morton showed up in my life and tried to find out about the pain I felt when Dahlia died. As soon as he opened his mouth to speak and his voice came out all thin and reedy, I knew I could never trust him. A whiner's voice.

Flashers seemed to be rampant in Bucharest. When the first one opened up his coat in front of me, I stopped, lost in my memories. The flasher must have been terribly disappointed. The first penis I ever saw was Toby's. We were fifteen and ensconced in our hay-bale cave drinking watered-down gin from his mother's liquor cabinet.

'Your father tried to have the birds and bees talk with me yesterday,' Toby had said to the two of us.

'Val?'

'My mother asked him to.'

'He talked to you about sex?'

'He asked me if I had hair down there.'

We fell into giggles on top of each other.

'Do you?' asked Dahlia.

'Want to see?'

We looked at each other. I knew what Dahlia would say. I answered before she could.

'Sure,' I said bravely.

He undid his belt, swiveling his hips and dropped his jeans. He stood there watching us in his bright white boxers. In one movement he pushed them down. His penis lay on top of a patch of black, curly hair. So much of it. His penis jerked and began to fill out, rising slightly.

I stood up. 'Okay, stop it now.'

He smirked at me as he leaned over and pulled up his boxers, one green eye peeping out behind his silky black bangs. My heart thudded. I wanted to walk away, but didn't want to leave the two of them alone. I stared back at him and raised my chin.

The second penis I ever saw was Trevor's. It looked small, but after I put my lips around it, it thickened and grew squat and broad. It was only when we tried to slide it into me that it deflated. We tried it again and again. The same thing — as soon as it got near my vagina, it wilted and we had to start all over again. I started laughing and he started laughing and then all the blood went to his face and that was the end of the loss of my virginity. We laughed and kissed and went out to drink a bottle of cava on the windy beach at Barcolonetta.

The night before I left Trevor, we went to a circus on the beach. We flew through the sky on a roller coaster and spun in circles on a giant disc and everything was perfect until we went into the fun house. At the end of the shrieking clowns and room of smoke, was the house of mirrors.

Dahlia everywhere: in front of me, jumping out next to me, chasing me, springing out to my left and right. I ran into glass walls, smashed into mirrors, blind with panic until I curled into a ball on the floor. Trevor appeared and covered my eyes and led me out. A crowd had gathered from my screams and looked at the fun house with trepidation.

On the way home from Thassos the Greek's office, hurrying through the heat-saturated streets, thinking of the next book I would read, sounds of splashing broke through my haze. I looked through a metal gate and saw a large pool I had never noticed. When I walked over to it, I saw that it was slightly murky, a dull green color.

A hunchbacked woman sat behind a desk with four bikinis and a pair of goggles for sale. I bought one of the suits and used the changing room. The bikini was too big and drooped in the crotch, but the moment I eased myself into the water all was forgotten. For the longest time I floated face down, eyes open in the over-chlorinated water. It was quiet and a few leaves drifted on the bottom, wafting in an unseen current. When I got out of the swimming pool, my skin shriveled and reeking of chlorine, I began to wail and I wondered if that was how babies felt when they left the womb.

At night I began to dream of underwater cities. I dreamt that I grew gills and the dreams were so vivid that I had to feel my face each morning to see if the gills were still there in my cheeks.

CHAPTER 19

OSCAR the III

The house is silent, the kind of silence that tells me it's empty. It is late morning in Nova Scotia, gloomy inside, drizzling outside where the dogs are barking excitedly. I look out the window and see Anabelle washing out the kennel with a high-powered hose surrounded by three dogs bouncing in the air and dashing in circles. One of the dogs stands to the side barking and biting at the spray of water with great snaps of its jaw. She coils the hose and blows on a long whistle tied around her neck and the dogs immediately sit in a row staring at her with focused intensity. She opens a large plastic container next to the kennel and measures a scoop of food into three bowls.

The dogs remain frozen, ears forward, saliva dripping. She blasts a single note on the whistle and they lunge forward, burrowing their muzzles in the food, tails whipping back and forth. Her movements are smooth and calm and I see she loves those dogs. She spots me in the window and waves for me to come outside.

I dress in the soft wool sweater that Anabelle left in the bathroom for me to wear and slip my feet into some rubber boots. Even my black designer trousers are now wrinkled and stretched enough to fit in with the countryside.

The air is chilly and clings to my skin. The dogs finish eating and trade around each other's bowls sniffing and licking to ensure no morsel goes missing. The dogs notice me approaching and rush at me, hackles up. I freeze until they smell me and conclude that I am not dangerous and then they swarm round me.

'Down, down you damn black bitches. Sorry about that. You sleep all right?'

Anabelle's pink skin is flushed and angelic. Her blond hair twists out of her braid in little white tornadoes.

I nod. 'It's very quiet here.'

Anabelle picks up a brush and begins to give one of the dogs an energetic brushing. 'She's done this before. The first time it was with pills.' She shoves away the dog and starts on another. 'Stupid cunt. Kills me to see Oscar suffer. They're at each other's throats all the time, but what can he do? She's his daughter, his only child.'

I realize she must be talking about Oscar's emergency, which must be his daughter. I think of her in her floating white caftan and thin skin, martini held dramatically high in the air.

'All he does is give her what she wants and she does this again and again. She will inherit all this — if she lives.' Anabelle sweeps her arm around to encompass all the land and the house.

I gaze around at the house and grounds and imagine being given all of it. It seems that the last thing you'd want would be suicide, but as I know, when someone decides to go, there is nothing holding them back.

A square Land Rover drives up, honks its horn and a tall man gets out. 'You ready?' he calls as he heads around to the back of the house and disappears.

'Now where's he going?' she folds her arms in annoyance.

'Can I help with something?' I ask.

'Ah, there's an idea. Since Oscar will be indisposed for some time, we could use a wee bit of help herding the sheep.'

'Herding? I don't know anything about sheep.'

'This is all you need to know.' She jumps into the air, waves her arms and yells. 'That's it. Can you do that?'

I throw my arms in the air and jump and shout. She nods approvingly, the dogs bark wildly.

'Good girl.'

I'm not sure if she's talking to a dog or to me.

'Let's get you dressed,' she says and walks to the house.

Anabelle stops by the front door and grabs a large stick out of a canister.

'Choose your own,' she says.

The sticks are actually beautiful wooden canes with curved handles. I choose one with a carved bone handle and smooth base. Anabelle eyes my feet and takes off the boots she is wearing and drops them next to me. She rummages around in a wooden chest next to the door and tosses out a thick pair of socks. I pull on the socks and boots, still cozy from her feet. She wraps a scarf around my neck, hands me a pair of heavy-duty gaiters and takes off down the hallway and through a door. Her muffled voice floats toward me past the gilded mirror, past the floor to a ceiling tapestry of Hercules prying open the jaws of a lion, past the vase full of lilies until I hear a remnant of her speech.

'Waterproof...bog...fast...'

I walk down the hallway to her and she bursts out of the doorway with an armful of coats and hats. She sticks a hat on my head and thrusts a green jacket into my arms and stomps down the hallway and out the door. I put on the jacket and look at myself in the mirror. Transformed into a herder, perfectly blended with my new environment. A chameleon of the world and I wonder how many of us are around, people who move from country to country, from life to life, forgetting themselves and creating themselves with each move.

We get into the Land Rover, Anabelle in the front with the man and me in the back. We take off with a spin in the gravel, the driver's head grazing the top of the car. His skin is wind-toughened and his cheeks are ruddy with health.

'This is my brother Neil,' Anabelle says.

He waves a thick, tanned hand at me and makes eye contact in the rear view mirror. He is the male version of Anabelle. The seats springs are sprung and I am tossed all over the back seat and up and down. I hang onto the door and try not to whack my head on the roof. The Rover drives through several gates and over metal cattle guards. The car winds slowly through an enchanted forest with stunted juniper trees and twisted oaks carpeted in dark moss.

Toby comes to mind and I wonder what he is doing right this moment. He could be making coffee, packing a lunch for Lorna. Does he write her notes on her napkins? Has she been better about eating her fruit? A quick sting travels up my nose and I have to clench my eyes together.

When I open them we are crossing over a stone bridge and breaking through the trees into an open field. A ray of light streaks through the clouds and illuminates a man striding through the field, surrounded by a dozen black and white dogs, circling and bouncing toward us. He meets up with Neil, who jumps out of the car, and they start talking, waving their arms around and pointing up at the hills. I can't understand a word they are saying.

'Gaelic?' I ask Anabelle, shaking my head.

She gives me an odd look. 'English. We need to move the sheep from the hills to the pens at beginning of the road, where we came through the first gate.'

'That's a long way back. Where are the sheep?'

'Out there.' She vaguely points off in the distance. 'Normally Oscar would be here, he hates to miss any of the herding.' She heads off and starts striding up a hill, then turns and motions for me to follow. 'So, we're really desperate for another body.'

I run to catch up. The ground is rocky, covered in lichen and moss and thick bristly heather. It feels as though I am walking on a bumpy carpet.

'Oscar loves it out here. Says it keeps his wheels turning, all this hill walking. Breaks my heart to see him like this, after all the trouble she's put him through.' She stabs her cane into the ground. 'Stupid cunt.'

'What did she do this time?' I ask.

'Razor. Smart enough to cut herself the right way. You cut your strongest arm first so you have enough strength to cut the other one. Then you cut diagonally along the arm. Lost a lot of blood. Went into shock. She did it right this time.'

So it *was* suicide. Poor Oscar. I see the hospital room, the blanched light, the tubes, the thin blanket piled from too many times through the dryer. Eyes twitching, but no one's home. I see Oscar's hand over hers, her face loose under her tight skin.

I rub my fingertips along the raised scars on my arm. Oscar's daughter cut herself to die. I cut myself to be alive. When I felt that sharp stab and watched that trickle of blood, I knew it was my blood, it wasn't any redder or thicker than Dahlia's, but from the pain in my arm, I knew it was mine.

Oscar did not ask why I could take off from New York on a whim and stay on the farm without any complications.

He simply doesn't care. The wealthier or more famous a person, the less they care about your past or even your present. It's all about them and how you fit into their world. He presented the option to me and I could take it or leave it. I took it.

'When we come upon the sheep don't startle them. Neil and my other brother will spread out on either side of us and we'll meet there. The goal is to bring them down the hills to the pen at the bottom.'

She points off into the mist. I squint to see through the swirling cloud to see the vague outline of a ridge. It looks an impossible distance away.

'The idea is to gently move them along, without panic. If they panic, they'll run the wrong way. You need to understand the mentality of a sheep.'

I have gone from being robbed by a transvestite named Ignacio to understanding the mentality of a sheep. I smile and trudge after Anabelle through the heather, stepping in her tracks. I suppose this is what I have done all along. I began by stepping into Dahlia's life and then Toby's and with one giant lunge, I hurdled out of them all and into Roza's, then Peter's and now here I am in Oscar's. Will I ever have my own life?

'How long have you worked with Oscar?' I ask.

'About three generations. My father, my grandfather and who knows, probably before that.' She laughs and holds her hands up in the air. 'We're shepherds. Always been shepherds, even before we immigrated.'

We are nearing the top of the hill, the sun breaks through the mist and a rainbow appears above us. Half a dozen sheep spy us and trot down the hill where we know Anabelle's brother is waiting. A fat rabbit skitters in front of me and disappears into the scrub. Intense light cuts through the birch trees, reflecting slivers of the blowing leaves. Autumn has hit Cape Breton.

I am envious of Anabelle. To be so certain of who she is and what she is. I watch her striding up the hill, confident, happy, knowing that today she will herd her sheep. At this moment I feel envy, but I know if I were given the option of taking her place, I wouldn't. I want to find out where all my steps are taking me. Me, Hetta.

Anabelle shouts suddenly and waves her cane around. About a dozen sheep have spooked and are running up the hill toward us.

'Run along the ridge!' she yells at me. 'Stop them from going back into the open.'

Anabelle takes off in one direction and I run in the other. It's like running in a knee deep snow bank on a steep hill. The sheep run up the hill until they see Anabelle at the top waving her cane and then they veer to the left toward me. I run along the berm and down toward them yelling and waving my cane. They slow down and mill about nervously. One of them, a big ram with curled horns, heads directly to the right of me, in between the two hills where Anabelle and I are jumping up and down. With one more surge of energy, I run down the hill and try to turn them away. Behind me are acres and acres of open land.

The ram ignores me until he is ten yards away and I trip on a large branch of heather and fall down the hill toward him, cane flying through the air, my body crashing and rolling until I am stopped by a ledge of ferns. I smell the damp of the bog, a smell of earth and fresh rain, and the color of the lichen up close is an explosive yellow-green. My hands are a bleeding mess of scratches and I can feel some on my face, maybe a big one on my forehead and my eyes start to tear. Then I see that the ram and herd have taken off in the right direction and Anabelle is yelling encouragement from the top of her hill.

I lie in the heather and smell the dank earth. Water is seeping through the knees of my trousers, my body lies on top of the heather, suspended above the bog. It is so quiet I can hear the water trickling down the hill. I feel like a kid again, scratches on my knuckles, my face planted in the fresh smelling bushes, knees wet and muddy. There is a cracking in the bush and one of the dogs appears and sits in front of me. His tongue hangs pink and wet between his pointy teeth, his breath comes out in white clouds of condensation.

I know I should stand up, but it's so peaceful laying here in the middle of this misty bog with the sheep far down below. The dog is not threatening, he seems to be guarding me like a little angel. The whistles of the shepherds float over the hills. There is more crunching in the brush and someone appears down the hill calling, 'Roy, Roy!'

It's Oscar. Out of the grey fog I see him far below, at the bottom of my hill, striding toward me, coat flapping open, hood tight against the mist. His sure steps crash through the brush and I can already feel the heat of his twinkling eyes on me. The dog ignores Oscar's calling. He lies down across from me, paws delicately crossed under his chin and smiles.

CHAPTER 20

CHLOE SPEAKS AGAIN

Every year Dahlia would send three or four postcards. Celia had convinced me that after Hetta's death, it would be good for Dahlia to go to Europe, with a close friend of Celia's as a chaperone. A gay chaperone named Trevor. As soon as the suggestion was out of her mouth, I felt pressure building in my head...I hung up the phone.

The next day Celia called back and explained that it would be like *rumspringa*, the Amish sabbatical that adolescents participate in. The teenagers go live in the real world for a year, to see outside life and get it out of their system, then they return to their community to settle down and be outstanding citizens. You would think those kids would run far away never to be seen again, but almost all of them return to the community. Celia figured Dahlia would do the same. I never believed she would actually go. We are not a traveling family and I have always had this fear that if I leave my life to go away, I won't fit back in when I return.

She told me Trevor chewed his food and spit it out so he wouldn't gain weight. As if this confirmation of his gayness would lay my fears to rest. Instead all I could imagine was Dahlia in restaurants looking the other way as he daintily spit into his napkin.

She disappeared from their last stop in Barcelona. One day she and Trevor were visiting *La Sagrada Familia* and the next day she was gone. I always thought Trevor knew more than he told us, but he insisted she simply disappeared. Poof. She took her luggage and her ticket and left the guide to Spain on his pillow. Inside the front cover was a bright pink lipstick kiss. I had to admire her for leaving...she did it.

The Amish way of thinking was so far removed from someone who had been through something like Dahlia. The next week, the cards began arriving, one at a time. I followed her travels through Europe: Greece, Bulgaria, Montenegro, Croatia, Serbia, Hungry and finally Romania. For the past four years, none of the postcards have been about her or her life, instead they were comments on events or happenings. No greeting, no Hello or Dear Chloe, simply a snippet:

One of the street dogs bit my neighbor and when the dogcatcher came to take the dog away, all the neighbors, including the one bitten, surrounded the man and pelted him with rotten vegetables. One old man even threatened the dogcatcher with a samurai sword...

Or

A teacher at the school (this is how we knew she either studied or worked at a school) *had his car stolen three days ago and*

*the police told him they
had recovered it. When
he went to the station, it
was the wrong car. They
handed him the keys and
tried to make him take it
anyway.*

No signature or love Dahlia. All written diagonally across the postcard and never any mention of what was on the postcard itself. The card would be of a communist monument or two men playing a board game or a cat sunning itself on a faded green window frame. I used to stare at those cards for hours trying to decipher a meaning. I thought there was a message included meant for me...would she be waiting for me at the monument? Had she taken up backgammon? Had she adopted a dog?

After Hetta died and Dahlia vanished into Europe, all I could think about was having another baby. Val was gone and I kept my distance from Toby, so one night I dressed up and went for a drink in the next county over. A woman alone with cherry-red lipstick will always attract the attention of men. I felt ashamed afterwards, yet hopeful that somehow one sperm had fought its way up my tubes. It didn't. It took one look at my immoral biochemistry and shriveled up and died.

For a while I thought Toby might be the catalyst for the crack in their twinship. I have a suspicion that something happened between them that they never spoke of or possibly acknowledged. Toby was not an evil person, he was simply a boy driven by his hormones. Not many young boys would have the nerve to kiss their best friends' mother. With teenagers it's all about testing your boundaries and

Toby tested his with the wrong adult. I didn't give him the boundaries a normal adult would have. I needed him at that time in my life.

Sex with him reminded me of what it was like to really want someone, when it is a madness. A total loss of sensibility. When you feel it against you, hard, and all you can think about is having it inside you. There is no sense of anyone or anything around you. I see it in musicians when they become so involved in the sound that they lose touch with the world. Eyes shut with sweat beading on their forehead, body moving in rhythm. That's what sex with Toby was like, a complete loss of myself.

After, when we finished and lay with our breath moving in rhythm and the taste of each other in our mouths, I felt debased. Not by his age, age doesn't matter to me, but by the fact that he was the twins' best friend. I felt as though I were stealing something from my babies, yet I was powerless to stop.

In the beginning the three of them equalized each other as they grew taller and braver. There is such a fresh beauty in youth, whether it is oily and pockmarked or peach perfect. They have yet to be molded by life's disappointments. When they drew into their teens, I could see the shape of their adulthood. Toby slipped into the minute crack that began between them and I watched it wedge deeper and wider.

When I saw Toby watching Dahlia on the swing, I saw what no mother should ever see: her own lover watching her daughter with the same lust he had imparted on me only that afternoon. I wasn't thinking clearly about my reactions, I had to get those girls away from Toby before a disaster annihilated our family. It happened anyway and I have a hard tumor of guilt lodged in my body...it never diminishes, it is alive and growing.

I arrived in Bucharest at the end of summer. After
several years of postcards from Romania, I decided Dahlia
must be there and that she was not sending me messages or
signs and if I wanted to see her, it was up to me to find her.

I understood her draw to Romania. Her curiosity about
her heritage. Look how many copies of *Roots* sold. It even
won the Pulitzer Prize. Val hated and feared Eastern Europe
and she wouldn't take that fear on without seeing for herself
where he, and ultimately she, came from. He couldn't help
his hatred, it was the leg irons of communism. What did
any of us know about Romania? Ceausescu's assassination,
Count Dracula and sex slaves.

I'd never been anywhere outside the US. Never had the
desire to see the Eiffel Tower or the Thames. It seemed to
be a lot of hassle and complication when it was easier to
read about it and look at photos in a travel guide. How do
you find a hotel, how do you talk to non-English speaking
people, what if I insult them by not knowing their customs?
What do I pack? How many shoes? What kind of suitcase?
Do I take the whole bottle of shampoo?

It took me months to prepare. First there was the passport
and that required paperwork and applications. Flights had
to be researched and hours in the air and stopovers and
how to check in. Then I bought the ticket and proceeded
to change the departure six times before finally packing my
suitcase and arriving at the airport. I wasn't afraid of the
flight, it was overshadowed by the apprehension of what I
might or might not find in Romania.

When the airplane landed in Bucharest, a rickety staircase
was attached to the exit door and after we descended, we
had to take a bus to the airport terminal. There was a long
wait in the customs line and finally I arrived before a grim

young man. He took my passport and eyed me as though he wasn't sure it was me, as though I were trying to enter Romania illegally.

'How long do you stay in Romania?'

'I don't know how many days. My daughter lives here. Two weeks?' I asked helplessly.

'Where does you daughter live?'

'I'm not sure.'

He peered at me and narrowed his eyes.

'I don't know her exact address.'

'Where will you stay?'

'At a hotel.'

'Where is the hotel?'

I handed him a printout of my reservation. He did not look it at, he pushed it back at me.

'You tell me. Where is the hotel?'

'Hotel Rivoli, Strada Sperantei,' I read from the paper.

'What does your daughter do here?'

'She is with a school.'

'With the embassy?'

'No...I don't...no, not with the embassy, a school.'

He lost interest at that point and stamped my passport.

'How long can I stay?' I asked.

'Ninety days.' He dismissed me with a flick of the wrist. 'Next.'

I took a taxi into town looking at all the billboards for massage and sexy times.

Was it possible my daughter was a hooker? She could be like one of those girls in Japan that become hostesses, caught up in money and furs.

Bucharest was a buzzing city with hordes of traffic and plenty of packed outdoor cafés. The Hotel Rivoli was in a grand three-story building across from a small triangular park. My room was large with old wooden floors that creaked and a bathroom with black and white checkerboard tiles. I opened two glass doors and stepped out onto a two-person wrought iron terrace. A tram ran along the side and across the street, next to the stoplight, stood a boy with thick black hair hanging over his eyes. He lounged with an unstudied arrogance that clenched at my heart and I felt an ache for Toby so strong I had to clutch the guardrail. Two cars stopped at the light and the boy approached them, hand held out, lips mumbling. As soon as the cars moved on, he raised a plastic bag to his face and inhaled the glue before resuming his pose.

Toby was one of those boys who never should have been born with such looks. Dark shiny hair, green eyes ringed with black lashes. Brando in *Last Tango in Paris*. He had a smoldering sexuality that he learned to use far too young.

For some reason, with all my intellectual pursuits and emphasis on brains over brawn, I've always been susceptible to good looks. It's taken me a long time to admit this folly to myself and if someone pointed this out to me, I might deny it. How can I though? Look who I married...and look who was the father of my children and who I spent my life with. In the end, I despise Val for these very things and wonder how I ever got involved with a man for whom I have no respect.

It is hard to love someone beautiful. You want to love them for something other than their physical attributes, but it is impossible to move beyond that. Beautiful people never need to develop their character, it is enough for them to stand in front of an admiring audience...the world is infatuated with perfection. Better they were born ugly and you would know they had substance.

What did Val see in me in the beginning? I was an adoring audience for his capers and a mirror for his charm. I never knew when he was bullshitting or lying, I believed it all. Later when I discovered how hollow he was, my world caved in and he dropped off his pedestal like a lead weight. After the girls were gone, one buried and the other so far away, Val and I lived our own lives. My hands grew thick and splayed from sanding the floors and circles spread under Val's eyes, swelling into eggplant-colored bruises.

Sometimes I imagine that if I had been a different kind of mother, everything would have been okay. Hetta would never have died, Dahlia would have stayed in the US, Val would have stayed home more. Maybe if I had loved Val a little more and the twins a little less, maybe then we would have been a normal family.

For the next week I spent most of my days walking the city and running after girls on the street who looked the way I thought Dahlia would look. The country was in the middle of a gypsy summer and the unbearable heat sapped my energy.

I surprised myself by adapting so easily to a foreign city. I learned to point and nod. Romanians don't smile much and at first it was hard for me to approach them, but I became skilled at finding the few who spoke English. Generally they were the younger, hip ones with Western clothing and dyed hair in varying shades of red. They were always helpful and amused to find a foreigner in their city. Every one of them wanted to know what I was doing in Bucharest.

I finally saw Dahlia across a busy street, in the middle of rush hour. I knew by her walk that it was her, my Dahlia, and without thinking I stepped into traffic to cross the street. A

car screeched to a halt, another crashing into it from behind
with a horrible grinding of steel. The driver of the first car
jumped out, cursing at me, the other driver screaming at him
from behind. Soon they were in a shouting match allowing
me to escape across the street. But of course Dahlia was gone.

I asked a few people if there was a school in the area and
there was. A school that taught English to Romanians. A
private grade school. The school was housed in a baby-blue
villa behind pointed iron gates with a uniformed guard who
stood in the front smoking and glaring at pedestrians.

When I married Val, I was pregnant and still a baby
myself. Eighteen years old. My mother begged me to have
an abortion and continue to study at college. I wanted a
husband and a baby. Who listens to their parents at that
age? I had everything none of my friends had: a monstrously
handsome husband ten years older who worked at a movie
studio, a two bedroom apartment and a grocery account at
Eco Foods.

Be careful what you wish for...a husband and two babies
equals a domestic life. It's no one's fault but my own, I
thought this was what I wanted. I have no idea what I did
want, I just didn't account for babies getting in the way of
whatever it was. Or how I would feel about a perennially
happy, charming, good-looking husband who was never
around, even when he was around. His optimism wore me
down. Every day was sunny for him and if it wasn't for you,
he didn't want to know about it. Don't rain on his parade.

We had a two bedroom, bay-windowed apartment in
Cow Hollow before Cow Hollow was trendy. Before the frat
boys and cappuccinos appeared. Back then there were still
the dive bars and local grocers. My favorite bar had a hand
burnt wood sign that exclaimed *Hark, Cocktails!* The patrons

were old and lively and welcomed newcomers with a pat on a barstool and the shake of a hand.

I sat in a café across from the school and drank cup after cup of black coffee, there was no milk, only those tiny round plastic packets of fake cream. By the time I saw Dahlia stroll out of the school gates, my nerves were jumping out of my skin and my heart nearly split in two. She looked so small and defenseless, it was all I could do to stop myself from rushing out to her and taking her in my arms. I had to remind myself that she had made this life herself and that she had grown into a capable young lady. She didn't look happy, yet she didn't look sad, sort of neutral, content.

My eyes gobbled up every detail, the short black skirt she wore, the flat sandals with rhinestones sewn on the straps, the paleness of her legs, her long thin neck like a Modigliani painting. My initial thought was too cover up some of her skin, there was so much exposed. But then I remembered the girlish dresses with puffy sleeves my own mother dressed me in. I used to purposely wash my sweaters in near boiling water so they would shrink four sizes. After my mother scolded me and put them in the give-away pile, I would sneak them back into my drawer. That's how I liked to wear them, shrunk down, buttons straining. I decided Dahlia looked just fine.

I followed her down the street, away from the heavy traffic and congested air, through a park full of stray dogs and children playing. She stopped at a fruit and vegetable vendor and I saw her choose several peaches and a melon. She entered a rundown, beautiful old building with bay windows, just like in San Francisco.

I stood down the street and saw the windows open on the top floor and glimpsed her cropped red hair as she went from window to window, throwing them open. A black cat jumped up on the windowsill and rubbed against her and I felt my stomach drop, painful jealousy of a cat. Before Hetta died, when she was young, I found her talking to Bird many times. And it was the strangest thing. He would stare back at her making little rumbling noises and wiggling his whiskers. I wondered if Dahlia spoke to her cat. Music wafted down to me, a woman singing in Spanish or French and I marveled at her international taste.

I wondered how she could not look down and see me...I felt my love for her was so intense that she must feel the waves pulsing through the air. It's impossible not to love one child more than the other. The first twin head emerged round and perfect, the second had to be suctioned out and was pointy. Did I love that pointy child more? I do love an underdog. Is that where it all went wrong?

I hoped she was living her life with vigor, not in the shadow of grief. I wondered if I should leave her alone, if I would trigger something in her that brought back the past and bring her unhappiness.

When I was her age, I was pregnant, I never went to college, I missed parties, satin prom dresses, booze fueled gropings. I never knew how important these things were until I saw my own daughters growing up and I realized how much they still had to learn. Both socially and scholastically. Even the most clever autodidactic will have holes in their learning that traditional schooling would have filled. At the age of eighteen, my full personality hadn't even emerged.

The problem with no education is that you come up with these ideas that you think are brilliant, but when you talk about them, someone else has always come up with the idea first. What's the use of all this book reading and self education if I can't even come up with original ideas of my own? One day I was reading an article about Eugene Debs and I had this brilliant idea that Jesus was the first socialist. He was the first one to tell everyone to give away their wealth and treat everyone equally. It all made sense. When I tested my idea at a dinner party that evening, the man next to me raised one of his eyebrows and told me that theory came out before my grandparents were born.

The next morning I woke up early and waited down the street from her house. I leaned against a fence and watched the neighborhood. Next door to her a door opened. A neighbor, a woman in a shocking blue suit and heels, came out with a little boy and they drove away in a black foreign car. A man across the street walked his dog, a huge shaggy one that lumbered down the street on its massive paws. The dog squatted right in front of Dahlia's doorway and I wanted to shout at the man. I glared at him as he strolled by me.

I tore a leaf off a tree and snapped off a branch and a few leaves and went to her door...I was ready to turn my head and walk away if she came outside...and I tried to scrape the dog's mess into the gutter. I gagged and scrubbed at the sidewalk with the leaves until it was clean enough for her to walk on.

I returned to my post and then her door opened. Today she wore a gun-metal grey dress with short sleeves and platform shoes. The dress clung to her figure and I wanted to weep, she was so beautiful. The little black cat ran out from between her legs and I saw that it only had three legs. The cat followed her for about a block and then sat and watched her disappear. She turned around and smiled at it and it hopped back to the house and climbed up a tree onto the neighbor's roof.

Years ago, I spent all my free time reading anything and everything I could find. The problem was that I didn't have anyone to talk to. The twins were always so busy with each other, and Toby, even as a young boy, was a more interesting conversational companion than Val. He debated and argued and came back the next day with more facts and answers, whereas with Val, it was all a joke.

Toby was seventeen, actually it was the day after his birthday, when we first slept together in my matrimonial bed. No one ever knew. He was a kind, willing lover. He went to the library and researched the vagina. He knew all the technical terms: the mons, the vulva, the inner and outer labia, and most important, the clitoris. When he first went down on me, I could hear him muttering and when I asked what he was saying, he repeated the words for me and touched each part. He even knew about the elusive internal Grafenberg or G-spot. His research was thorough. There are those who dispute the existence of the G-spot and I am not one of them.

I followed Dahlia for days. I become more uncertain of contacting her. She had chosen to live away from me and I was invading her life. She was my daughter, but family does not owe family anything, as Celia was fond of saying. Blood was merely a life substance we needed for survival, not something that bonded us to each other.

She had few friends. After work she walked to a swimming pool and spent a lot of time under the water. The first time I saw her, I thought she was dead. She hung there like a corpse and I stood there frozen, certain I was seeing the end of my last daughter. But then she surfaced, gasping for air.

Once a week she met up with a young man for dinner and came home late, unsteady on her heels, always alone, her and her black cat. I had begun to feel I was an intruder, an obsessed outsider. Dahlia's independence and vitality forced an awareness of my own deterioration.

I didn't know Val was a pathological smiler. In the beginning I thought his smiles were for me and only me until I discovered he smiled the same at everyone. At me, my father, or a beggar. He smiled when he spoke about politics, money or the church. He smiled when he orgasmed, stubbed his toe or vomited in the toilet. The more he pleased others, the less he pleased me. And when, for a brief moment, he stopped smiling, he cried. There were two modes, smile or cry.

Val made a great show of loving me. But that's all it was, a show devoid of any mental connection. A pretty spectacle. He was affectionate in public. Hugged me, held my hand, touched my cheek with his long, perfectly formed index finger. I am sure he was looking at the nice shape of his nail when he did that, not my skin, not me.

The parties he arranged. His motives were always off. He didn't have parties to be with his friends, he arranged them so he could be the center of an activity, Master of Ceremonies, life of the party. I would shift around the party and try to find someone interesting to talk to, someone who was not interested in sharing the limelight or waiting for the beam of Val to fall onto them and give them their fifteen seconds of fame at the party.

I began bringing the three-legged cat treats, crunchy smelly things I bought at the local market. He, I determined it was a he, loved those treats, snapped them right up and jumped in my lap for more. He had bright green eyes the color of grass and his fur was entirely black except for six white hairs on his stomach. For a cat with three legs, he was remarkably agile, climbing up trees and along fences, didn't seem to miss his fourth leg at all. When I buried my face in his fur, I could smell Dahlia on him...a whiff of lemon soap and spicy perfume.

CHAPTER 21

A FUNERAL IS NEVER ABOUT THE DEAD

Chloe's funeral day was bright and sunny. I leaned out the window, closed my eyes, and inhaled. Damp grass, acrid smell of smoke from a pile of leaves, the pungent aroma from the eucalyptus trees. Val said that when Chloe returned from Romania two months earlier, she went straight to the garden shed, put on her gloves and sharpened her shears. She hadn't touched any plants since the death: the death of Hetta...or Dahlia...as only I knew.

After I ran away to Celia's, Chloe insisted they move to a new house nearly identical to their old one. Val had all her favorite flowers transferred to the new yard, but she wouldn't touch them. Apparently, until she returned, the garden had been overgrown and tangled, the kind of garden people throw empty bottles into and neighbors hate.

The day of the funeral was peaceful and fresh, dew on the lawn, flowers shimmering in the early light. When I thought of her preparing this garden before her death, the day turned a shade darker, as if the sun had hidden itself behind a cloud.

I didn't know Chloe had been in Romania until Val told me the previous night. She didn't contact me, even though she was there for over three weeks. She told Val all

about my job with the Greek and the school and the tall
house I lived in and how nice I looked with my short red
hair. I didn't tell him I never saw her.

She hadn't told Val she was going to Romania, only that
she was going away for a bit. That's the kind of relationship
they had in the end. Val would have tried to stop her, he
wanted nothing to do with that country. *A city of peasants.*
That's what he says about Bucharest. I knew he'd never
come to Romania searching for me and I never thought
Chloe would. Val said that when he found her passport,
he knew that she had gone to Romania to find me. The
embassy in Bucharest put him in touch with my school
and they called me out of class one day. It was only Chloe's
death that brought me home, otherwise I would have stayed
in Romania forever.

That funeral morning, there was something red sticking
up in the middle of the lawn. I went outside and looked at
it. A newly planted bright red dahlia. One plant, one flower,
in the middle of the lawn, fresh dirt trampled flat around
the base. I looked around for someone watching me from
the street, but it was empty. No note.

Chloe's shears were hanging in the shed, same as they
always did. I headed straight for the dahlia and chopped it
off at the base. Then I went into the flower garden and cut a
few of her exalted roses. A perfume, achingly sweet, drifted
from the peach-colored rose bush. I cut another. Then a
couple of chrysanthemums, some daisies, amaryllis, posies,
and her favorite, the purple bearded iris. I remembered
her, in her faded gardening dress and straw hat and gloves,
bent over, humming to herself, happy, entertained, as she
rarely was around people...Bird lunging after her toes, Val
lounging in the sun, keeping one droopy eye on her.

I straightened my back and looked around. The garden was devoid of color, I now held every flower in the garden in my basket.

In the kitchen I recut the stems to fit the vases and filled the house. My father had still not appeared. This was highly unusual as he was an early bird. I trudged up to my room thinking that this would be the last of the silence for a while. I expected loud exclamations and drama. The door to his room was open and when I peered in, I saw he was on his knees, praying, his long hands pressed tightly together in front of his face.

This was a shock. He had never been religious, in fact he often laughed at the way people clutch at God in difficult times. Yet there he was murmuring prayers interspersed with Chloe's name. He had a towel folded beneath his knees and the sides of his face were wet. My breath caught and I hurried to my room to smother my face in a pillow.

There was a great void about my father. He was affectionate and interested in everything when he was around, yet somehow it was never personal. We could have been anyone.

Val doted on Chloe, ignoring her moods and expanding the times she would muster some enthusiasm and they would laugh together like two kids, the way they must have laughed before us. It never lasted long. He would unintentionally do something silly and irritate her. Only the good times and the laughing made an impression on him, the rest quickly forgotten.

He was the one to organize the raucous dinner parties, down to the flower arrangements and wine delivery. Chloe would attend the parties, but as I got older I realized she was always dressed slightly wrong. On purpose. Val never noticed, he always thought she looked gorgeous – any effort on her part made him giddy.

He would grill some meat for dinner, casual supper outside on the big wooden table and she would wear a silk chiffon cocktail dress and pearls. Or he would have a few of his movie buddies over and she would dress in high heels, miniskirt and outrageously red lipstick. He would be the life of the party and she would talk to the same person all night.

She didn't want to be with someone who was the same with her as he was with all the other people. She wanted to be special. She never felt special with Val because he was the same attentive, loving man to every gorgeous blond woman, old withered granny, or fourteen-year-old boy.

Black seemed too gruesome to wear for Chloe's funeral. I chose a frothy dress with flowers in honor of Chloe's garden I massacred. Val wore a black suit. I was sure it was a suit he had his whole life, his weight never changed. My father had always been a beautiful man. Physically gorgeous. Eyelashes that should be illegal on a man. A perfect man blessed with extraordinary genes, but lacking in the ability to love. He loved us as much as his own self-love would allow. Not enough for two daughters and certainly not enough for a wife.

He was always laughing, happy. My mother resisted. Resented. He went on without her in his joyous narcissism. He had no right to be that happy. Life was not that happy. Babies cried. People died. Bad things happened. Then bad things happened to him and this last blow took its toll. He was still a striking man, a full head of hair and erect posture, but for the first time I saw a looseness on his face, weighing down his cheekbones and jowls.

'Thank God you're here, Dahlia.' He hugged me with one arm. I started to pull away, then relaxed and I hugged him back. He smelled like toothpaste and the same deodorant he had used my entire life. Grief is a great one for pushing people into each others arms.

A black car came to pick us up. It looked threatening, why couldn't they have those cars in lighter colors? We slid inside and the first thing I saw was a full box of tissues in the middle of the seat. I threw them on the floor.

'I've arranged a special service,' Val said.

'Service?'

'We're going to St. Anthony's.'

'The church? I thought we were going to the crematorium.'

'We're going to the church two blocks away.'

'Did she ever go to that church?'

'No.'

'She was an atheist.'

'Your mother was a very spiritual person.'

'She hated the church.'

'Don't say that.'

'She wanted to have her ashes spread in the garden.'

'She is going to be buried.'

'She wanted to be cremated.'

'She was a beautiful person, and I want her to have the best ceremony.'

I began to cry. This is not what Chloe would have wanted. Then Val started to cry and both of us were sobbing in the back as I scrambled for the damn box of tissues on the floor.

I was in a daze of grief and fury throughout the funeral and I purposely didn't listen to anything the man up front had to say. He never knew Chloe. Near the altar sat the coffin. I ignored the looks of everyone in the church. Pity again. After the service, I avoided the people lingering in front of the church and went to sit in the ugly black car.

Val had his boisterous friends around him, but he didn't acknowledge them. They kept patting him on the shoulder and touching his arm. He stood, eyes downcast. They didn't know what to do and stood clustered together looking at him and whispering.

After the funeral, it occurred to me that the line of cars following us with their lights on were coming back to the house. If this were a real funeral, that is what they would do, and so far, it had been a real funeral.

I hated the thought of these people seeing Chloe's garden stripped bare and I wished I could put back some of the flowers. So many people came to me and I felt like a robot saying the same words over and over again. The last time I saw most of these people, I was Hetta.

People's faces blurred together and I stopped seeing them as individuals, they became a flesh-colored crowd all talking and touching and crying and through the crowd I saw a man leaning against a tree drinking out of a silver flask. The light caught the metal and I was momentarily blinded. It was Toby. Toby as a man. He looked different all grown up. Tall and disheveled. He did nothing but stare at me with those intoxicating eyes. My stomach clenched and I bent over, too much sadness and stress. I never went to Dahlia's funeral, this was my first one ever, if I don't count Bird's service.

Toby's eyes were at half mast, slits of emerald. He ambled up, took me by the arms and pulled me away from the crowd. He held my shoulders and looked in my eyes and stuck out his tongue.

'In honor of Bird,' he mumbled.

We breathed each other's breath, he kept repeating the words. I stuck my tongue out and touched his. The people around us became silent. He swayed backward and I grabbed him. He was completely drunk. I put my arm around his waist and helped him to the house and into the study. He sank to the couch and closed his eyes. He opened them again, focused and saw me.

'Hetta. Will you marry me?'

I could still feel the pressure of his tongue. I crouched down next to the couch and rested my head on his chest. 'Yes,' I said.

'Thank God,' he said as he closed his eyes.

This seemed appropriate, marrying Toby and therefore losing my virginity to him. I sat on the couch and drank my gin and tried to join Toby in his oblivion. What was the big deal about having a penis inside you? Fingers and tongues do much the same thing? Made you be more creative about your sexual escapades. What was virginity anyway, but the snap of a hymen?

Hetta. He called me Hetta. Did he know? Had he always known? Or was it a drunken slip? I pried open his eyelid and the greenness focused on me. He stood up and looked around the room. He walked out without looking at me again or saying a word. He was so drunk he would never remember he called me Hetta. Or that he wanted to marry me. For all I knew he was already married. I stood and made another drink.

Someone was ringing a bell incessantly, then talking. There was a hushed clutter of voices, a few claps, one cheer. I looked out the window. Toby stood on the deck with a bottle of champagne, good French champagne, talking to the remaining funeral guests. The people saw me looking through the window at them and I could see from their expression that Toby did not forget.

CHAPTER 22

VAL TALKS

I assumed when Chloe returned from her mother-daughter trek to the 'dark land' and began tearing up the weeds in the garden — that all was fine and dandy. Our lives would go back to the way they were before all the heartbreak. She had healed herself in Romania, of all God-forsaken countries. Romania was not a land of healing, it was a land of destruction and I should have remembered this. Physically she looked stunning: bronzed skin, her hair grown wild with thick grey streaks. She seemed back to her old self, the one I fell for over twenty years ago.

She worked like a devil every day in her garden. One baking hot night, when the moon was huge, I saw her fertilizing the roses in her nightgown. Her hair floated around her shoulders, the white cotton stuck to her body with sweat. She still looked like a young nymph and Shakespeare's quote popped into my head:

> Or like a fairy, trip upon the green,
> Or like a nymph, with long disheveled hair...

She stood gesturing and at first I thought she was talking to herself, then I saw a figure, standing in the darkness under the tree. A pale body that glowed, it looked as though she were communing with a ghost. I'm pretty certain that if I had investigated, it would have been Toby talking to her... but I prefer to believe in the ghost.

When Chloe stopped noticing the redness of her skin from sunburn or the collection of dirt under her nails, I should have sat her down and made her look in my eyes and brought her back to me. The morning I found her cold body next to the irises, I brushed her hair and scented it with rosemary from her garden. Then I soaked her nails in a pan of warmed water and scrubbed out the grime before I let the paramedics take her away. She looked so peaceful in the early light, as if she'd lain down to take a quick snooze in the flowerbed. It was the hemlock behind the azaleas that she chose to swallow.

As a high-schooler, I was the lead in the senior play — Arthur Miller's *Death of a Salesman*. It didn't help much with my popularity, only dweebs were in plays, but it convinced me that I was destined to be a Hollywood star. That one play and my whole life changed. It was the applause. The adrenaline, the buzz, the adoration that spread out from the audience wrapped around me so warmly. They loved me. I couldn't get enough of it, the sound ricocheted in my head all night. I couldn't hear music or voices or even my own thoughts until the next day.

The lesson I learned was that actors have to be willing to ignore shame in order to gain glory. Most people would be embarrassed to dress up and pretend they were someone else and talk in false voices. Or too uptight to put on makeup and wear a wig. Actors take the risk of being absurd.

Those old people in parks who go every day with a bag of stale crumbs for the pigeons or wormy nuts for the squirrels bought at a discount from the local store — I understood them! They felt needed and loved – those birds loved them. They flocked around and flapped their love. They crowded around to be closer. They cooed their adoration.

The week after graduation I deserted my family in the mid-west and took off for LA in my father's big old Chevy. It broke down twice and I jerry-rigged it when the clutch cable snapped. I didn't have time to waste in some damn hick town to have it repaired. I was in such a rush to get to Hollywood that I cut out a section of a farmer's wire fence, patched the cable, and on I went – Hollywood here I come!

I was still gangly and awkward when I arrived in LA, my adolescence lasted a long time, however I was a quick study. After a few months, I learned how to use the power of my smile and when to move my eyes and how to touch someone's arm...upper arm, lower arm and how to brush the back of a hand. My chest hair curled out of the top button of my shirt and my skin was a rich dark color from catching some rays on the beach. Women and men reacted to me with intense eagerness...I never was any good at saying, no.

Susie, whom I met at a coffee shop, offered me her guest cottage until I got settled. She lived in the main house with her husband, who traveled all the time, which suited us fine. She would ring my bell, vintage bottle of burgundy in one hand, basket of French cheese and baguette in the other, robe tied loosely under her free swinging breasts.

Susie's friend, Douglas, invited me to come on set with him and I did, certain that this would be it! I would be spotted immediately and turned into the star I should be. Nearly every day I would go to the set with Douglas and lean against one building or another, hip thrust out, cigarette between my fingers...think James Dean, Marlon Brando.

Douglas was a gay hairstylist who worked on all the big stars. He fit every cliché. I would watch the actors arriving drab and ordinary, disappear into the hair and makeup department, and walk out a star. Stars liked to talk to me, they thought I was one of them.

I became a sound engineer by accident. Most people don't think about sound. They may think about music or noise, but not sound, not Foley sound effects, as they are called in the industry. The sound of footsteps walking up stairs or the difference between a zipper on a ski parka and a zipper on a pair of pants or a dog's nails clicking across a wooden floor. If these sounds are off, the brain registers that something is wrong, it may not know what, but it will throw people out of the movie, out of the story and that is one thing a movie maker never wants.

Bad lip-synching or lip-synching in another language makes an unwatchable movie. I find myself looking at the actor's lips instead of watching them act. Lack of sound can be just as powerful as sound. Sound changes everything: enhances moods, emotions, turns a drama into a thriller, a sob story to a drama. Walter Murch was the first sound editor to use silence as sound and won his first Oscar for it with Apocalypse Now.

Big Bernard, the sound engineer, put me to work. He wasn't impressed by my big, brown eyes and flashy smile and I wouldn't have dared to have touched his arm. He was a big ole brut of a man, but he wasn't very tall and he needed someone with height to help with the sound equipment. Also, he had a strong work ethic and couldn't stand to see me standing around idle. So I may not have been a star, but I was in the movies.

Susie heard I was spending all my time with Douglas and told me I would have to get out. I met Chloe the same day I moved out. She was as unimpressed with my looks as Big Bernard. She liked me for me — or should I say, she liked me despite me. I felt real around her, she grounded me with her rationalism and strong fingers. She was no slouch, she wore deep red lipstick and tight cashmere sweaters. I used to run my fingers along those sweaters and get goose bumps. We were married within six months.

Chloe used to cry after we made love. She sat on my lap every morning for breakfast while we drank our coffee and ate our toast. Then she got pregnant and I had to work longer hours and still no one asked me to star in a movie.

I didn't deserve to be married to Chloe. She should have married an intellect, a writer or a professor. Even an engineer. I loved her and after I met her, all I wanted was her approval...which I never got.

My life was a total ruin. I had believed that if I stayed optimistic and laughed as much as possible my world would continue along its merry route. Look what life brought me: A daughter run over by a truck and a wife dead by suicide. And the other half of the twin unmoored in Romania, a country I loathed with all my heart. When my parents escaped from Romania with me, as a boy of fourteen, they vowed never to return and they injected me with stories of family betrayal, prison and paranoia.

I tried to be the best father I could, I really did try. I tried to be a friend to my kids and to understand them. I wanted them to like me. I have a hard time connecting with people, sometimes I feel as though I am a hollow shell. I laugh the loudest, I stand the tallest, they all stare at me, they touch me, the women and the men. Everyone wants Val around — *he's such a hoot* — for a while, until they realize there's nothing inside me. They realize we have never spoken about anything real. I know all about where they are going on their next holiday and how many kids their sister has and their business plans for the year and what they think about global warming...but I don't know their hidden loves or their dreams or how they feel about their lives and what they are missing.

It's karma that ultimately destroyed my life. Which means that it's all my fault. It was me, my actions. I hadn't been faithful to Chloe. Not even a little faithful. Oscar Wilde said:

> *Those who are faithful know only the trivial side of love: it is the faithless who know love's tragedies.*

How I would love to only know the trivial side of love. It must make life so sweet. There are a lot of us out there: the sexually aware. Men and women, men and men, and women and women. We recognize each other easily. The adventurers with ambiguous sexual orientation. Our greying hair and slight paunches hasn't slowed down out hedonistic actions. We mingle at business cocktails, chat at Little League games and then meet in basements or garages or public bathrooms.

Our lies do get discovered. There are always stories of the man caught in the closet or the woman seen naked in the bushes. Yet, we are good fathers and attentive husbands. We bring flowers and make love to our spouses with tenderness, but it's not the tenderness we are after when we meet with the others. It all boils down to narcissism. Besides masturbation, how much closer can we get? We don't need foreplay and soft words. It's often violent and fast and there is no lounging in the bed in each other's arms whispering sweet nothings.

It's the guilt that makes us better husbands and wives. There are no Mickey Mouse games to play next time we see each other, no winks or coy looks or reminders that we never called. We are back to our jovial selves, laughing about the weekend football game or the newest scandal at the PTA meeting.

Oh, and we love our spouses. Loyal Chloe, it would have crushed her if she had known the affairs I've had. It all had to stop. The doctor said impotence can be caused by trauma and this is the only good thing to come out of the disasters of my life. I thank God for this.

The night Bird was run over was only a warning. I couldn't face any of them after that night. I never spoke to Tommy again, we couldn't look each other in the eyes. If only I had paid attention to that warning. If only I had taken a moment to think about what I was doing to my family. When Hetta died, my world imploded — It was my own adulterous actions that had killed her.

CHAPTER 23

TOBY REMEMBERED

Toby and I sat in our bathrobes in front of the fireplace on a chilly summer day, nearly two years after our marriage. There was no fire in the fireplace, just a television set with a recording of a fire. The recording snapped and crackled and would have looked quite nice if it weren't on the television. It was 2:00 p.m. and we were drinking hot toddies as the rain poured down outside. We sat and stared at the big cardboard box in front of us. The postman had delivered it in the morning and after unwrapping the brown paper and miles of clear plastic tape, we found an electric baby Jesus from Val.

The hot toddy started to smell rancid and, as I ran to the bathroom, my stomach twisted and I threw up just as I reached the sink. I splashed water on my face, careful not to look in the mirror. I walked back into the room fanning myself, suddenly so hot that I could feel a red flush wash up my face. Toby looked at me and raised an eyebrow. I turned down the volume on the fire and slumped in the chair. Out of the corner of my eye I saw Toby staring at me.

'You're pregnant.'

I had told myself he didn't remember that horrible night. It was easy to convince myself that it had been the champagne and then the vodka and then the joint, but he was talking about it. He remembered. The bastard.

'No, I'm not.'

'Goddamn it.'

He hurled his drink at the wall. He walked over and stood before me. 'Don't leave me,' he said. 'I love you.'

Then he slapped me, not hard, but hard enough. I froze. He froze. His face contorted and he dropped to his knees and put his arms around me.

He had never said those words to me before, not as children, not as spouses. And I'd never said the words to him. I didn't think we needed to, we'd known each other since we were twelve. Love was an overused and abused word and why should we fall into the same trap everyone else did by repeating a word that had long lost its meaning? We were different, the two of us. But when those words came out of his lips, my heart beat faster and my skin tingled. I felt split wide open, raw.

Then I realized he had said it to Dahlia, not me.

The room spun and I ran to the bathroom to be sick again. I rinsed out my mouth and snuck a quick look in the mirror. Dahlia. He appeared behind me. I whirled around and slapped him. As hard as I could. We had never hit each other before either. That day was a day of firsts.

He ignored the slap. He stood over the toilet, unwrapped the lump of hash and held it over the bowl. He crumbled it into the water, pushed the handle and it swirled around disappearing into the sewers of San Rafael. I wondered if he would come back in a few moments and pick up the crumbs along the seat. As if reading my thoughts, he took a wad of toilet paper and wiped along the edges, tossing it in. We both stared into the white bowl not quite believing what he had done. He took my hand, his twitched in mine and that was it, the end of the hash.

I didn't have the guts to tell him that I wasn't going to have the baby.

A week later I walked out of the house, got in my car and drove to the doctor's office. There was no guilt about what I was doing, it was the right thing. Kids didn't fit into the way we lived and I didn't see things changing any time soon. And the way this poor baby had been conceived, I couldn't imagine a happy beginning for it. Although Toby had quit all the drugs, *bam, no more*, his drinking quickly increased and he was a bad drunk. Hash and weed had kept the effect of alcohol in equilibrium. Without them, he was sloppy. I couldn't even drink a beer, the smell of alcohol made me vomit.

I never told Toby when I lost my virginity with him, somehow I felt it would give him an upper hand. A week after the funeral we were in his living room, on the couch, smoking some hash when he pounced on me and we slid to the floor. It was a frantic, frenzied shedding of clothes and tongues and I didn't hesitate, I shoved it right inside me. My eyes popped open and there she was, staring right in my eyes — Dahlia leaning over me, eyes wide, mouth in a big O. I screamed and even as I screamed I knew that she was in a mirror propped against the wall.

The doctor's office was in a bland rectangular building with a row of those ugly little sculptured bushes in front. I went inside and checked in with the reception. D&C, they called the procedure. Sounded like a cocktail.

In the waiting room there were three women in various stages of pregnancy and two others who nervously looked around the room and flicked through the gossip magazines. There was only one man in the office. He sat next to a young pregnant woman, stroking her hand and looking at her with worshipful admiration. She kept her face averted from his and she looked worried. A dried up fern drooped next to the magazine rack. The door flew open and Toby walked in. He sauntered over and sat down next to me. He smiled pleasantly and leaned close to my ear.

'Not here for a check-up, are you?' he asked.

I stood up and walked outside and sat on the curb. He followed and sat next to me, lighting a cigarette.

'You weren't going to tell me?'

I didn't answer, I busied myself filing one of my fingernails against the concrete curb.

'Why? Look at me. Why?'

'You remember.'

'Remember what?'

He was going to deny it. In his head he had already filed it under: harmless play. He had filed my tears under: too much booze, and his laughter under: too much hash. I had always thought men couldn't have sex when they were so messed up, but I was wrong that night.

I had returned home after a week of visiting Val. I was exhausted. Val the Charmer turned Val the Devout. It rankled me. Val had moved to New Mexico where he knew no one. He attended nightly church meetings and lived in a tiny house full of crosses and emaciated figures. He seemed content for the first time in his life. He didn't have the need to show off or tell stories.

Toby had flowers and champagne waiting, and he wouldn't let go of me. I sat on his lap as we talked and drank. The house was clean, as clean as it had been when his mother was alive. He had even fixed all the little things that bothered me, like burnt-out light bulbs that never got changed and the kitchen faucet that dripped. He had been wandering around the past week, drug fueled, dusting and wiping and scouring, so when I returned the house gleamed.

He turned on the fire TV, we finished off the champagne, moved on to screwdrivers, took a few tokes and started fooling around. The sex was still great after two years. Our clothes were off, heavy breathing and when I asked for a condom, he kept going as if he didn't hear me and I told him to stop and pushed him away, but he grabbed me and shoved it in and I spit in his face and screamed '*rape*' and I was crying and he was laughing.

I could see from his face now that he knew what I was talking about.

'No more weed,' he said.

As if that explained what had happened that night.

'And I got a job.'

'You what?'

'At a newspaper. I studied journalism, I can write.'

'But we have enough money.'

'That's not the point. We need to do something. We need to set a good example.'

'Don't start with that parenting jargon.'

'I want this baby. I need something in my life to ground me. This is it.'

I thought about Toby without a father and our parents all dead, except for crazy Val. I imagined Val going into a store for ear swabs or shoe polish and seeing the dumb baby Jesus box, the fluorescent lights shining off the plastic front. He would have turned the box around reading all the print and asking the store clerks a million questions. He would have carried it home and wrapped it in plain brown paper, taping the edges around and around. He would have found the thick blue flat pen and addressed it to us, almost the same address he had with Chloe. That would have stopped him for a moment.

Then he would have gone to the post office and stood in line grinning at the thought of us opening the box. The woman up front at the counter would have been grumpy and in a hurry and he would have chatted with her about the box. He wouldn't notice her down-turned mouth as he told her about me, his daughter. Perhaps in the end, she was dazzled by his enduring good looks and engaging smile and he was able to jolt her out of her disgruntled expression.

'Baby, no more booze.'

I wasn't sure if Toby was talking to me or the baby. No more booze. What would life be like with no more booze? Sobriety, the new high. Funny, I did feel as though no booze was a high for me. Maybe it was the thought of something growing in me or simply the knowledge that if I let these little cells grow, my life would never be the same. Maybe it was the future of change that gave me my high these past days. Whatever it was, Toby and I, we both felt it. His enthusiasm caught. I imagined our lives smoothed out, calming blues and greens instead of chaotic yellows and reds.

And by the time I finished all this thinking, this little alien in me was a child, not a seed and I knew I couldn't get rid of it anymore.

That was it, the booze all went down the drain, the smell of it gagging me. Toby looked pale for another reason all together. First we took the open bottles: the whiskey, gin, vodka, tequila, vermouth, triple sec, Cointrou, Kahlua, absinthe...and poured them down the kitchen sink. Then we went to the drinks cupboard and pulled out all the reserve bottles and those went down the sink too. We drew the line at the wine in the cellar. Too many old bottles of wine down there. But we bought a big padlock and destroyed the key with a hammer. When the right time came, we would saw it off.

The first couple of days were fresh and new without the booze or drugs. Like when I first moved in with him after Chloe's funeral. I never did go back to Romania, I dropped everything to marry Toby. I spoke to the Greek who kept my little three-legged cat, and he said, 'I was waiting for you to crack. Now you'll end up like me,' and laughed uproariously. He said, 'Give me your address and I'll send you a calamari for your wedding.'

Sobriety was the new high. We had sober sex and it was as if we had forgotten the moves. We avoided each other's eyes, the only position we knew was missionary. It was quick, awkward and soul destroying.

I couldn't sleep at night. I slipped out of bed and headed downstairs to the Baby Jesus. I opened up his back and inserted the bulb before plugging it in. Baby Jesus lit up, 100 watts, and I basked in his glow.

CHAPTER 24

A TRICKY STAR

It's dark and I'm in bed. The air has a biting chill that reminds me I am in Cape Breton. My muscles ache from the shepherding, the trudging up and down the hills and my spectacular fall into the heather. Even though the room is quiet, I sense a presence. I am not afraid, I only hope it is Oscar.

I lean over and switch on the light.

Oscar is propped against the doorway, a towel wrapped around his waist, drops of water running off his head. I am glad to see him, but the purple half circles under his eyes concern me. One eye droops more than the other giving him a lop-sided derelict look. He hasn't shaved and dark hairs pepper the lower half of his face. He sits next to me on the bed and I see the dark hairs are interspersed with many white ones. The smell of chlorine stings my nostrils. His shoulders and neck slump forward.

'Anabelle told me,' I say.

'My daughter has a propensity for drama. Deadly drama.'

'I'm sorry.'

'I tried to swim. Can't...couldn't get my rhythm.' He rubs his eyes and wipes his hands over his head. The color is so silver, it is nearly gold. 'You were a huge help today, I completely forgot...and... I have to ask a favor. You can say no.'

'Ask away.' I feel as though I would do anything for this man.

His lips curl into the shape of a smile, but his eyes stay straight. 'I almost hope you will say no. Tomorrow I have to meet someone. I can't leave now and Roza won't be here for a few days still. The meeting is for a delivery.'

'Yes, Oscar.'

'I can't leave now...'

'I'm saying yes.'

'Jesus. I'm sorry. Thank God you're here. And you're a good distraction.' He flattens the tip of my nose. 'We need it. My driver will come for you in the morning...Roza trusts you. And I trust Roza.' He is so relieved he leans back against the headboard and closes his eyes. 'She's in a coma now. My little girl. What have I done to her?'

His breathing slows, his face relaxes and he is asleep. I cover him with my blanket and curl next to him. I touch him with two fingers and leave them there resting on his chest and close my eyes. I wake up several hours later and he is lying flat with both hands crossed across his chest and the blanket has fallen away. I tug it back over him and drift off to sleep again.

In the morning, the blanket is tucked in around me and Oscar is gone. I go to the bathroom to shower and see that someone, the cleaning lady, has washed all my underwear and socks. Bless her bones. And Anabelle has left me a fresh shirt, socks, and another thick green sweater. What a luxury to be taken care of. There is a knock on the door and Anabelle pokes her head in.

'The driver is here.'

I dress quickly and go outside. Anabelle gives me a hug and says in my ear, 'You will be picking up some stones. Take care when you talk over the phone. It's something we all adhere to around here.'

She pulls back and looks me in the eyes gravely. Meeting with the Kunas in Panama was entirely different from dealing in stones in Canada and I can imagine the authorities closing in on me. The memory of Oscar standing in my doorway takes over and I see his bruised eyes again and I want to do this for him. I nod at Anabelle and she steers me toward the big black car with the same bald driver. I get into the car and she pats me on the leg and closes the door. The driver points to a cup of steaming coffee in a sectional on the door and hands me a phone.

'Oscar here. How are you?'

'No, how are you?'

'They tell me she's out of the coma, I am on my way to her room. Thank God. I would have given anything to trade places with her.'

He is brusque, energetic and I am glad his voice is robust again.

'You're a doll. The driver will take you to Halifax and you will meet with Suri. She will have twelve pieces for you. On the seat next to you is a sheet of paper with all the details and an envelope with the cash. Please read it before and check each piece. Remember the other night when we spoke about color and clarity? Keep all that in mind. These are high quality: in particular, the big one. Look for twelve rays. It's not rocket science, just keep your eyes open and act with confidence.'

'You don't trust her?'

'We're all sharks in this business.'

The Nova Scotia countryside is stunning with the violent fall colors of chartreuse and magenta and white sheep dotting the hills like clouds in a hot summer sky. I look over the sheet of paper Oscar left me and see that I am going to pick up twelve stones, gems, from a dealer. Three rubies, three sapphires and six diamonds.

The car is nearing Halifax. We pull into a one-story sordid hotel with chipped white walls and dying rhododendron bushes along the front. I am nervous and hope I won't let Oscar down. I want to erase the bruises under his eyes and bring back the rhythm in his swimming.

The dealer is seated at a table inside a room. She is a woman with thick glasses and a mannish suit. A large man with broken blood vessels on his cheeks stands behind her, to the side, arms folded. She peers at me over the top of her glasses with tired eyes. I can't imagine this woman believes that I know what I'm doing.

She lays out the stones. These are polished and cut and the light flickers from each of them. I am astonished by their beauty. I pick each of them up the way I saw Roza do with the diamonds on the island. There is a list with all of the recorded sizes and clarity. I check them against the list and find that I do know what I'm doing, they all correspond with the list. The biggest one is a sapphire, similar to my stone, the same cool blue. It feels slightly heavier than my stone and when I hold it up to the light, it appears there is something alive inside. When I move the stone, the rays move, a little starfish inside. I look more closely and count six rays. I tip it to the right and left and I hear Oscar's voice saying twelve rays. I move it to my left hand and look at it from another angle. Still six rays.

I inhale deeply and say, 'This is not a twelve star.'

'Of course it is.'

She takes it from me and tilts it sideways. She slaps her other hand on the table and curses at the man. He snarls at her behind her back and walks to a safe in the closet and unlocks it, taking out a clear plastic bag with another stone inside. I see piles of bags and stones inside before he slams the door and locks it. He wears a gun under his jacket. He hands her the bag and she takes out the stone and examines it. She laughs so hard that she snorts as she hands it to me. I don't know if I should laugh: is this a joke she plays every time? I look at the stone. This time there are twelve rays and it looks like a sun from a tiny planet complete with its own streets and mailboxes.

I hold the stones in my lap on the drive home and stare at my reflection in the dark window. I look unfamiliar and I wonder if my new life has changed my face. I think about Chloe's two stones I buried the night of Dahlia's death. The night I sawed off the swings and sat for the last time in our tree. I'm glad I never dug the stones out, it's better that they were left together.

It is late when I return and the house is empty. I go into the kitchen and find a plate of dried sausage and cheese and fresh bread. I wander around the house munching on the food trying not to leave a trail of crumbs. The swimming pool looks long and black and the fact that Oscar is not in the house makes me afraid. I go to my room and close the door, but leave it unlocked. I put the stones under my pillow, relieved and hopeful that I have done a good job for Oscar. Just as I am drifting off, the house creaks and I jolt awake. I get up and lock the door.

In the morning, I look out the window and see Anabelle brushing Roy. I have learned to distinguish him by the extra thick mane around his neck. He has rolled onto his back, four paws in the air. The dogs are calm, almost melancholy, as they sit in a circle around her, close to her feet. Anabelle drops the brush and does not pick it up. She sits there staring at it until Roy sits up and sticks his muzzle into her lap. I open the window and she looks up. She walks slowly over to the window and stands below looking up at me, her jaw clenched.

'Oscar is in the hospital.'

'I know, you told me.'

'No...it's him...'

I picture him in the pool, sturdy, vigorous. I feel the strength of his arms around me. 'His daughter?'

'He...he...' She stops and can't talk, she is breathing heavily. She still can't talk so she points with a finger to her heart.

'His heart?

She looks at me, eyes wide and tears spilling silently over her eyes.

'Oscar had a heart attack?'

She covers her face and I feel my stomach lurch as if the ground under me has dissolved.

CHAPTER 25

OSCAR TALKS

My daughter lies in front of me, tubes coming out of her hands and one out of her nose. There are bags dripping liquid in her and bags dripping liquid out of her. Her pink nail varnish is so perfect it looks out of place on her shriveled, dried-out hands. She never has unchipped nails due to her obsession with horseback riding and competitions. The knowledge that she had a manicure before she slit her wrists sends a spasm of pain into my stomach and my head becomes so weighty that I have to rest it on the edge of her bed. I am weary. I would give anything to have our places reversed. I am older, I am her father — I should be the one on the edge of death. My failure makes my chest ache and I gasp, clutching at her arm, dislodging the tube... and I sink to the ground.

My eyes open with a dry click and I am blinded by white. My vision slowly focuses. I see the ugly square telly strapped to the wall and I feel the stiffness of the over-bleached sheets and I can't understand what I am doing in a hospital bed attached to a bleeping machine. A rush of images plays through my mind. My daughter's nails, myself sinking to the ground, clutching at her fingers. I look down at my hands lying on top of the sheet, sun spotted, wrinkled around the knuckles.

When you get old you begin spouting grey hair down below and then it starts growing in odd places: ears, noses. And for what genetic purpose? I've got this Turkish barber in London who burns all that unnecessary hair away with a fire wand. Some ancient technique brought over from Constantinople. He wraps the end of a pointed stick in cotton and dips it in alcohol before lighting it on fire. Then he quickly flicks it into your ear so it singes all the hairs away. Smells horrible, burning hair and Lord knows what.

First time he did it to me, I leapt out of the chair and bashed him against the wall. He stammered and explained and when I looked in the mirror, I saw the hair was gone. I apologized and tipped him a fair bit, but had to come back the next day, he was shaking too hard to burn out my other side. Had to spend the night with one ear clean and the other hairy as a monkey dick.

Men feel so useless when their wives are pregnant. I wanted to do everything for mine to make up for the fact that nature had assigned the task of pregnancy to women. She was not one of those women who bloomed during pregnancy. She was ill and bloated and hated the way she looked no matter how many times I told her she was lovely. I'd known her for years and I didn't love her at first. Love came later with a loosening and commingling of our selves. It was a surprise that nearly bowled us over.

It's the fear of death that has made me fall in love again. I am not one to ruminate on the encroaching years, but when the age of fifty has passed, there are moments of panic.

Until now I lived my life with no regrets. How is it that I regret it all now? How is it that suddenly I can see I have wasted my entire life chasing a quid? And what good does that do me now as I lay between these cold sheets staring at the grey television screen? All my accomplishments bequeathed to a daughter who hates me. The realization that love is the only thing of any value at the end. A bloody cliché to sum up the failure of my life.

At first I was drawn to her Zanzibar box. I hadn't seen one for a long time, never in Panama City, and this one was exquisite. It didn't take more than a split second to see that the box was the least interesting thing about her. I watched her on that jetty for quite a while and when she went into the water, it was as if I had expected it. I didn't really think she was a suicide, but I had to ask. Suicide would have been unpardonable.

The moment I saw her in the light of Roza's café, I could see she was at the beginning of a life. People live several lives within their life, most of the new lives brought on by marriage, divorce, birth, death or God. I envied her. I saw straight into her, I saw no past, only the moment, the beginning.

Every once in a great while you meet someone you can see straight into, no curves or mirrored corners or rabbits in a hat. I wanted to give her everything with no strings attached so she could follow that life unencumbered. Money traps some people, nails them in a coffin and hands them a bitter smile. With her, it would be freedom, the way it should be, the way it guides the lucky ones.

She could easily have disappeared from my life. One step and she would be in Argentina or Portugal or Vietnam. Gone. She's filled my head and my heart and for her to vanish would have left a desperate void.

All youth has its beauty to an old man like me. I took a drastic measure, a barking mad maneuver, preying on a young woman, a spider weaving its web. God help me. I didn't want to love again, not after so many years, not at my age. Love is for the young — a vain, futile emotion for the old.

I can't even say what it is I hope to find in her. I don't believe she would ever fall for an old codger like me, yet I want her to be around. I want to watch her. This sounds dangerously close to a stalker, but I would never harm her or change her. I am like those *National Geographic* photographers: they observe, not intervene.

Part of me wants to yank this tube out and walk out, bare arse protruding, there is no dignity in a hospital, and head straight for my swimming pool where I will swim until my injured heart bursts. But the other part fights to live and maintain what I have left.

The only thing of value from my life are those dogs. Lord help me, I love them. I've transferred a lifetime of love onto four creatures that can't even visit me in this damn hospital.

Their kennel is heated, their food the most expensive, real goose down beds, and the most absurd thing of all: I keep a huge herd of sheep for them. Shepherding is a form of art requiring patience and a deep understanding of the dogs. It's a profession as old as prostitution. My top dog, Roy is his name, used to live in the village with a family. They came to my house one day and told me that they could not keep Roy, that he was nervous and paced the house like a wolf in a cage wearing a hole in the carpet along his trail.

I took Roy as one of my own and the moment he saw the sheep, his whole body quivered with joy. Usually it is difficult to train an older dog, but Roy had some special instinct in him and he learned the hand signals and the whistles faster than any pup.

Shepherding is instinctual, you either have it in your blood or you don't. Quite a lot of the actual herding is done by humans. If you use your dogs too often, the sheep will get nervous and bolt back into the high country. It's the burning of leg muscles, the smell of the wet bog, the alertness of the dogs focused on the tiny white dots down in the valley that winds me up. As I stride up the hills, dogs swarming close to my legs, mist melting down my cheeks, the distant bleating of lambs, I feel part of the land and part of my history as I never do anywhere else.

Sheep aren't as daft as most people think. A few years ago, near Baddeck, the sheep found a way to get over the cattle guards by rolling over them on their backs, to get to the greener grass on the other side.

A good dog never hassles the sheep, he stays a distance and rounds them up gently. Roy tends to be a bit deaf when I call him in...sometimes I think he ignores me because he's having such a grand time. These days he rests peacefully at my feet in front of the fire instead of wearing a trail in the carpet. It's the same with humans. If a man's lifestyle doesn't fit his temperament, he's likely to go batty – or even worse, give up entirely.

The happiest moment in my life was when this bloody, mucus-covered newborn slid from between my wife's thighs. Five weeks later, the greatest tragedy in my life occurred when my wife killed herself. After that, I couldn't trust another girl or woman. Kept thinking they were going to die on me and I couldn't stand it again. Got hooked on prostitutes. Who gives a toss if they die on you? I tried not to see the same one twice. There was always fresh blood on the streets, especially when those Eastern European hookers started coming into England. Lovely girls. Knew

their business. Some of them had those fake boobs – never
liked those, felt as though I was squeezing a ball of Dutch
cheese. As I got older I realized that I paid them to not wake
up next to me. I paid them to not talk to me and to not fall
in love.

It was jail that guided me to a life of law breaking. There
was no going back, not with all those connections you make
behind those walls, under barbed wire and AK-47s.

I didn't start out in diamonds. It all began with arms.
Machine guns, grenade launcher. When I had my daughter,
I had to get into something safer. Art was next. 'Ordered
art.' Some rich sod would put out the word that he had a
craving for Munch's Scream or Picasso's Blue Lady. I never
understood why they couldn't just enjoy the painting in a
museum, the way you enjoy live music.

If you decide you want the real thing, you have to nick
it, then you find a room for it – one that's temperature
controlled, your own room that guests can't go into. You
can't have people sniffing around. A guest might tip
someone off, someone like the police. Some of those rich
wankers have morals and you don't know which guest it
might be. So there you have it, a masterpiece in a locked
room with you and your glass of wine. Sorry cunts they are.

I never worked the ground, I brokered the deals. Made
a lot of money. Never liked taking art like that, so the
average bloke couldn't see it. And all those kids missing out
on a piece of history. Might have changed one of the little
squirt's lives.

I wept the first time I saw Sir Edwin Landseer's painting,
The Old Shepherd's Chief Mourner. I know that was his intent
and it bothered me, but I couldn't help myself. It's an empty
dark room with a corpse in a bed and a dog sitting next to

the bed, its head resting on a quilt, a paw curled under in sadness. I felt for that dog and his unloved master. I thought everyone who ever owned a dog should see that painting and realize what a dog's life is about. It's a crime to hide something away for one person's viewing.

After art, I got into smuggling artifacts out of poor countries into rich ones. Rocks and old glass and chipped pottery. Amazing the kind of things the rich want to collect. I had a whole business: scouts, carriers, deliverers. I could get a fake ID made in a couple of hours. 9/11 changed all that. Now it takes a few days, once it even took me a whole week. Anyway, a fake ID or two means nothing. It is your face that counts and gets you past the controls. It's hard to not look like a thug when you are one. There's a look, a whole dress code you have to follow or you lose respect.

Using my devious mind, I invented a way to keep her in my life. I instructed Roza to give her the apartment, then I had the apartment searched and gave the order to steal her ID. I had to laugh when I heard she had five of them. She was one of us. I waited in anticipation of our next meeting. Roza kept me updated on her life, the trip to the islands, her perfect basketball shot, the pouch the Kuna witchdoctor gave her.

The US government banned me from their country for a good many years, following my jail sentence. I got pardoned. Those Americans love a title – all it took was a little time and a paid for Sir before my name. Roza has been the one positive constant in my life. When I was sentenced, my life went tits up and most of my friends disappeared. Not Roza. She kept my business running and when she had her own trouble years after my own, I shipped her out of the US, she skipped bail, and I set her up in Panama. There is loyalty in humans just as there is in dogs.

After my stint in the jail, it was only half a year or so, I turned to moving stones. I never tire of the beauty of stones, the intensity of their color. I find the same colors in my beloved Scottish hills: the emerald green of the brush, the ruby red lichen, the sapphire loch under dark clouds.

I didn't want to know anything about her, all I cared about was who she was at that moment. She filled the room so completely with her intensity and curiosity. She bounced around the room like a ewe in season, handed me my diamonds and bolted out the door. Gone. I knew where she was of course, shacked up with some half-wit pillock. I've experienced enough in life to know that if you want something badly, you have to let it go.

When she walked through the door of the airplane, I almost thought there might be a God. In fact, in my mind, I found myself repeating over and over *thank God...thank God.* She had arrived in record time and looked different, new hair, posh clothes. For a moment I didn't recognize her until I saw the movement of her eyes and the wonder in her expression. The box was under her arm and I knew she was coming with me. It was all I could do to stop myself from seating her in my lap and eating up every detail of her. I didn't. I knew I had to play it cool and not be over eager. I'd done a good job over the phone getting her onto the plane.

Lord, she did something to me, made me feel as though my life were starting all over again, cranky geezer that I am. Anything became possible.

When I touched her with my ancient, spoon-splayed fingertips, I was ashamed. How is it that I am one of these old men clinging to youth by loving a young woman? I, who have scoffed at these pathetic men with their grey pubic hairs and wrinkled necks and saggy buttocks. How can they parade the onset of death in front of such youth, such freshness and firmness?

My father was a hard man. When I was fourteen we were stag hunting far back in our hills. Neither of us had shot anything that day when suddenly the most glorious stag bounded out in front of us, a twelve pointer. I shot him straight through the eyes. Perfect line-up. My father walked straight to the Rover and got in and drove away. I was left on the hill with a massive stag and the sun setting.

I gutted it and by the time I finished it was so dark I could barely see the glistening of the blood in the bog. My hands were stiff with cold. I dragged it down the hill, nearly sobbing. By the time I reached the house and hung it in the blood room, my father was in bed. The next morning when I saw him, I was still angry and crashed around the kitchen making a cup of tea. He sat down at the table.

'Do you know why I did that?' he asked.

'You wanted to see me suffer.'

'Exactly. I wanted to see you suffer in the way that the stag could have suffered. If you had missed that mark by a centimeter, you would have only wounded that beautiful animal. He would have run off and you could never have found him by dark and he would have bled and roared all night.'

'I...didn't realize it was so close to dark.'

He stood and walked to the doorway. 'Next time you will.'

He was right of course, I never shot an animal so close to dusk again. It's these lessons in life that make us who we are and suddenly I see that I have broken the *National Geographic* rule: I've intervened with the observed specimen.

CHAPTER 26

A PROPOSAL

I drive to the hospital in Oscar's car following a map from Anabelle. The car is big and black and rattles over the uneven roads, the windshield wipers squeaking across my vision. Anabelle said Oscar asked for me. Does he just want the stones, or does he want to see me? I realize how attached to him I have become, how quickly I've been swept up in a new life's crisis. Complete with suicide and illness. Shakespearean themes and Freudian undertones.

Then there's me: the observer, the watcher, the narrator of their stories, according to Hetta. Everyone is the narrator of their own tale, but in my version of the story, there is Oscar, the good-bad guy undercut by the Machiavellian son-in-law and manipulative daughter.

I want to bring something to Oscar. Out of the gloom jumps a bright field of flowers. I stop the car and back up to find a field of narcissus. I walk out to the field and stand in the middle. Their smell haunts the heavy fog, the scent itself creates a condensation on my skin.

I peer into the room and see Oscar sitting up in bed, reading a newspaper, a cup of tea steaming beside him. His color is back and he smiles at me, but I can tell he is embarrassed at the breakdown and betrayal of his body. I hold out the flowers to him. There are no other flowers in the room.

He takes them and they look miniature in his hand. He examines the stems.

'You stole these.'

'I did not. They were growing by the side of the road.'

'These are Gregory MacDougall's.'

'If you don't want them, I'll throw them out the window.'

'I love them. Did you know they are toxic?'

'Don't eat them.'

'If you put them in a vase with other flowers, they'll kill them off.'

We stare at the flowers for a moment.

'Don't you want to know how the meeting went?'

'Doesn't seem important anymore.'

'She tried to give you a six star.'

'I told you to watch her, that's her trick. I bet she cursed at the big guy as if it were his fault.'

I take the stones from my purse and hand the bag to Oscar. He smiles wryly at it and sets it next to him on the table without looking inside.

'My daughter, she's out of her coma and giving the nurses hell,' he smiles wryly, 'I've landed three floors below her. Never even knew I had a bad heart. Doc says stress set it off. What a father...useless.'

I compare Val and Oscar as fathers and although I would like to think Oscar was a better father, I know this may not be true. I think Val did as well as he knew how to. He simply wasn't fatherhood material. I suspect the same for Oscar.

'I hardly think you are a useless father.'

'A gangster does not usually make the best father. Her mother died and I tried...'

'I am sure you took care of her. Protected her. Provided for her.'

He lowers his chin and looks at me from under his brows. 'Provided, I did. Is that what I am? A provider?'

'More of a protector. You did save me.'

'A superhero.' He mock-flexes his arms.

'A superhero on a drip.'

We laugh and his tubes jiggle around and I get worried so I hide my smile.

Dale walks in and frowns at us.

'Be a dear,' Oscar winks at me, 'find me a newspaper.'

I wander through a maze of corridors until I reach a small store. It is full of tiny stuffed animals, candy and papers. I am unable to decide which paper Oscar would like, so I purchase one of each: *The Globe, The Sun, The Post* and *The Wall Street Journal.*

I return to his room and collide with Dale as he hurries out. He grabs a hold of my arm with a wire-like grip. I twist away and hold the papers protectively under my arm so he can't take them and bring them to Oscar himself.

'What are you doing here?'

'Bringing Oscar his papers.'

'Leave him alone.'

'That's his choice.'

I can hear him grinding his teeth. 'The only reason he is interested in you is your extreme unsuitability.'

I walk back into the room and roll my eyes.

'Marry me,' Oscar says.

I hand him the papers and he takes them and tosses them on the floor.

'Marry me,' he repeats.

'You obviously overheard that conversation and have taken leave of your senses.'

'My mind has never been so clear. I'm on my deathbed, humor me.'

'You had a heart attack, lots of people have heart attacks and recover.

'It's my last wish. Say yes and the judge will be here in an hour.'

'My God, you're serious. Why would you want to do this?'

'To piss off my bastard son-in-law. I like to rattle his cage a bit. You see, all this is a game we have been playing for years and frankly,' he sighs, 'I'm tired of it. Say yes.'

I laugh. 'Well since you put it that way, yes.'

I have just agreed to be a polygamist. Or have I? Dahlia is dead and although it was me married to Toby, it was her name, so technically I'm not married. Easy to rationalize. I look into his mischievous eyes and they twinkle at me and I nod, yes. I will marry Oscar, not just to piss off his Dale and upset his daughter but because, at least to me, he is really something extraordinary.

'So, you called yourself a gangster — will I be marrying a criminal?'

Oscar pauses. 'I have aspirations in that direction.'

'Don't make this a deathbed confession that you live to regret.'

'My dear, I don't think you have to worry about that,' he says sadly. 'I have to tell you something: I lied about why I sent you on that job yesterday.'

'You lied to me,' I say, delighted.

'Don't look so happy.' His eyes glitter at me. 'You're an odd bird.'

'And I lied to you.'

'About what?'

'My name is not Jillie. Or Lucy.'

He starts laughing until he starts to cough. 'Oh bullocks,'
he says. 'I knew that.'

I shake my head. 'There's more.'

'Lassie, I don't give a rat's ass about any of that. But if
we get married and you have no proper ID, you have lied
yourself out of my will. You know that daughter of mine will
sniff out anything not in order.'

'I don't want anything in your will, Oscar.'

'You don't, do you? Jesus, I should have found you years
ago.'

We are silent.

'How did you lie to me about the pick up yesterday?'

'I'll tell you, but first do something for me. Run back to
the house and get your Zanzibar box. Go now and then I'll
tell you about my lie.'

'Sure.'

'Promise me you will be quick.'

'I promise.'

'Not lying?'

'No. Not lying.'

'I was always curious to see if I'd turn religious at the
end. Thank God,' he chuckles like a naughty child, 'it hasn't
happened. Now if you can just do one more thing for me.'

'Yes.'

'Please gently lay on top of me for a moment.'

And so I carefully spread myself out flat on top of him.
Amidst all the tubes and wires. We don't move for several
minutes, we just lay there with the ticking of the machines
and the clicking of heels in the hallway and the nurse's
rubber shoes squish-squishing in the rooms. And then his
heart. The erratic beating of his heart.

His eyes are closed. I close mine too and my heart — for
once I am glad of my reversed heart — is directly over his and

it starts to beat in time until it seems there is only one heart beating. I whisper in his ear. I tell him my real name, my full name and I repeat it over and over like a mantra. *Hetta Esmerealda Carter*. His eyes are still closed, his face totally relaxed so that the wrinkles have become smooth and I swear a tiny smile flirts on his lips. I kiss his cool lips and go.

I drive back to the estate. This time every light in the house is lit, the windows are open, curtains fluttering into the cold evening. I close the windows and from the living room I see Anabelle in the dog kennel crouched in a corner, the three dogs around her with Roy draped across her lap. Another licks her face and I can hear her sobbing from the house. One of the dogs raises its paw toward her and licks her face. She doesn't push it away, she just stares ahead into the darkness, her voice hoarse.

My stomach jumps and I feel a sharp pain. I run upstairs and grab the Zanzibar box and dart out the front door. Back in the car, driving too fast, a horrible feeling grows in my head, crowding out any thoughts. I hurry back into the hospital, run through the doors and stab at the elevator key, but it is too slow so I run for the stairs and bolt up and up until I come to the fifth floor and there is Oscar. He has fallen asleep and his skin looks pink and fresh.

I touch his hand to make sure he is sleeping and find it warm. I quietly set the Zanzibar box on the table next to him and smile. I touch him again. He's warm.

'Oscar?' I say. 'I'm back. I have the box.'

I open the Zanzibar box's door to make sure my stone is inside and I hold it tightly in my palm, feeling the stone warm to my hand. I carefully lie down on his bed and arrange myself along his side. 'I want to explain something to you. You are the only one who knows my true name.

Not even my husband or daughter knew. Or my mother or father. I told you because it doesn't matter to you. My name never mattered.

'I had a twin. She was my best friend and I killed her. I don't mean I stabbed her or strangled her, I told her to do something and that killed her, it caused her death. Families can get complicated, I think you understand that. Then I married the boy she loved. In a way he was the cause of all this. It was more though, I couldn't stand the way she was changing — the way she was separating from me. Me, her twin. I loved him too and he wasn't a boy when we married and we weren't happy, but I tried to live her life as she would have.

'Of course, that didn't work.

'In the end, I couldn't live as her anymore and I killed her...over the cliff she went. And then I found myself free, but who was I after all those years? I still don't know, but I do know I'm me and not her anymore. You liked me as me and it meant a lot.

'Lying doesn't mean anything. Good people lie. I thought I was bad for years because I lied to everyone, but I didn't lie to be bad, I lied to be good. I wanted her alive. I wanted her alive so badly I buried myself.

'So you see, Oscar, you didn't ask me anything about me, but look, you are the only one I am telling these secrets to. You. You know everything about me now.'

Someone walks in the room behind me.

'I'm sorry.' I look up to see the nurse. 'His daughter has asked that he be moved to the...downstairs.'

She pats my back and it dawns on me that he is gone. And I knew he was gone. She pulls the sheet over his face, just like in the movies. She gives me the sympathy face, it's a pretty good one, and rolls him out the door.

There was no deathbed confession he lived to regret. He loved me in the way that a man looking at the face of death can love a young woman. And me? Could it be that I fell for him the moment there was a splash beside me in the water next to the underwater stars?

I sit in the room and stare at my stone. I open the drawer to put it inside and find an envelope jammed in sideways. I wiggle it until I manage to wedge it out and open it. Inside are two first class tickets to Zanzibar and hotel reservations for two weeks. My eyes flood until the tickets blur into misshapen lines.

CHAPTER 27

DEAD DOGS AND NO SEX

I was out late for the fifth night in a row. There was a full moon, a red bubble that filled the sky with a burnished glow. I turned off my headlights and cruised for several moments guided by reflections from the road. The past few nights, I had gone to the library, a movie, the zoo, a dive bar and tonight a long walk on the beach. Toby hadn't said a word about my lateness and Lorna didn't seem to notice I was gone.

If I were to talk to Dr. Morton, he would tell me to examine my own feelings. Would I care if Toby came home late every night without telling me where he was? Part of the problem is that I knew exactly where Toby was all the time, and the other part, the biggest part, was that I didn't care. Neither of us was interested in the slightest where the other was or had been. That was the crux of our dilemma. But if Lorna went to a friend's house unscheduled, Toby had a panic attack the moment he walked in the door.

I'd have liked to hear Dr. Morton's analysis of what that was all about, especially in light of Toby and the sick relationship he had with his mother. Running around as a young boy with a permanent lipstick mark on his cheek. We found it amusing the first couple of times, but as teenagers do, we turned cruel, me and Dahlia. We called him Mommy's boy, little lover and when we overheard her call him Pumpkin, he was spitting angry with her. He was Pumpkin for the rest of the summer. She hated us after that, although Toby says she hated us all along.

Just as I switched on my headlights, there was a bump. I slammed on the brakes, looking in the rear view mirror. In the middle of the road there was a dark shadow. Moonlight shone on the asphalt and tiny dots sparkled like fireflies. I scanned the bushes on either side of the road, thinking of serial killers: Bundy, Manson, Zodiac. I locked my door. The shadow moved, formed a shape. It was an animal, an injured animal.

I got out of the car and stood for a few moments until the crickets started up in a deafening chorus. The animal looked like a dog, or a fox. It was badly hurt and trying to crawl off the road with its front paws, dragging its hindquarters. I whimpered and held my head in my hands. It heard me and turned in my direction, growling, baring its teeth. A coyote, an older one. Silver glinted from its muzzle in the soft light. I leaned against the car, moaning. I knew what I had to do. Dahlia was tough and she could do it. I stood up straight, got back in the car. I turned up the music loud. Beck – *Odelay*. I threw the car in reverse and punched the gas pedal, tears flowing, wailing. Bump again. I went forward. Bump. The shape didn't move.

I opened the car door and stepped out to make sure it was not still alive. The coyote lay, legs sprawled, a trickle of blood coming from its open mouth. Its eyes were open and non-seeing.

'I'm so sorry, I'm so sorry...,' I whispered over and over.

I grabbed the coyote by its tail and pulled it toward the side of the road. If it were alive it would curl around like a snake and attack me. It didn't. The tail fur was coarsely thick, soft like a mountain dog. It is possible, but rare, for coyotes to mate with dogs and make coy-dogs. This one was a male, which I knew were only fertile once a year and even then they didn't play around much, they mated for life.

I dragged it into the bushes and left it under a sage bush. Broken branches from the sage filled the night air with pungent aroma. The smell was wild and I closed my eyes to inhale the heady scent. I broke off one of the branches and put it into my pocket.

Near the coyote's head was a single lupine flower, the purple glowing delicately.

I drove home slowly. I pushed eject on the stereo and Frisbeed the CD out the window. The house was dark and I found Toby and Lorna in the den watching cartoons, dozing, heads fallen towards each other on the couch, bathed in the blue light of the television.

When I first moved into Toby's house, after Chloe's funeral, his television was sideways on the stand. I didn't ask him why. A few days later, I saw him watching the weather channel, lying on the couch, so that the screen was properly oriented. As soon as he quit drinking the television went straight up. I hate television, but damn, I missed the sideways screen.

Now Road Runner raced a train, beep-beeping and caught the attention of Wile E. Coyote. Wile E. licked his chops and prepared a dozen mouse traps on the road. Road Runner flashed by and all the traps snapped into the air and attached themselves to Wile E.

Wile E. lost the plot and forgot that he wanted to eat Road Runner and focused on destroying him instead.

Next he read a hypnotism book and learned to make other animals walk over the edge of a cliff. When he tried it on Road Runner, Road Runner held up a mirror and he hypnotized himself...over the cliff he went. Wile E. turned fanatical and hid behind a rock on a four cornered cross road. Road Runner bee-beeped as he approached the road crossing. Wile E. stepped out from behind the rock and stood in the middle of the road to catch him. Beep beep, Road Runner ran him over. Flat on the road. Road Runner zipped by again and once again zoomed him over, double flattened...I ran for the bathroom and locked myself in.

My reflection in the mirror was pale, damp looking. Dark eyes that flitted from eye to eye trying to see something three-dimensional in two dimensions. Brown hair pulled back with curly baby hairs springing out from the sides. Mouth pursed, trembling. Where was I? It wasn't me in the mirror. I looked at my arm, it looked fake. If I wasn't there in the mirror and my arm was fake, where was I? I slapped my leg. I felt the slap. But the eyes in the mirror, they weren't mine. They were hers. Dahlia's. I took a razor from the drawer, my legs were weak, I sat on the counter and drew the razor down the inside of my thigh. There was pain, it was my leg. Me, not Dahlia. Blood peeped through the cut in fat drops. My head stopped spinning.

I blotted the blood and put on some antiseptic cream and left without looking in the mirror. Toby and Lorna had leaned towards each other so that their black heads were touching. I clapped my hands and Toby jolted upright and Lorna blinked her eyes.

I crunched the sage in the palm of my hand and inhaled the smell. I knew that I had to leave them, my husband and daughter, or I would die.

'Bedtime,' I said and smiled sweetly.

One of the world's greatest lies is: *people don't change.* They do change. Toby changed. I watched him change. Crazy irreverent Toby disappeared and in his place was a man his mother would have approved of: polite, gallant, generous and irritating as hell. He quit booze, drugs and sex.

He stopped knowing what was fun. He would ask me, with all sincerity, did we just have fun? I would tell him, yes, it was fun. Later I would think about it and wonder if it was really fun or not. Maybe I didn't know what was fun either.

He asked me to describe fun. 'What does it feel like?'

'You smile and laugh,' I said. 'Sometimes you might not smile and laugh on the outside, only on the inside.'

'Inside?' he asked, as if he had no inside.

After Toby quit drinking, he forgot how to have sex. He remembered the basics, the missionary position and where to put his penis, but no more. He didn't look in my eyes, he didn't look at my body, the covers had to be over us, no talking. And it was fast. He wouldn't use the word sex. He called it a thrill. 'How about a little thrill?' he might say, looking down. And as I lay under him I thought about the misuse of the word and how it had become that way.

Before, he knew exactly what to do and how to do it. We had sex in cars, forests, on the kitchen table, under the table. He knew what he wanted and he knew what I wanted. He would grab me with one arm and flip me over and enter me from behind or he'd stand up, my legs encircling his body and rub me up and down. When he came, he closed his eyes and smiled so gently and genuinely. He looked like a boy raising his face to early morning sunshine. That was before he turned back into a sixteen-year-old kid with no technique and plenty of shame.

Last week, we sat watching a movie, an old Marlon Brando, the one where he rubs the butter all over his French mistress. I was embarrassed for us. I glanced at him his eyes glistened with tears.

He began to chew differently. Methodically, noisily and too many times. I could hear his teeth come together with a solid *clack clack clack*. I began to turn up the music when we ate, suggest we watch a movie. *Clack clack.*

He stopped listening to music. He'd become afraid of it, the emotions that might bubble up, the feelings that might burst out. When I turned on the stereo, his foot would start to jitter up and down and he then he would leave the room. He didn't want to go out of the house, he just wanted to watch TV and work on his magazine articles at home.

He never really liked people. He wasn't sure what he liked and didn't like at all. There was no high peak from the drugs anymore, so was this low monotone life fun? He didn't know when he was angry. Was he really angry or was he angry because there were no drugs?

At the time, when he quit smoking hash, I was glad. His personality had undergone a transformation that became stronger with each lungful. He became a slick over-confident asshole. Which did I prefer, the asshole or the wallflower?

What I thought was Toby was the drugs, and what he thought was me was Dahlia. As much as Toby had changed, I changed. I changed into Dahlia. I did it so successfully, no one knew I wasn't her. Even Dr. Morton didn't realize I was lying. Wasn't he supposed to figure those things out?

We lay in bed together, as separate as two in bed can be. I heard his breathing and I knew he had fallen asleep. I went downstairs and turned on the television and watched the rest of Wile E. Coyote. I knew he would never win against Road Runner, but I kept watching and hoping and each time he tried something new...I couldn't help thinking that maybe that time he would win.

CHAPTER 28

A BAD DOG IN AFRICA

The air in Zanzibar smells of cloves and sweat. Exactly what I'd expect a spice island off Tanzania to smell like. I must be the only person to arrive in Zanzibar, box already in hand.

A crowd of tall men with skin so dark it reflects light descend upon me as soon as I step out of the airport doors. Nothing in all my travels could have prepared me for this chaos, this madness. The crowd shifts, moves, they jostle and yell. They are confused about my lack of luggage and when they see the box, they point at it and step away. I feel so white, pale. So vulnerable.

I picture Oscar in the midst of this turmoil and I smile, the crowd immediately smiles back. It's hard for me to accept that someone so bursting with energy could die in a matter of days. Someone who made such a strong impression on my life in a short time. I feel all the deaths around me: Dahlia, Chloe, Toby's mother, Bird, Oscar — and I feel I have thwarted fate long enough.

One of the men in the crowd pushes to the front and picks up my box. No one argues with him, he is an immense man, both tall and wide. He grins widely.

'Welcome to Zanzibar, my lady.'

We get into his taxi and there is what looks like a monkey paw hanging from his mirror. When I tell him the name of my hotel, his eyes flicker for a moment and he eyes me in the rear view mirror.

'You will want to go to the house of Freddie Mercury.'

'Freddie Mercury? From Queen?'

'He was born here in Stone Town. We will go to his house.'

'I don't want to go to Freddie's house. Anyway, he's dead.'

'Yes,' he nods sadly, 'he's dead. We will not go to his house.'

We drive through the outskirts of the town where the houses get smaller and smaller until they are huts with plastic tarps for roofs. Ragged chickens dig in the hard dirt. Schoolgirls wearing full robes run along the road in the heat, holding onto their head coverings and waving at my pale face peering out at them. They are swathed from head to toe in white polyester. It shines in the sun.

The front of the hotel is nothing special, but once I walk through the reception area, I see green water covering massive reef that stretches as far as I can see. When I check in and the hotel asks where Mr. Whitehall is, I lie. I tell them he will arrive later.

The bungalows are built on a rock cliff that looks over the crystal water where hermit crabs scuttle from nook to cranny, leaving their trails in the pale sand. I stand and look at the hermit crabs for a long time, until the sun's reflection burns my eyes and spots float before me in wavering lines.

In the afternoon the cook comes to me and hands me a menu. He wears a white double-breasted chef's coat with no spots or stains. He stands tall and erect, pen poised above his notebook.

'What will you and the mister be having for dinner tonight?'

I peruse the menu and think of what he would order.

'One coconut calamari for me. And... one fish in island curry for the mister.'

The other tourists trail by at cocktail hour, two by two. They sit at their tables set out on a rock patio, lit by hurricane lamps. I sit at the open bar and look at my table set for two and watch as the sun begins its descent. I have a Zanzibar Sling for Oscar and toast him. The guests laugh quietly among themselves and talk about swimming with dolphins and spice farms. I think about nothing, my mind skitters along the surface of what I see. Hunger drives me to my table. I am the only single person.

I sit gazing out at the dhow boats. The waiter brings me two cocktails and the second one sits pointedly across from me. I look away, out at the water and don't think of Oscar. I don't think of him swimming in the dark or his fingers tickling Roy under the chin. I don't think of him in a crisp white shirt or lying under me in the hospital bed. I wave to the waiter.

'My husband is tired after all the walking we did today. I will take him his food in the room,'

'Of course,' he says.

'Lala salama,' the waiters call, as I walk to my bungalow.

I walk inside and stand with the plate of fish in island curry, the smell making me ill. I set it on the chair and pace. A couple of ants find the food. There is nowhere to hide the plate, they can crawl anywhere. If it were the middle of the night, I could sneak out to the ocean and toss it in. I cut the fish into smaller pieces and scrape it down the toilet. I feel really sick now. The noise of the flush makes me miserable. As I watch the food disappear down the hole, I cry for the pure waste of it all: I cry for the hungry Africans, I cry that my life is now this.

In the morning, I feel empty, as though I have already died. The reminder of all the deaths in my life follows me like a hangover in the glaring light. Shards of aquamarine and turquoise water move along the shallow beach that stretches out into the ocean for infinity. A crab, missing one of its orange claws, scuttles in front of me waving his remaining one threateningly. The hotel is empty except for the Swahili woman serving me my juice and eggs and she does not ask where the mister is.

Heat floods the restaurant as the sun rises higher. My eyes ache, staring out at the blazing sand, a band of pressure increases against my forehead. I find a faded and torn guidebook in the reception. I learn that Zanzibar is not just Muslim, it is conservative Muslim. Most of the uncovered women are Swahili and they wear colorful sarongs they call kangas which are bright and printed with personal sayings that can be either fortuitous sayings or slanders and curses.

The tide creeps out as an underwater desert appears before me, the sea receding into the far distance. A couple of crows screech insults from the top of the thatch roofed restaurant. The north winds have brought in massive mounds of seaweed which piles up against the rocky beach.

I go to my room to put on my bathing suit. My blue stone is soothing in the palm of my hand, cool and it gives me a bit of hope that life is something more than death. I will take the box and the stone with me. I can't stand losing them, I imagine fire, flood, theft. I adjust the straps of my

bathing suit top and get redressed to walk twenty steps to
the pool. The guidebook warns not to offend the villagers
with too much skin. *Cover your knees and shoulders*, it says.

The pool is cool and overflows when I step in. I lie
back in the water and close my eyes. I remember my pool
in Romania, my own underwater world. I imagine that I
don't exist, my body is not here, my mind floats to the blue
sky...my heart stops beating. I sink slowly to the bottom and
touch the cool tiles. An involuntary moan racks my lungs
and I inhale water. I come up choking and coughing and
have to blow my nose on my towel.

A small boy with the richest dark skin stands next to the
pool with a bag of wares. He places a carved wooden box on
the wall near me.

'*Jambo*, hello my friend. Zanzibar box for sale.'

The box is impressive, polished, exotic. He is wearing a
T-shirt ripped under each armpit and shorts with the elastic
worn out so that he has to keep hitching them up.

I point to my own much bigger box. 'No, thank you, I
have one.'

He stares at it solemnly and runs a finger down the side
reverently. 'This one is special.'

'Yes, do you know who made it?'

He shrugs and holds out the small box. 'Small souvenir
for holiday?'

At the thought of a holiday, my nose starts to run and
the boy looks aghast at finding this pale tourist weeping in
the eternity pool. He looks around for help.

'Come back tomorrow,' I manage to get out.

He regains his showmanship. 'My friend, I will see you
tomorrow.'

I don't want any friends.

In the evening, I sit above the ocean and listen to the soft movement of the water until it fills my veins with its slow liquid noise. No one mentions Mr. Whitehall again, they must have had a group discussion. Behind me, there is the sound of sweeping along the rock path. The sweeper is a small Rastafarian man with dreadlocks all the way down his back. He walks over to me and stands close, pressing his penis against me as he gazes silently out at the water. I slowly move my body away so as to not offend him. He sadly resumes his sweeping. That night I stay in my hotel room, I lie in bed and check my pulse. It seems to have stopped.

The next morning, I stand above the beach, on the hotel wall and look along the shoreline, nothing but rotting mounds of seaweed and a million hermit crabs. I am afraid to go to the village, afraid of my pale body standing out against the green water. Afraid of my whiteness against the black of the villagers.

I sit on a rope swing and stare out at the sea. The intensity of the translucent green makes me shiver. A gang of children play in the seaweed piles, jumping on them and scattering them as if they were autumn leaves. The girls wear dresses from a forgotten era, full skirts, puffy sleeves. I walk closer to them and can see the dresses are filthy, the backs split open and shredded hems.

Late afternoon, I stand at the back of the hotel, at the gate and look outside. It is another world. A rocky dirt road, coral and cement houses on either side, scrawny chickens pecking at pebbles and grit. A herd of goats stands on a pile of rocks, mothers and babies.

I lean against the white plastered wall, shuffling my feet in the blanched soil. Two men crouch on stools playing a game with round stones and a narrow wooden board with scooped-out holes. A newborn goat stands in the middle of the road, bleating into the fading afternoon light, his umbilical cord trailing in the dust. The bigger goats ignore him. I hold out my hand. I want to inhale his sweet baby breath and look into his trusting eyes.

A gust of wind slaps the road and sand twists into the air. Thunder shudders in the distance and shrieks pierce the air. A dark dog with a white face runs haywire, excitement or rabies, chasing children. The goats scatter. For a moment, I think it's Oscar's dog, Roy. It's not, it's too skinny and has a demon look on its face. The tiny goat runs the wrong way and the dog follows. It bites the runt goat. Villagers pelt the dog with stones and yodel a primitive ululation. A man appears, grabs the goat and darts off.

I turn and run back into the hotel. Horizontal rain floods the gutters. I duck behind one of the coconut trees and howl into the tempest. I howl until my throat hurts. The storm vents its fury and abruptly stops. Total silence. I walk slowly to my room, saturated and shivering, numb.

I put on dry clothes and sit on my dark terrace. Music starts up from the outdoor bar again. The demon dog gallops by. I follow it. It goes to the bar and lies at the feet of a dark man, a dark man with a tiny goat curled in his lap. The goat is quite happy in the man's lap, it looks around and snuggles against his arm. The man pets the goat and talks to it.

'Thirty thousand shillings I had to pay the herder for you. Look, it's not even hurt,' he says to me. 'See where my dog bit it.'

He shows me the saliva marks from the dog, no blood.

'He's not a bad dog.'

He continues to pet the goat. Even in the heat, his skin is still wet and beaded from the rain as if it has been oiled.

I want to pet the goat, but I feel spoiled, ruined, like I will taint its purity.

'I came to see you,' he says.

'Me?'

'The white lady alone. You have something special.'

I think about the stone. How would he know about my stone?

'Your chest.'

'My Zanzibar box,' I say with relief.

'May I see it?'

I retrieve it for him, taking out the stone and putting it around my neck in the leather pouch. He takes the box in his hands. They are the same color as the wood. He rubs the brass and opens the drawers and sniffs inside.

'There is a history to your box. It was made by a very famous carver, my great-grandfather. It was called the box of lies.'

'Lies? That's what the boy said who sold it to me.'

'It carried false plans for a fight against the slave trade in the eighteen hundreds to trick the slave masters into believing one plot, when there was an entirely different plot.'

'Did it work? The trick?'

He opens a drawer and feels around with his finger until he finds the smooth knob and releases the drawer in the back where I found my stone.

'This is where they hid the plans.'

I take my stone out of the pouch and hand it to him. 'And this? I found it there too.'

He takes the stone and holds it tightly in his hand. He rubs an edge on his tooth. He holds it up to the light and squints. He sets the stone on the bar counter, lifts the box high above him, and brings it down on top of the stone.

I scream. The stone shatters easily into a thousand blue splinters.

'Glass,' he says.

He stands and nods briefly at me. 'No, it didn't work.'

He and the dog and the goat, still cradled in his arms, disappear along the shadowed beach. I stand motionless and watch the dark swallow him.

Somewhere down the beach, the ancient sound of Africa drums into the night. The slapping of hands on taut leather. A chanting that fades and wanes in the breeze. I press my finger into the glittering shards and a piece lodges in my skin. I pull it out and a drop of blood pushes through, falling onto the floor. My head pulses with the beat of the drums, my heart slows down.

I step down the stairs to the beach and trance-like, follow the man, trudging through the piles of seaweed, spongy and soft, like a feather mattress. The moon lights the way, reflecting off the beach. The sand is white, ultra-fine, yet is clay-like where the ocean has seeped in.

A dozen men sit around a fire pit pounding on drums. I stand outside the light. The first civilization was from this area and this scene could have been 150,000 years ago. I am so white and new. The men are sweating from the heat, from the fire, from the drums. Whites of eyes flash as the beat picks up. Skin glistens.

I walk into the circle, my paleness shining, reflecting the red of the fire. The shattering of the stone has made me bold. The men are so intent, they hardly notice me. A few nod in my direction. I see the man with the goat. I sit on the log next to him. He is stroking the goat in time with the drums. His dog sits next to him in the sand.

Their hands move faster and faster. The man hands me the goat and takes one of the drums, pounding and vibrating into the flames. I embrace the goat and feel its heart beating against my knee. It looks up at me and makes a soft noise I can't hear. The pounding grows louder and louder and the dog leans back and rests its warm head on my foot and through the heat I feel my heart start pulsing with the beat of the drums. It beats and beats until it feels as though it will burst in my skin and I fall to the sand, cheek against the cool granules, goat still in my arms. The dog pants nearby. I see its glistening gums and dripping red tongue and I shiver into the sand which has turned to ice and the flickering of the fire freezes.

CHAPTER 29

I AM A PLANNER

It was Ken Kesey who inspired my plan. A year after Lorna's birth I volunteered at the local library, and when I read about Kesey faking his death by drowning and then fleeing to Mexico, I felt I had chanced upon the perfect plot. I got a copy of my own death certificate, *Hetta Esmerelda Carter*, and applied for a driver's license. Then I registered my mobile phone in my new name, after that, it was easy to get a bank account and then a passport. Once I had one, I made four more. Little by little I deposited money into my security box.

Once I had twenty thousand dollars saved, I began to search for Toby's new wife. I thought about gardeners, housecleaners, a new best friend of mine...in the end, I decided a nanny would be best. This way she'd already be installed in the house. It shouldn't take much to push it any further. Robin Williams did it. Jude Law did it... Ethan Hawke. She had to be pretty, but not in an overt way. Someone he would fall for slowly, in his own time, in his own mind. Otherwise he would put a barrier between the two of them immediately.

She would have to be different from me. Someone who would evoke underground feelings, a hidden turmoil for a woman who would reveal all of my shortcomings and make him certain he was not in love with me anymore.

In the local newspaper, I found a tall Croatian girl, Maja. Tiny hips, long legs, and curvy bust...eyelashes, abundant and black. What man wouldn't fall in love with her?

I decorated the downstairs bedroom, modern and sophisticated. She moved in and the whole atmosphere changed. There was a charge in the air. Lorna followed her through the house and clung to her shapely legs. Surely Toby would fall for a woman his child obviously adored.

I watched them and was careful not to push them together. I noticed that whenever Toby encountered Maja, he would avoid eye contact, his eyes sliding over her sleek coiled hair and bristly lashes to escape out the window or onto a newspaper. This sly avoidance I took to be a good sign and I arranged for Toby to teach Maja the rather complicated rules of Lorna's favorite game, Princess and Alien. It was a game that had developed over the years and the rules had become unwieldy. I was always getting them wrong, so it would have to be Toby to teach her the correct version.

I left them sitting in front of the fireplace, on the couch, the game board on the wooden table in front of them. Toby had a pad of lined yellow paper and a pen for her to take notes. Maja looked lovely, thick hair falling over her face, cheeks flushed from the fire. I came into the room with my coat on, jingling the keys in one hand. Her perfume assaulted my nose. I wished she hadn't put the perfume on.

'Need anything at the store?'

Toby looked up and stood, panicked. 'Wait, I'll come with you later.'

'Don't worry,' I turned and jingled the keys again, 'I have a lot of shopping to do. I'll see you in a couple of hours, I know how you hate grocery shopping.'

In the grocery store I drifted between the avocados and pineapple, floated through the pork chops and sirloin, tossing one of everything into the cart. I stopped at the café and languorously sipped a green tea while munching on a crispy cookie.

The house was quiet when I returned. And empty. Toby's car was gone as were Maja and Lorna. Had he run off with her, abandoned me? Had my plan worked better than I ever imagined? I pictured a life on my own and waited to feel regret, but all I felt was relief.

I ran a hot bath and lowered myself into the steaming water, listening to the silence the way a classical music aficionado might listen to the most heart-wrenching version of Rachmaninoff. I floated in the bath with my head under the water, only my nose sticking out and imagined I had gone back in time, way back, into my mother's stomach. I touched myself and heard the movement of the water and felt my skin as Dahlia's skin. She was there, I felt her presence so strongly. We were two again, not one as two.

The front door closed. Toby took Lorna to her room and I heard him preparing her for bed, brushing her teeth, singing the bedtime song. My eyes flew open and I saw that I was only one and that the bath had turned very, very cold. I got out and stood shivering before the mirror. Dahlia looked back at me. Never me, always Dahlia. She smiled at me and I threw the ceramic soap dish at the mirror, cracking a diagonal line through my body.

Toby came into the bathroom and looked at me naked in front of the cracked mirror. He took my robe from the hook and wrapped it around my body and gently moved me into the bedroom. He sat on the bed next to me.

'Next time *you* explain the rules to the nanny.' He

twisted his lips and looked disdainful. 'I took Maja to a hotel for the night. I didn't want her in the house anymore.'

'What did she do?'

'You can imagine.'

'She...touched you?'

'Enough, I'm not going to go into details. She'll be back tomorrow to pick up her things.'

'She's a pretty girl.'

'What? What's wrong with you?'

So Maja had the same idea I did, Toby was not one for aggressive women. He liked to be the pursuer, it had to be his idea. I knew the perfume was a bad idea. The next one will have to be more subtle. Eastern European women were not known for their sexual subtlety.

The next day the doorbell rang and Maja stood outside, looking at me belligerently. 'I need to pick up my suitcases.'

I swept my arm grandly and smiled at her to let her know, no hard feelings. She faltered. This was not the reaction she expected, but she walked by me, head held high, sneer on her lips. I followed her into her room and offered her a cup of coffee. She froze and narrowed her eyes, she expected tricks and poison in the cup. She threw sweaters, underwear, make-up and a book into a massive suitcase, shoving them in, in a frenzy. She snapped the suitcase shut and lugged it downstairs without looking at me again. There was a beat-up truck outside and a man leaning against the door. He lifted her suitcase into the back and they left, her sitting slouched next to the door, hair hanging in her face.

I took my time searching for the next nanny, she had to be right. I didn't want a succession of nannies, he might get immune to them in the house. I interviewed chubby-cheeked Russians, flat-faced Swedes, butter-ball Mexicans, but the one I liked best was from the good old U S of A,

Maddy Cormac. She had that thick wheat-colored hair that the Midwest breeds so well. She was not small or dainty, she was sturdy with strong Midwestern values, so I knew she would not come on to him, he would have to make the move on her.

When I was interviewing her she told me she took Tai Kwon Do at a gym close to our house. The next day I went and spied on her in her class. She wore uncomplicated grey sweats and bounded energetically around the room, kicking high onto a stuffed bag and punching it with vigor. Her hair was pulled back into a high ponytail and it swung wholesomely with each kick or punch. A red flush spread up her cheeks and I thought that if I were Toby, I might just fall for her.

There was always the possibility she was gay, hard to tell with athletic women. She was strong. Thick legs and hard arms. Bright white teeth. It was like I was shopping for a horse or a dog and in a way, I was. Someone to do what I needed done. To make my husband fall in love.

At the end of the hour I hovered around the door and as she walked out, I stopped and touched her arm.

'Maddy?' I asked, acting surprised.

'Well, hello, how funny to see you here.'

'I had some shopping down the street.' I held up my shopping bag. 'Listen, I know you haven't showered, but how about a quick coffee next door?'

She glanced at her watch. 'Sure.'

We both ordered regular coffees, nothing fancy, a good sign. She was a freelance copywriter, a few years out of college.

'My husband's a writer.'

'What does he write?'

'He has a column.'

She was impressed. Good. 'Where?'

'In *The Chronicle*. Toby McInnis.'

'Sure, I know who he is.'

His column had started out about cars. Then he moved on to new electronic gadgets mixed with local gossipy tidbits taken from the social pages. He had sort of a cult following and a fan website.

'You'd enjoy talking to him.'

'Wow.'

'How did you get into Tae Kwon Do?' I asked.

'In college, with an old boyfriend who was studying to be a cop.'

Boyfriend, not gay. 'And is he?'

'Actually, he is. I mean we're not together anymore, that was a long time ago, but we still keep in touch.'

Everything good so far: simple, still in touch with old friends, a writer.

'Really nice to chat,' I said. 'But I've got to run some errands before I pick up Lorna. I'll call you later on and we can talk about the job.'

'That would be great.' She beamed at me and flashed her healthy teeth.

Maddy fit into the household as if she had always been a part of our family. At first her hearty laugh startled Lorna, but after a week, she began imitating her and following her around like a puppy. I was glad to have the pressure taken off me so I was not the only mommy source in Lorna's life. Maddy bonded with Lorna in a way I never had. She even carried a photo of Lorna in her wallet and I overheard her talking to her family in Minnesota about the photo she sent them of her. The only photo in my wallet was of Dahlia and me sitting in a tree, on the same horizontal limb, sole of foot to sole of foot. It's the only photo I have ever carried with me.

In front of Toby, I complimented Maddy, on her hair, her straight teeth, her strong arms. He didn't appear to be listening, but that was his way. He was listening.

Weeks before Toby's birthday, Maddy, Lorna and I plotted a special surprise, with me plotting an extended plot none of them could possibly imagine. I couldn't believe I would ever have the nerve to leave my family. It seemed I would plan my whole life for an event that never happened, like the bride eternally waiting for the groom, or the actor always waiting for the breaking role. I would be eighty with no teeth and sunspots on the back of my hands and I'd still be thinking of things I needed to do before I left and depositing bits of cash in my account every week.

In my bedroom we dressed for the Mexican themed party, margaritas in hand. I picked through a pile of clothing on the bed and withdrew a few items as if they were there by chance. In reality I had spent days shopping for the right outfit for Maddy, something sexy, yet wholesome. And I had found just that item: a white off-the-shoulder dress with a flirty ruffle along the bottom.

'Try this. It doesn't fit me anymore.'

'You're tiny. Nothing you have will ever fit me.'

'I was pregnant when I wore this. Try it.'

She held it up to herself and smiled. She didn't mind that I was handing her outcast pregnant clothing. As I squirted myself with my perfume, I made sure to have my spray drift onto Maddy too.

Maddy, Lorna and I waited in our Mexican outfits for Toby to walk through the door. Lorna in a child-sized sombrero, myself in an over-sized adult one, three feet across with itchy straw band around my forehead. We had mariachi music blaring and Lorna looked adorable in her little red dress with the embroidered roosters. I braided my hair Frida Kahlo style and Maddy pranced around the room, twirling and calling out, 'Ole!' He would have to notice.

I wore tight matador-style trousers and a long sleeved, ruffled shirt, sedate, in line with the theme, nothing feminine. I drew on a black curling moustache. Ole Mole delivered tamales, black beans, salsa. I made another batch of margaritas with fresh lime, Grand Marnier and Tezon tequila. We were ready. Maddy shone, her cheeks red. Lorna skipped in circles, and me, I gave myself an imaginary pat on the back.

We heard Toby's key in the door and ducked behind the sofa. He walked into the room and we popped up like jack-in-the-boxes, yelling, 'Happy Birthday!' Lorna flung herself at him and he tossed her up in the air, her sombrero fluttering to the ground. She screamed and ran to get it, smashing it back on her head. Toby came to me and kissed me on my moustache and even grinned at Maddy.

More margaritas...Maddy and Lorna danced to the blaring music. Toby and I sat on the couch and watched them whooping and laughing.

We danced vigorously around the sombrero, kicking up our legs and shrieking until I hobbled off to the couch and held my ankle as if it were bothering me. No one noticed. The power of suggestion exceeds even my own understanding – if there's anything I believe strongly in, it's this. Toby continued to whirl the two of them around. Maddy's breasts bounced fetchingly and I smiled into my margarita.

CHAPTER 30

SAVED BY THE DRUMS

My mind meanders through time...faces appear and distort...my skin sheds oceans...the drums...black eyes watching...cardamom shaped fish...eyes open to shards of blue glass...thumping pain inside...a trickle of rain smells dark.

The black eyes do not go away. They are Roza's. Roza is in Zanzibar. She puts cold cloths on my shivering body. She forces pills, hard as stones down my sandpaper throat. She rubs my body with a cold cloth and it bruises me. I tell her I hate her and she laughs.

I open my eyes to a blue sky, shell-shaped clouds and a crystal-clear head. It feels as though I have been asleep for years, a modern day Rip Van Winkle.

'Hakuna matate,' Roza says. 'I'm learning Swahili.' She leans closer. 'And you had dengue fever. Bone crush fever.'

My brain cannot understand all of this...Roza, Swahili, dengue fever, my feet sticking up at the end of the bed, draped in a white sheet like a corpse. I sit up and feel fine, weak, but fine. I walk to the window, my legs shaking and I hold onto the windowsill to keep myself upright. It is a different beach outside.

'You have to wait out dengue fever. There is nothing anyone can do.'

I peer outside and see that the carpet of seaweed and miles of reef have disappeared and in their place is a pristine white beach that stretches into the horizon. The dhows, with their patched rag sails, charge across the ocean.

'The trade winds shifted. You missed it. In one day the monsoon winds went from north to south, from Oman to India. From rock and seaweed to pure white sand in less than a day.'

It's as hard for me to believe that this is the same beach, as it is for me to believe that I had dengue fever...or that my stone is in shards...or that Roza is sitting here in Zanzibar.

'Roza, how did you get here?'

'I arrived in Nova Scotia the day after Oscar died, but you had already disappeared. Anabelle bought the tickets for Oscar. He wanted to take you here to find the story of your box. He likes a good mystery. I didn't think you went back to Panama or New York when you had tickets to Zanizbar, so I bought myself a ticket and arrived to find you in the midst of a nasty fever.'

We walk down the street to the pier. I walk slowly, my muscles are tired, they ache in protest, yet my head feels clean, fresh. A pile of boys, some wearing baggy greyed underwear, others in neck-to-ankle white robes, play on the docks. The youngest boys have empty water bottles, full of air, strung together and tied around their waists to give them buoyancy.

I am so happy to have Roza here. I look at her and smile. She smiles back, quick and tight and takes my arm.

'I have a confession to make.' Roza squeezes my arm. 'I put that stone in your box.'

'What stone?'

'Your blue stone.'

'My blue stone was glass.'

'I know.'

My heart starts to beat faster in my weak body. 'Why would you put a piece of blue glass in my box? And let me think it was something else? You knew I thought that stone was something special.'

She takes a deep breath. 'Let me start from the beginning. Oscar...he didn't want you to disappear, so I...I...'

'You put a stone in my box?'

'I...and...the robbery was planned.'

'You? You took my IDs? And my money?'

'I set up the theft of your ID. I didn't know you would have five of them.'

'You had me robbed. Jesus.' I drop her arm.

'I didn't know about that. They weren't supposed to steal your money.'

'I thought you were my friend.'

'I am your friend. But you have to understand, Oscar was my friend before you. For many years. He saved my life.'

I turn to leave. My head is spinning. Roza pulls me down onto a bench where I sit, numb. The cement bench is still scalding from the afternoon sun, but neither of us moves. Next to us is a barren park covered in raspy scrub grass that catches wind-blown plastic bags, straws and ripped cardboard.

'He was afraid you would disappear. I've never believed in that kind of love and especially from someone like Oscar, but it happened. I saw it. That day he saved you, from the beginning, that first day you arrived in Panama. He asked me to give you the apartment. But I figured the only way to keep you around was to make you dependent on me.'

'So you robbed me and then offered me the job. And got me the passport.'

'When Oscar heard that your money was stolen, he was furious. I didn't care — I saw his face when he watched you and I knew I had to make sure you didn't leave.'

As evening approaches, men begin setting up impromptu restaurants furnished with lopsided wooden tables, on the edge of the dusty park. The sugar cane men are the first in business with their bundles of neatly piled sheaves, ready to be shaved and crushed for juice. The coal fires start burning and the park is covered in a low eye-stinging haze. Plastic bags cartwheel into the sea. Groups of children gather in colorful circles, riding rusty bikes that squeak with each rotation of the wheel. The noise level increases.

'I have something for you.'

Roza hands me a US passport. I open it and read the name: *Hetta Esmerelda Carter*. I drop it as if it stung me.

She picks it up and flicks through the pages. 'It was the only one the police recovered. The others were gone, sold I'm afraid. This one is a good fake. One of the best I've seen.'

'It's not a fake. None of them are fakes. They're all dead...most of them infants. It's just me alive...and that's my real passport.'

I start to laugh at the irony of being restored to myself and then I remember that I too am dead — officially dead at the age of seventeen. I laugh until I choke and Roza pounds me on the back.

Behind me there is a shriek of rage and I turn to see a barefooted man tipping over the grill of a tall skinny man. Hot coals drop onto the ground and scatter. The skinny man picks up a hot coal that landed on his foot and throws it at the other man. All of the food vendors join in the ruckus. Instead of hitting the culprit with their fists, they throw anything they can get their hands on: a bent hubcap, firewood, chunks of concrete. A crowd gathers ululating bloody war cries and they chase after the man. The swimming boys join in and run, trailing air-filled bottles and damp robes. I desperately want to join these men, running and yelling into the wind.

Soon the park is empty except for a child or two and me and Roza. I am weak from laughing and my illness and the spectacle of Zanzibar.

'I told you that I left my family, but I didn't tell you that I faked my death. Twice. Pseudocide. Ken Kesey did it too, except he was running from the government.'

'What were you running from?'

'My twin. My dead twin.'

She widens her eyes. 'Well you did something most of us only dream of doing. At a certain point everyone looks at their stained sinks or Persian rugs and wants out.'

'It took an earthquake to make me leave.'

'Most people never feel the earthquake.'

'No. I mean a real earthquake.'

'Ah, so you are from California....But the fact that you did it, and they haven't, will condemn you.'

'I am condemned.'

Roza touches my arm. 'I have something from Oscar.'

She hands me a small satchel with a gold tie. I open it and there is another blue stone. It looks the same as my old one, it even feels the same in the palm of my hand, same color, same roundness. I throw it in the dirt. Roza bolts up and snatches it off the ground and rubs off the dust and inspects it between two fingers.

'This is the stone that Oscar wanted you to have. When he heard that your money was stolen, he had me put the fake stone in your box, thinking it would be switched for the real one at a later date, after he made the deal with Suri, the woman you met. Look at it closely and *please* don't throw it again.'

I take the stone from her and look at it. Intense blue, I turn it in the sunlight and suddenly see the twelve rays branching out from the center of the alternative universe.

'This is the stone from the pick-up for Oscar?'

'Yes.'

'He had me meet with her so that I would recognize it when I saw it? *Everything* was planned...'

The drums have stopped. The crowd slowly returns to their fires and tables. I am detached from the shouting water boys and the sizzling octopus and Roza, who sits in front of me talking and talking. I see her mouth moving and the tip of her tongue, but nothing makes sense to me.

I have lived so many lives since I left San Francisco without Dahlia. I have discovered that people like me as Hetta. Roza trusted me and lied to me, a handsome druggie took me in, a tough old man fell in love with me. I have lived so many lives in such a short time. Roza's mouth curves and opens and closes, but I am inside my head and it is only me in there and I know I will have to go back.

CHAPTER 31

THE END

I arrive back in New York as Hetta Esmeralda Carter. Me. I followed Roza's instructions and struck up a spontaneous friendship with some 'camels,' a wholesome tour group, until I was through the security check. It's easy to make conversation with a frazzled teacher and ten students. The teacher was more than happy to chat with an adult and complain about the rowdy nights and bickering among the students.

I go straight to Celia's house, passing the church with the cowardly pastor where I saw the seagull eating the dove. My ears can still hear the cries of the dove. When I think back on my bus ride, I had to have been out of my mind to obsess over the amount of time for the trip, stabbing the wheel with a letter opener and screaming 'rat.' Even my time with Peter seems a lifetime ago.

Celia's house looks exactly the same. I walk up and down the street several times before climbing the stairs to her door. I stand there, shaking, just as I did so many years ago after Dahlia died. I put my finger up to the doorbell. It hovers there for a few moments before the door is yanked open and Celia comes barging out, shrugging on her coat.

She stops and looks at me and shakes her head. Her purse drops to the ground, her nostrils flare until the edges become red.

'Celia, it's me – I didn't die.'

Her mouth opens, but no sound comes out. I doubt my decision to come here and tell her everything.

'But it's not the me you think it is.'

I hand her a stethoscope I bought in Stone Town. She doesn't talk or move so I guide her back into the house and shut the door. The house is quiet. I put the tongs gently in her ears. She looks petrified. I take the end and put it on my heart, on the right side of my chest. She listens, her eyes widen. I move the speaker to the left side of my chest and she listens again. She yanks the tongs out of her ears and throws the stethoscope to the floor. Her hand moves to her left chest and her mouth hangs open. I realize that I've given her quite a shock. I go to the liquor cabinet and pour her a Scotch.

She takes a deep gulp. She stares at me shaking her head. 'Who are you?'

'Hetta.'

'I don't believe in ghosts.' Her skin has turned a dull pale color. She looks around the house as if to reassure herself where she is.

'Let's sit down.'

Celia nods her head. 'Yes, I think we should sit down.' She sits limply on the couch. 'Are you a ghost?'

'You heard my heart. I'm alive. Hetta didn't die, Dahlia did.'

'But Dahlia died in the earthquake. And Hetta died when a truck hit her. I went to both of the funerals.'

'I took over Dahlia's identity when I was seventeen. No one noticed. It wasn't Dahlia who died in the earthquake. Anyway, no one died in the earthquake. I faked it.'

'My God. What have you done?'

'I couldn't stand that she had died, so I pretended I was her. For over ten years.'

'Who are you?'

'Listen to me, I am Hetta — I didn't die when I was seventeen.'

'You are not the Hetta I knew.'

'I have been living my life as Dahlia and I couldn't do it anymore. She was stronger than me and I had no control over my life.'

'You've done a horrible thing.'

Somehow I thought she would be more accepting of what I had done. I didn't expect her to jump up and hug me, but I thought she would understand. Maybe what I've done is impossible for someone to understand unless they've also lived a life of total lies.

'I know. I want to try and fix it.'

'It's not possible. Don't even think of going to Toby.'

'No?'

'No. Do you have any idea what they've gone through, your husband and your daughter?'

'I have some idea.'

'You have no idea, or you would never have done this.'

'Celia, I thought about it for years. I planned it all. I had to. Try to imagine your twin, the closest person in the world to you, dying...you'd do anything to keep her alive.'

I stay with Celia for the night. She keeps me at a distance, afraid of what I have done or what I might do. She does not call up Trevor or ask me if I would like to see him. I see now that sometimes truth is not the best answer.

In the morning she is waiting for me in the kitchen, dressed, coffee made. She nods to greet me and sits at the table waiting until I have made myself a coffee and seat myself across from her. She looks straight at me. Her face is tired, but her eyes are clear and I can see she has been thinking for hours, maybe all night.

'I do not believe in family for the sake of family. Blood means nothing to me, it is no different from a friend or acquaintance or a random man on the street.' She takes a deep breath and looks away from me. 'I want you to leave my house. I can't forgive you for what you have done. And I order you to stay away from Toby and Lorna.'

She leaves the room. I stand and walk to the sink and pour my coffee down the drain. This is what I deserve. It was a mistake to come back and think I could tell the truth. I splash water on my face, gather my things and go to the door. Celia does not appear. I walk outside and stand on her doorstep.

I've changed. Toby's changed. Val's changed. People *do* change. The lock clicks into position behind me.

Despite Celia's warning, I get on an airplane to San Francisco. When the airplane begins it descent, I look out the window, waiting for the wash of energy I have always felt. It doesn't come, I only feel jittery and nervous.

I rent a nondescript car and head into the city. As I near downtown, I find off-ramps and freeway junctions closed and detour signs posted everywhere. I have been so wrapped up in my own world that I forgot about the aftermath of the earthquake. My breath is painful and I have to pull the car over to the side of the road. In front of me is a massive detour sign where the 280 exit used to be. In my head, this whole earthquake has been about me, while the reality of it is that I am microscopic compared to the enormity of what has happened to the city and its people.

Cars are driving by, blasting their horns. I pull back onto the freeway and make my way downtown, straight to my old street. I drive by a block away and stare down the street at my old house. No one is around, but it is dangerous. Toby or Lorna could walk by, or a neighbor. I drive to Castro Street and buy a long black wig, Jackie O sunglasses and some makeup. I cover my skin with dark foundation and dress in a fur stole, tailored suit, and pearls that I find in a vintage store. My lipstick is cherry red. Then I sit across and down the street from my house, engine running.

Lorna appears first, her regular time after school. She is walking down the street toward the house, holding hands with a woman, a nanny I assume, but not Maddy. She skips happily and clings to the hand. I catch a glimpse of my face in the mirror and see tears running through my dark foundation, leaving pale trails. I blink rapidly and reapply the foundation. As I pat on the powder, I catch a glimpse of Toby walking by the car. He glances at me — my heart spasms in the right side of my chest — and then he is past. In the rear view mirror, I watch him crossing the street, oblivious. He walks into the house.

I have to leave. Toby has taken note of me and the car. Yet my hands do not put the car into drive, my foot does not move to the gas pedal. I sit with my eyes glued to the doorway in the rear view mirror.

I am rewarded for my stupidity and the three of them emerge from the house and walk down the street away from me. This time it is Maddy. My stomach twists for a moment and I have to take slow, careful breaths. Isn't this exactly what I arranged? Precisely what I wanted?

Part of me wants to shove Lorna out of the way, jump into the air and throw my arms and legs around Toby, wrap them like a boa constrictor, hold onto him tight until he sees me, not Dahlia, me Hetta. Children are not born naïve. They have deep rooted survival instincts and Lorna's instinct to prefer Toby was so right.

Toby is to blame for the rape. That night wounded me and ultimately hurt our daughter. It became me against her. I thought that by having a child, something in Toby and me would bond, we would heal beyond the blame and hate. Of course it didn't. Lorna only forced us further apart.

I slide over to the passenger side of the car, shove open the door and lean out over the gutter. I retch a few times and press my knuckles into my eye sockets trying to relieve the pain inside me.

Maybe I should have done this the other way. The honest way. Told Toby I wanted a divorce. He could have custody of Lorna. Tell him I had to leave them. Tell him I didn't love him...and if he loved me...it wasn't me. Tell Lorna I was not the mother she thought I was. And then tell them it wasn't me — it was my dead twin and I couldn't let her live in my skin any longer.

I am too cowardly to have left them like that. Society doesn't accept mothers who abandon their children. They become outcasts, shamed by their actions. Men habitually move from family to family, but women are condemned, monsters to be abhorred, ostracized. They become the gossip at dinner parties and the fodder for talk shows.

Do men lie more than women or women more than men? I think about lies and truth a lot. In order to tell the truth, the issue has to be seen clearly from all sides involved whether it's the world, one other person, or simply yourself. It's easy to convince yourself you are telling the truth. It's an innate act to rationalize your version of the truth. Self-preservation.

When the president of the United States declared, 'I did not have sexual relations with that woman,' he knew what he had done, but in his mind he rationalized that it was not sex. A blow job was not sex. And is it? Or is it inappropriate relations, as he later admitted? It's easy to deceive oneself.

The truth for me has been hard to face. The truth is that I would have left Toby and Lorna anyway. It was only with time that I have been able to step back and see my own distortion of reality. Dahlia became the reason nothing worked in my life. She became my scapegoat.

Smuggling diamonds had given me the adrenaline bug and Roza hired me permanently. Oscar's daughter fired Anabelle as soon as she got out of the hospital. Anabelle tried to take Oscar's dog, Roy, with her and was arrested for theft and thrown in a Halifax jail until Roza had me fly over and bail her out. Now the three of us: Roza, Anabelle, and myself — all continue Oscar's trade in Panama.

Just as Roza said, there are shades of morality. Some people would judge me harshly for leaving my family, or condemn us for selling Angolan diamonds, but when I feel the newfound buoyancy in my misplaced heart or see the photos Roza's husband sent us of the villagers, standing around their new well, toasting with tin cans and paper cups, I know everything is the way it should be.

Anabelle still misses Roy and after we have a couple of drinks we plot ways of kidnapping Roy and bringing him to Panama. We talk about buying him his own herd of sheep and how much we enjoyed trudging up those Nova Scotia hills waving our hands at the sheep like a bunch of idiots. Six months ago we bought a collie, black with white paws and a star on his forehead. He has one brown eye and one blue eye and Roza named him Racso, Oscar backwards. She believes that if Oscar were reborn, he would want to be reborn as our dog.

When I throw a ball for Racso, he whirls in circles and leaps and I see the excitement in his brown eye exactly like Bird. And I can imagine I am a kid again and Dahlia is alive. Other times when I sit on the stone wall above the ocean, watching the scuttling fish, Racso cocks his head and looks at me from his blue eye, and I swear it is twinkling in just that way, and I wonder if both of them haven't ended up together in that damn dog's body.